IT'S A FABULOUS LIFE

Also available by Kelly Farmer

OUT ON THE ICE SERIES

Out on the Ice

Unexpected Goals

Calling the Shots

IT'S A FABULOUS LIFE

FABULOUS

LIFE

A Novel

KELLY FARMER

alcove
press

Published in the United States by Alcove Press, an imprint of The Quick Brown Fox & Company LLC.

Alcove Press and its logo are trademarks of The Quick Brown Fox & Company LLC.

Library of Congress Catalog-in-Publication data available upon request.

ISBN (trade paperback): 978-1-63910-604-2
ISBN (ebook): 978-1-63910-605-9

Illustration and cover design by Louisa Maggio Design.

Printed in the United States.

www.alcovepress.com

Alcove Press
34 West 27th St., 10th Floor
New York, NY 10001

First Edition: October 2023

10 9 8 7 6 5 4 3 2 1

For all the fabulous drag performers bringing joy to the world.
You truly are magical.

THE ANGELS

The old RV turned onto Main Street and chugged past a large, cheerfully decorated wooden sign. Clara Angel bunched the top of her gold silk robe to ward off the chill seeping in as she braced herself against one of the windows.

"*Welcome to Lanford Falls*," she read. "Cute."

A smaller sign announced *Home of Winter Wonderfest*.

Clara took in the sights: Tall evergreens. A narrow wooden bridge spanning the river. A dog park filled with happy pooches romping on a Sunday afternoon. It didn't look as though it had snowed recently, but here in Upstate New York, that was only a matter of time.

"What do you suppose happens at Winter Wonderfest?" she asked Gabriella.

Her drag mother focused on the road, muttering encouragement to the transmission to hang on just a bit longer. The brightly patterned scarf tied around her head and faux fur red coat made her ebony skin glow.

Clara turned to her drag sister in the passenger seat. Jovanna was touching up her eyeliner and sighed dramatically when they hit a bump. Her curly, brassy orange wig was not the most flattering against her pale face.

"Do you think they need to book some entertainment for the festival?" Clara wondered aloud.

"I'm sure they've had everything lined up for months," Gabriella said. Always the voice of reason as the mother of the House of Angel.

"We could use another gig," Jovanna said. She waved her liquid liner at her poinsettia red A-line dress. "This all doesn't come cheap."

"Your appetite doesn't come cheap." Their mother gave Jovanna's ample frame an up-and-down glance.

"Don't be jealous of my curves, old woman. Watch where you're going."

Gabriella clucked her tongue, then squinted at the road ahead.

"Where are your glasses, Mother?" Clara asked.

"I don't need glasses," Gabriella snapped. "You mind yourself and get dressed."

"Won't wear glasses even though she needs them." Clara shook her head. "Once a pageant queen, always a pageant queen."

They drove into a charming small downtown. Lush green garland hugged every lamppost. Each storefront was decorated with wreaths and lights and evergreen swags. It had a cohesive look, as though it had all been carefully planned to match. A group of teenagers wearing blue-and-white striped scarves stood on one corner, their harmony on "Greensleeves" beautiful and melodic.

"This place loooves the holidays," Jovanna drawled.

A Progress Pride flag waved in the breeze outside a coffeehouse. Beneath it, a young person with spiky green hair shared a warm beverage and conversation with an older Black woman and an East Asian man, the three of them holding sketchbooks and art supplies.

Gabriella flicked the turn signal to where a sign pointed out a public parking lot. The faint scent of rich chocolate wafted into the RV.

Clara smiled at a mom and dad and two kids exchanging hugs with a middle-aged white man and woman carrying full shopping bags.

As the RV rumbled into the lot, a variety of folks waved and greeted one another from their cars. "What a friendly place," Clara said.

"That's what happens when Christmas vomits all over you," said Jovanna.

They parked at the far edge of the lot so as to not take up too many spaces with their large ride. The jovial metal sign at the lot's rear exit declared *Thanks for visiting Lanford Falls. We'll see you again soon!* Even that was wrapped in garland.

Clara perused their overflowing clothing rack for something day-appropriate. She held the sleeve of a teal number against her warm beige arm. Hmm. She wasn't feeling teal today. Maybe the purple tea-length with a smattering of rhinestones. Or the royal blue jumpsuit with the sequined belt.

She touched the gold lamé gown she wore for their splashy final number at most gigs. It shimmered in the sunlight streaming through the windows.

Clara ran her fingers down the silky material. It was beautiful, but was missing something. One very important thing.

"Are you sure this is where we're needed?" she asked Gabi.

"This is where I was drawn to go next," Gabriella said.

Jovanna fluffed her wig. "Why couldn't we be drawn to someplace warm?"

Clara tiptoed in her fuzzy leopard-print slippers until she stood between them. "Do you think . . . If we've been called here, do you think there's opportunity for me? To wear the wings in our final number, I mean."

Jovi groaned and rolled her eyes.

Gabriella waved a hand. "You'll get your set of wings when you do what needs to be done."

3

Clara's heart sank. She knew what she had to do in order to wear the dazzling wings. "I have to prove my Christmas spirit shines brighter than the moon," she mumbled.

"Which is *exactly* why you haven't earned them yet. That kind of attitude."

"I've tried," Clara insisted. "I try so hard. I rescued that cat—"

"That was a raccoon covered in mud," Jovanna laughed.

"I helped that nice lady find the perfect gift for her granddaughter. And there was that time I talked that girl out of getting bangs." Clara nodded sagely. Those bangs would have been tragic.

"Small potatoes." Her sister glanced over her shoulder. "You need to do something *big*. Something to prove you're worthy of wearing the wings."

"I just don't know what that could be," Clara said.

All drag queens were enchanting, but some possessed a little more magic than others. She'd felt it the first time she'd donned a wig and heels, like Gabi and Jovi. Empowered and fierce. Only she had yet to do anything truly life-changing with her magic.

Jovanna groaned out of her seat. "I have been sitting way too long. These legs need to get to dancing." Her Latin feet cha-cha-ed past Clara.

Gabriella stood, placing her hands on her lower back and stretching with a moan. She followed Clara's line of sight out the front window to the parking lot exit sign. It was so welcoming, a visitor would never want to leave.

"Everyone here must really love the holidays," Clara said.

Gabi snapped her fingers. "I've got it."

"Use the special cream from your doctor, honey," Jovanna called from where their coats hung beside the door.

"You know what we haven't done in a while? A good old-fashioned life transformation."

4

"Ooh, a makeover?"

"No," Gabriella said. "Though that might be fun." She turned to Clara. "Do you want to get your wings this time, Clara Angel?"

"More than anything," Clara said, clasping her hands.

Gabi pointed in the direction of the shopping district. "Somewhere in this town, there's a person in despair. They don't love the holidays anymore."

"In this town? That's hard to believe."

"There's one person in particular. I can feel it." She touched below the knot on her goldenrod yellow wrap dress. "They want to get out. Leave this town behind."

"Is it an adult? A child? A moody teen?" Clara hopped from foot to foot, giddy with the chance to earn her wings.

"You know I can't tell until I know for sure."

Jovanna shrugged into her shaggy off-white jacket. "When Mother knows, Mother knows."

"We'll find that person, and we'll help them." Gabriella nodded at Clara. "You'll help them see what a gift the holiday season can be."

"And then I can get my set of wings?"

Her mother clasped a warm hand on Clara's shoulder. "If you help them have a change of heart, you can wear the wings in our final number."

My wings. My very own set of wings.

"That's what I've always wanted," Clara said.

"Well then, let's go." Jovanna waved both hands impatiently at the door.

"Your sister isn't dressed yet, and I have to freshen up." Gabriella dismissed her with a wave. "I'm gonna revoke your wings if you don't cheer up."

Jovi grumbled and sank onto the cushioned bench at their tiny dining table. "Sorry, Mother. You know it's my favorite time of year."

Clara hastened to grab the purple dress. This was going to be fabulous, and she needed to look fabulous. She wouldn't mess this up. Not again. No more muddy raccoon mistakes.

This time, things were going to go right. She'd show her Angel family just how bright her holiday spirit shined. This lucky person was about to become the most Christmassy Christmas person ever.

She couldn't wait.

CHAPTER ONE

Bailey George waited outside one of the large windows at Caffeinated Corner, as she did every morning. The usual Monday crowd filled the café tables, chatting or reading the newspaper. The actual *paper* newspaper, since Lanford Falls was all about being old-school.

She bounced her knees, trying to get blood to flow down to her cold feet inside her tall rubber boots. The rest of her was nestled in her long, tan wool coat and green knit hat and gloves. Anything to ward off the chill on a dull, overcast December day.

Lulu propped her front paws against the brick exterior. She craned her canine neck as she sniffed.

Kurt finally noticed them from behind the counter. He shared a wave with Bailey and snagged a to-go cup.

Lulu whined and dropped back to the sidewalk. She shook in her blue plaid doggie coat. Being a shorthaired, soft coated wheaten terrier mix meant needing a little extra protection. Besides, she knew how cute she looked.

Yvette passed by on her way to open the florist shop. Her cheeks were almost as red as her hair. She gave a cheery, "Good morning, Bailey."

"Morning," Bailey said.

"Looks like we're in for some snow. We sure could use it for Winter Wonderfest."

"We'll see." Glee washed over her. Whatever happened this year was not her problem.

The café door opened to the warm scent of coffee and pastries and a jazzy rendition of "The First Noel." Lulu wiggled in anticipation.

"The usual," Kurt said as he handed off the coffee cup. His bright crimson apron hugged his *I do yoga for fun* lean frame.

"Thank you," Bailey said.

Her lifelong buddy bent to give Lulu a homemade dog cookie. She inhaled it, then sat, knowing she wouldn't get any more without behaving.

"Piglet," Kurt teased, then gave her another treat.

"You know this is the only reason I stop by," Bailey said.

"I thought it was my sparkling personality." Kurt rubbed behind Lulu's ears and cooed lovingly to her.

"That, and dog treats."

"And free coffee."

"You can charge me any time, you know," Bailey said.

"It's all good. This place wouldn't exist without your help."

Now it was her turn to tease him. "True."

Kurt stood and scratched at his dark hair. "Are you coming to Wednesday night trivia? Christmas edition. Arnie's making his legendary red-and-green taco dip."

"I'll be in New York on Wednesday."

"That's right. I forgot." He grinned wickedly. "You never go anywhere."

"Not this time," Bailey said. "I'm getting out."

"Mm-hmm."

"For real. I've got everything in order. Five whole days to ignore the holiday season."

Kurt settled his hands on his hips. "Okay."

Irritation flashed through her body. "I'm serious. This time it's different. Nothing's going to stop me."

"I hope not. I'd hate to see you cancel another trip."

"That makes two of us." Bailey crossed her glove-clad fingers on the hand holding Lulu's leash.

Kurt glanced inside the café, then said, "Gotta go. See you later, gator."

Lulu tried to follow him, so Bailey had to gently tug her back before the door closed on her nose. "You can only go in when they're not open," she told her sad pupper.

They walked the few steps to the corner, where Main Street skirted along the large village green. The site where Winter Wonderfest would go off without a hitch that weekend. The enormous Christmas tree inside the entrance glowed like a beacon of good things to come.

She sipped her café au lait. Perfect, as always. Kurt could whip up a mean cup of joe. One of these days, she'd pay him back for all the free coffee. Though they tended to trade services in lieu of payment.

If she sat down and did the math, he probably owed *her* money from when she'd helped him start up the café. Not to mention waiving her commission when he and Arnie had bought their house. Such was life in Lanford Falls. Doing favors. Always doing favors.

They crossed Main Street, passing Gruber's General Store. The hand-painted signs in the windows advertising sale items were the only things that ever changed. The brown brick building had been around since the early 1900s. The wooden shelves inside, nearly as long. *Charming* and *vintage* would be how she'd describe it in a listing.

Bailey shielded her face with her cup so Mr. Gruber wouldn't spot her. She had things to do. Getting stuck talking with her old boss was not on the agenda. Mr. Gruber loved to wax poetic about when she'd worked there during her high school summers.

Martin exited his diner and set out the placard listing the daily specials. The fifties-inspired graphics on the door and antique plastic snowmen on either side matched the vibe of the place.

"Morning, Bailey," he said.

"What's good today, Marty?" Bailey asked.

"The Merry Meatloaf sandwich."

His wife made the best meatloaf. "I'll probably be around later to get one."

"I'll save you a seat," he said with a denture-filled smile.

Bailey made a vague noise of agreement and continued down the sidewalk. They both knew she'd get it to go.

Lulu pulled on the leash, trying to head back to the diner. "No, baby girl," Bailey told her. "We have to get to the park. You want to go the park, right?"

Her folded-over ears perked at one of her favorite words. She trotted back to Bailey's side. The only thing Lulu loved as much as food was the dog park.

The imposing dark wood entrance of Potter Real Estate loomed large up ahead. Its single plain evergreen wreath contrasted the lush swag cascading down a nearby lamppost. No doubt Felicity was already at her desk, plotting ways to rip off unsuspecting homebuyers. Bailey resisted the urge to stick her tongue out as her navy blue boots clomped along the concrete.

She nearly choked on her coffee as Miss Josephine stepped out from nowhere. She was a shrunken, tiny pale lady with short, curly, snow white hair and thick glasses.

"Good morning, Miss Josephine," Bailey said, mustering up a smile.

"Good morning, my dear." Her thin lips upturned. Miss Josephine had been perpetually, just, *old*, even when Bailey was a kid. She'd been carrying that same black handbag forever. It was like time had stopped for her at some point, like it had for the whole town.

"How are you?" Bailey asked.

"I'm doing very well, thank you." Miss Josephine patted Lulu's head with a wrinkled hand. "I'll bet you're excited about the festival this Saturday. You always do such a wonderful job."

"Thanks, but I'm not in charge this year."

"You're not?" She blinked, her watery blue eyes magnified behind her glasses.

"Nope. Ten years was enough." *More than enough.* "I passed the torch. Susan's doing a great job. It'll go off without a hitch."

"Oh, that's too bad you're not running it." She pursed her lips, then brightened. "The good thing is, you'll be able to enjoy it as an attendee."

Bailey opened her mouth to say otherwise. Nah. It wasn't worth another conversation about missing the town's biggest event of the year. She glanced down at Lulu and said, "We've got to get to the park. Lulu's friends are waiting for her."

She took two steps down the sidewalk, but Miss Josephine didn't get the hint. "You're still on the Beautification Committee, I hope," she said. "You haven't given that up?"

Not that it was any of her business, but Bailey said, "Still on that committee."

"Good. You have such wonderful ideas. The dog park, revitalizing the wooden bridge over Lanford Creek . . ."

"Okay, Lulu." Bailey inched along, pretending like Lulu was pulling her. Even though Lulu stood patiently waiting. Damn well-trained dog.

"You do so much for this town. We appreciate everything you've accomplished. Especially when you stepped up to run your father's real estate agency after he passed."

Her heart used to twinge when people said things like that. It was so long ago, she simply nodded and said, "It had to be done."

Miss Josephine gestured across the street to George Family Homes and the white twinkle lights outlining the windows. "That was so good of you. You were so young, but you saved the business and everyone's jobs. And saved our town from . . ." She glanced over her shoulder at Potter Real Estate. "Felicity Potter."

They shared a knowing look. "That's a battle I'm still fighting, Miss Josephine," Bailey said.

"Indeed."

"Do you need me to do anything for you? Run any errands or anything?"

"Oh, heavens, no." The older woman chuckled. "I manage just fine."

"It's always nice to see you," Bailey said. "Have a great day."

"You do the same, my dear. Goodbye, Lulu."

They shared a farewell wave. Bailey tried to make herself invisible inside her fluffy blue scarf. At this rate, they'd get to the dog park by noon.

It would be nice to just once walk across town without getting stopped every five feet. Good thing Lulu enjoyed all the attention.

"Two more days," she murmured to herself. Two days from now, she'd be on a bus heading down to Manhattan. A place where she could blend in and just *be*. Hell, she wouldn't have to talk to anyone if she didn't want to. A rare chance for anonymity.

She guided Lulu toward the shortcut behind Town Hall and the library. No more people-ing until they got to the park.

They cut through the newest subdivision in Lanford Falls. Giant blow-up snowmen and Santas waved in the chilly breeze in a couple of the front yards. This was such a festive area. One of the best civic projects she'd been involved in. Helping lower-income families achieve their dreams of home ownership had been so rewarding. Being roped into heading up the project was worth it every time she handed the keys to an excited family.

They genuinely wanted to live in Lanford Falls. A place with festivals and events all year 'round. Neighbors who would snow-blow your driveway just to be nice. Established artist colonies and a laid-back spirit. Over the years, more than one homebuyer had told her they'd felt welcomed the moment they set foot here. If a person didn't mind giving up the amenities of a larger city, it was a very attractive option.

Lulu made a pathetic mewl that should never come out of a dog. She strained against the leash when she spotted the tall fence surrounding James George Park. Bailey jogged with her to the entrance, taking care not to spill her precious coffee.

She could barely unclip Lulu's leash, she was dancing so hard. The second it was off, Lulu dashed to greet a familiar pack of canine pals. Bailey closed the gate and sighed. Now her monster would burn off some energy so she'd sleep on her dog bed at the office.

She shared a hello with a couple of fellow dog owners. Most people stood in groups and talked the whole time, but Bailey liked to watch the dogs. Lulu play-wrestled with a bouncy chocolate Lab. Ooh, her coat was gonna get nasty. Better take it off the next time she ran by.

The cold air prickled her lungs. She sipped her rapidly cooling coffee before setting it on a nearby picnic table. In a month, she'd start her annual online search for what it would take to get her real estate license in states that weren't frozen for large chunks of the year. The ground inside the dog park was hard, and what little grass had been able to grow there had shriveled up weeks ago.

A big white boxer type of dog with tan spots galloped over to Lulu. She froze. The big dog froze. Then their butts wiggled in excitement. The big dog's thin tail whipped. She bounded to the side, and Lulu followed.

They chased each other in circles, hopping and bopping and leaping. This was a new park pal. Maybe the couple who'd recently lost their sweet old pit bull had adopted a new furry friend.

Lulu raced over, grinning up at Bailey like *Mommy! Mommy! I made a new friend!* The unfamiliar dog came up to Bailey and sniffed her. "Hi, buddy," she said.

The dog jumped and gave her a full body hug. Bailey grunted and tried to untangle the dog's long legs from around her. It was more like prying off a friendly anaconda.

"Rosie, no!" someone called. "Get down! Bad Rosie!"

A petite woman with shoulder-length blonde hair under a cream-colored cap came running over. "I'm so sorry," she said. "Rosie has the worst manners. We've been working on them, but . . ."

She snagged her dog's pink collar. Gave Bailey an apologetic smile. Then she squinted. "Bailey?"

That adorable upturned nose. Those big brown eyes and creamy, ivory skin. "Maria?"

"Yeah. Hi." A bright smile lit up her face.

Maria Hatcher.

Bailey's heart whacked against her ribs. "What are you doing here?" she asked.

"I just moved back to town." Maria released her dog so Rosie and Lulu could scamper off. Her mid-length green coat flapped in the breeze.

"I didn't know you were moving back." In Lanford Falls, people would have talked.

"I wasn't planning on it happening so soon," Maria said. "It all came about kind of fast. The perfect job opened up at the right time."

"You moved back for a job," Bailey said, nodding. That made sense.

"I did. I'm the new executive director at the library."

Right. Maria had been at a library somewhere in New Hampshire since college. Not that Bailey had been keeping tabs on her or anything. "Good for you," she said, then wanted to cringe.

Good for you? Really?

"I'm excited." Maria's big smile made her nose scrunch at the top. Which made Bailey's heart thump even harder. "Okay, I'm thrilled. It's a dream come true. I've always wanted to work at the place that sparked my love of books."

"That's great. Getting to do your dream job." Some people were lucky enough to have that opportunity.

"It is."

"How's Dan?" Bailey asked. "I haven't talked to him in a while."

Maria laughed. "You know my brother. Just as ridiculous as ever."

"Tell him I say hi."

"I will."

Danny Hatcher had been one of Bailey's high school besties, but that wasn't the cause of her cardiac palpitations. It was other memories. Secret, private memories.

Maria squinted again, like she was trying to peer inside Bailey's mind. "How's the housing market? Are things going well?"

"I guess," Bailey said. "You should've reached out before you moved. I could've helped you find a place."

"Oh, it's fine." Maria waved a mittened hand. "I'm renting a small house over on Sycamore."

Bailey did a mental drive down Sycamore Street. What house was available for rent? "Not the old Grant house, at 320."

"That's the one."

She tried not to wince. "That place is awful. I happen to know they're renting it out because they don't want to invest the money it would take to sell it."

"It's in perfectly good shape," Maria said. "And I've always loved that house. It's a cozy little cottage."

It was a dump, but a fresh coat of paint could make most places look livable. "When you're in the market for something more permanent, let me know. I'd be happy to show you a house that doesn't look like it was built by hobbits."

A peal of laughter rolled out of her throat. "You're so funny. I almost forgot how hilarious you are."

There was a time she'd thought Maria was funny. And sweet, and cute.

Something like a wistful pang resonated in Bailey's stomach. That was before prom.

She glanced at Maria through her lashes. She was really beautiful now. Like a joyful Christmas elf, but without the pointy ears. Though maybe under her hat . . . Maybe that was why she liked that tiny hobbit hut.

Bailey checked on their dogs, still romping around the park with carefree abandon. "I'm sure your family's glad to have you back."

"My parents are ecstatic. I finally get to put down permanent roots here, with Rosie." Maria smiled up at her, that bright, pretty smile. "It's just me and Rosie."

"That's good," Bailey said with a half smirk. "That house can't fit more than one adult at a time."

Maria laughed again, like the tinkling of bells. "Oh my gosh, *stop*! I love my little house."

Their dogs ran close enough for Bailey to snag Lulu's dust-and-drool-covered coat and pull it off. Rosie jumped to give her human a big, sloppy kiss.

"Yuck," Maria moaned. "Your training is still packed in a box, I swear."

"How old is she?" Bailey asked as the chocolate Lab came over to join the fun.

"She's six, if you can believe it. I adopted her a few months ago. We're still working on listening and not jumping."

"She's cute."

"How old is . . . What's your dog's name?"

"Lulu," Bailey said. "She's a spunky eight years old. I've had her since she was maybe a year old."

"Aww, that's so great. I remember you always had rescue dogs when we were young."

"My mom's wild about dogs. She likes having granddogs now. Less work."

"Granddogs!" Maria laughed and touched Bailey's arm with her mittened hand. "My mom refuses to call Rosie her grand-anything. She thinks it's strange."

That checked out. Mrs. Hatcher was nice, but kind of a stick in the mud. "Maybe she'll change her tune when she spends more time with Rosie," Bailey said, though that was doubtful.

"Rosie forces her love on people," Maria said. "She needs to behave better for my mom to love her the way I do."

Bailey nodded and checked her phone for the time. She had to get to the office soon. Tie up loose ends before leaving town.

"Ooh, what time is it?" Maria asked.

"A quarter to nine."

"I should get going. I have my first meeting with the library staff at ten."

"Be sure to wash that doggie drool off." Bailey mimed scrubbing her cheek.

"Oh no." Maria's big eyes rounded even larger. She tugged a mitten off and touched several spots on her cheek. "Do I have dirt on my face?"

"No. Sorry. I was kidding."

Her concern melted into relief. "You." She playfully slapped Bailey with the mitten. "I had a vision of walking into my new job with a dried strip of slime on my cheek."

"You look fine," Bailey assured her. "Very professional."

"Why, thank you," Maria said, and gave a quick curtsy.

She looked better than fine. Her excitement at starting her dream job radiated off her. She might've even been blushing, but it was probably windburn.

Maria called for Rosie. Then whistled and called the dog's name again. Lulu trotted over, so Rosie followed. "My embarrassing monster," Maria muttered.

"I call Lulu my little monster," Bailey said.

"Lulu is an angel." Maria bent down and made kissy-face with Lulu. "Yes, you are. Will you please teach Rosie some manners?"

Rosie buried her head in Maria's coat, almost knocking her over. Bailey reached to steady her. Maria grasped her hands. She used Bailey's leverage to pull herself up. Her bulky mittens flopped inside Bailey's thin gloves.

"Thanks," Maria said.

"No problem."

"I'm so glad we ran into you." She tilted her head. "Do you come here a lot?"

"We're here most mornings."

Her smile caused another pitter-patter in Bailey's chest. "Then we'll see each other a lot. Which is a good thing. Our dogs really seem to like each other."

Lulu and Rosie plopped onto the ground, tongues lolling out of their mouths. "Lulu loves making new friends," Bailey said.

"I noticed the park is named after your dad. That's so nice."

"It's something he would've wanted for this town." And her most favorite Beautification Committee project.

"It's so much nicer than that old abandoned farm that was here forever."

"Much better use of the land," Bailey agreed.

"I'm not sure if we'll make it tomorrow, but Wednesday? Maybe we could—"

"I'm going on vacation Wednesday."

"Oh." Maria's sandy blonde eyebrows met in the middle. "When you get back, then? Though won't you be busy with Winter Wonderfest?"

Joy pulled Bailey's mouth into a wide grin. "Not this year. I'm not in charge."

"But you'll still be there, right?"

"Nope. I'm going to explore New York. Midtown, the Village, SoHo . . ." She gave a little shrug. "The festival will be the same as it always is."

"Wow, I can't believe . . ." Maria lightly shook her head. "I'm sure you'll have a great time."

"I'm planning on it," Bailey said.

"I'm so glad to be here for it this year. Winter Wonderfest is my favorite event. I came back to as many as I could over the years."

She nodded in recognition. They'd run into each other a few times at past Wonderfests. But Bailey had been too busy. Always too busy to enjoy it.

"I have such fond memories from it," Maria said. "A lot of really great memories."

Her dark eyes sparkled with one in particular. The same one running through Bailey's mind.

Their kiss at Mistletoe Grove.

Rosie sneezed loudly on Bailey's boot and broke the mood. "You *are* a monster," she laughed.

"Mommy's little embarrassment," Maria said. Then she smiled up at Bailey. "It really was nice seeing you. And meeting Lulu. I hope to run into you before you go out of town."

"I'm sure you will." Bailey gestured toward Main Street. "It's Lanford Falls."

Maria tilted her head again. "The library *is* practically across the street from your office . . ."

Not quite, but Bailey nodded again. "Stop in if you want to talk about better housing options."

"Maybe I'll come by to say hi to Lulu." A teasing glint lit those hot chocolate brown eyes.

"That's fine too."

"Or maybe I'll try to convince you to come back early from vacation. I heard the band playing the Winter Wonderfest concert is really good."

"They are. I hired them," Bailey said. "It was the last thing I did before turning things over."

"Then I'm sure you—"

"I'm sure you don't want to be late on your first day."

"No." Maria's expressive face scrunched into . . . Frustration? Disappointment? She cleared her throat, then attached Rosie's pink leash to its matching collar. "If I don't get the chance to tell you before you leave, have a great time in the city."

"Thanks," Bailey said.

"See you when you get back?"

"Yeah. Sure." Bailey waved as Maria tugged Rosie toward the exit. Lulu walked with them until two golden retrievers ran past. She abandoned her new friend in favor of the unleashed ones running free.

Bailey headed for the picnic table. A strong compulsion to turn pulled at her. She snuck a glance at Maria and couldn't help smiling at the way she talked to Rosie like a mom explaining to her human kid playtime was over. Rosie hung on every word.

Maria Hatcher. She'd been an unexpected surprise on a wintry Monday morning. Seeing her again would be . . .

What would it be? Bailey rubbed at some tightness in her chest. There was history with Maria Hatcher she didn't particularly want to revisit.

Plus, as much as this new job seemed like a great opportunity, Maria had been able to get out. Had made a life for herself someplace else. Why would anyone who voluntarily left Lanford Falls want to move back? They'd seen all the other possibilities out there.

Bailey sipped her now cold coffee. She'd see Maria again at the dog park. Around town. After Christmas, because she had more important things to do.

She was getting out.

CHAPTER TWO

That night, the multicolored lights on the Christmas tree bathed the living room of Bailey's childhood home in a warm glow. She crossed her arms over her tailored royal blue blouse and admired her mother's handiwork. Every decoration was perfectly placed, from the large burgundy bows fluttering down the windows to the evenly spaced stockings on the fireplace mantel. Even the snow falling gently outside seemed to be carefully coordinated.

"Mom, you outdid yourself this year," she called.

From the kitchen, Mom said, "I took the time to do the tree lights the right way. It makes such a difference versus when I just throw them on."

"I can see where Hannah got her penchant for interior design."

As if on cue, her little sister came in with an after-dinner mug of tea. Hannah pretended to study the mantel. The red-and-white pattern on her mug almost matched the one on her thick cotton sweater. Hannah loved it when things matched.

"I would've put Lulu's stocking in the middle," she said. "But other than that, it's exactly what I would have done."

"Lulu's already the center of attention," Bailey said. "And wouldn't your dogs be offended?"

"Nothing offends them." Hannah laughed to herself. Her husband Reuben was at home in Syracuse with their two elderly Lab mixes. The three of them were probably enjoying a long winter's nap on the couch.

Their mother joined them with her own mug of tea. She and Hannah looked so much alike: light brown hair, light brown eyes, a dimple peeking out of one cheek.

Bailey pushed her heavy dark hair behind her shoulders. Gazed at an old homemade paper ornament with a photo of her and Dad at Winter Wonderfest. She was Jim George's kid, all right. In looks, in dry sense of humor, in career, in everything.

"Boy, am I pooped," Mom said, sinking onto the couch. "Talk about power Christmas shopping."

Hannah joined her with a groan. "We kept the Lanford Falls economy booming today."

Lulu trotted out of the kitchen and plopped at her feet. She loved her Auntie Hannah and the steady supply of treats she usually had in her pockets.

"Thanks for making dinner," Bailey said to her mother. "You didn't have to."

"It's not often I have both my girls at home," Mom said with a smile. "And you should have a home-cooked meal before you go off and eat out for a week."

"It's not a full week," Bailey reminded her yet again. "I'll be back nice and early on Christmas Eve to help you prepare a magnificent feast."

Hannah shot her a wicked grin. "If you're helping, the feast will not be magnificent."

"Ha ha." Bailey wandered over to one of the comfortable armchairs.

"I'm still in shock you're deliberately missing the Wonderfest. But I get it. If you were here, someone would rope you into helping out."

"Exactly." Bailey pointed at her sister. "This is the only way to send the message loud and clear. It's not my responsibility anymore."

Mom cupped her mug in both hands. "You really did put in your time. Though without you, who knows what would've happened with the festival. If you hadn't stepped up . . ."

"Someone else would have done it," Hannah said.

Bailey gave her a look. "No one did. For ten years, no one did. I don't blame them. It's a year-round job with zero pay. But it's the town's big moneymaker. Our businesses need the annual boost."

Someone had needed to head up the festival when its planning fell into disarray. A series of unexpected events—an out-of-state job transfer, baby triplets, an ailing parent—had effectively disbanded the previous committee. The scrambled-together event twelve years ago had locals worried about its future. Bailey was good at working on committees and volunteering for worthwhile causes, so she'd taken on the mighty task.

Okay, she was just bad at saying no. Every year, she'd sworn it would be the last. Every year, nobody else stepped up. And every year, she disliked the holidays a little bit more because of it. But the town needed Winter Wonderfest, and it'd been satisfying to watch it grow. She'd built a strong foundation for it to thrive for years to come.

"My amazing big sister." Hannah's smile softened. "You've earned this vacation."

"I really have," Bailey said.

"You have," Mom agreed. "It'll make up for the Alaskan cruise you had to miss this summer."

"True." Who would've guessed the office manager at George Family Homes would go into labor six weeks early? "And the long weekend of leaf peeping in Vermont."

"When was that?" Hannah said.

"Which time?" Bailey couldn't help saying. Something always came up.

"Yikes." Her sister cringed.

"Go enjoy yourself," Mom said. "But not too much. I'm so afraid you'll fall in love with the city and never come back."

"I have to come back." Bailey quirked her eyebrows at Lulu. "At least to get Lulu and all her toys."

"Duly noted." Mom looped a leg around Lulu's body. Lulu rolled over and demanded a belly rub.

"Oh, Mom, I forgot to tell you." Bailey lightly slapped her thighs. "I heard back from Samantha Wright. We're meeting up for lunch on Friday."

The worry lines on Mom's forehead deepened. "That's nice," she murmured.

"Don't look so concerned. It's just lunch with an old friend."

Hannah gestured with her mug at Bailey. "Your old friend who's always trying to get you to move to the city."

"We like to talk shop and commiserate. The real estate markets are different, but our basic problems are the same."

"Sammie's done very well for herself," Mom said, staring into her mug.

"Have you seen where she lives?" Hannah's jaw dropped. "She has a view of Central Park."

"Bryant Park," Bailey corrected.

"Whatever Park. She's loaded."

"It'll be fun hanging out with her." She knew Mom worried about Sammie stealing her away. But Sammie had stopped trying to persuade Bailey to move to New York years ago. Now it was occasional video chats while Bailey quietly yearned for the life she possibly could have had.

"Lulu is also pooped," Mom said as the canine lump beneath her foot moaned in belly rub ecstasy.

"She ran extra hard this morning," Bailey said. "She made a new friend at the park."

"A new friend?" Mom cooed to her granddog. "Who was that?"

"A big boxer mix, I think. A total goofball named Rosie."

Hannah scrunched her face in thought. "Rosie? Like, a big, goofy white dog with brown spots?"

"Yeah." Bailey scrunched up her own face. "How do you know that?"

"Maria Hatcher's dog?"

"Yeah."

"I saw a picture on Instagram this morning of Rosie at the dog park. She just moved back to town. Maria, I mean. And Rosie too, obviously."

Bailey opened her mouth to ask how they knew each other, but . . . Lanford Falls. And Maria was between them in age, so she'd gone to school with Hannah as well. "It was Maria and her dog. We chatted for a minute."

Mom perked up. "Maria moved back? Oh, her mother must be thrilled. First Dan moved to Arizona, and then Maria never came home from college."

"She was hired as the new director at the library," Hannah said.

"How wonderful."

"I can't believe no one said anything," Bailey said. "When someone moves back, it's practically front page news in the *Gazette*."

Hannah set her mug on the coffee table. "It kind of seems like it wasn't planned. Like it happened quickly. At least that's what I pieced together from snooping on social media."

"How do you mean? The job?" Bailey found herself leaning forward with genuine interest.

"There was a breakup at some point. She had a partner for years. Nancy, I think. I met her once. She seemed nice."

"But . . . ?"

"I got nosy when I noticed she hadn't been in Maria's mentions for a while. No tagged photos or anything. And then Maria said she'd gotten this new job and was moving back. So, yeah." Hannah tilted her head. "Why are you so curious?"

Heat spread across Bailey's cheeks. "Dan was one of my best friends. Just wondering about his sister."

Also wondering about the girl who kind of broke my teenage heart.

Mom nudged Hannah with her elbow. "So Maria Hatcher's back. And *single*."

Hannah leaned into their mother's side. "Yeeeess. And she likes dogs. That's very interesting."

"Stop." Bailey held her palms up to deflect where this was heading.

"She's such a lovely person, inside and out." Mom set her hands on her chest. "So pretty. I've always liked her."

"Me too." Hannah mimicked the hands-on-chest pose.

"Don't get any ideas," Bailey half warned.

"She had such a nice singing voice," Mom said. "I remember her from choir concerts, and when the madrigal singers would walk around town during the holidays."

"Bails, you love to sing." Hannah grinned like the evil little sister she was.

Bailey crossed her arms. "I haven't sung in years."

"You sing to Lulu all the time. Wouldn't it be nice to have someone to sing with?"

"Not someone who wanted to come back to Lanford Falls. She's actually excited to be here." Bailey rolled her eyes.

"Then she's not going anywhere." Mom beamed with visions of a match dancing in her head.

"Plus, it sounds like she just had a breakup. One big enough to make some major life changes. I don't need that kind of baggage."

"Ugh," her sister groaned. "Don't be so dramatic."

"I'm not being dramatic," Bailey said. "I'm too b—"

"If you say 'I'm too busy to date' one more time . . ." Hannah shook her head.

"I don't want anything right now. I'm going on vacation. That's all I can think about. And Maria's going to be focused on the library. Quit trying to make me settle down."

Her mom and sister pressed their lips shut, twin images of wanting to say a lot of things but wisely choosing not to. They knew it was a losing battle. Bailey wanted a partner who dreamed of travel and adventure, not putting down roots.

They didn't know about the other reasons for not wanting to reconnect with Maria. No one did.

Mom cleared her throat. "Well, it's nice she's taking over at the library."

"Apparently it's what she's always wanted to do," Bailey said.

"It's almost too bad she moved away," Hannah said.

"You moved away," Bailey pointed out.

"Only because there aren't as many interiors to design here as there are in Syracuse." Hannah gently kicked Bailey's leg. "And I wouldn't have gotten the chance if you hadn't stepped up for me."

The gratitude in her sister's eyes dissolved the pang of resentment in her gut. "I did what I had to do."

Lulu stood from her belly rub and shook from nose to nubby tail. Then she snuffled at Hannah's jeans in case there were any treats hiding in her pockets.

Hannah scratched at the dog's head. "Your mama gave up the chance to go to college for me. She's sacrificed a lot so I could pursue my dreams." She cast Bailey another grateful look. "You stuck around even when that wasn't what you wanted."

"Totally worth it." Bailey forced a smile. "You turned out to be a rock star interior designer. And met a dorky but sweet guy who swept you off your feet."

She'd helped put Hannah through college with the plan that she'd return the favor. Only Hannah had thrived and found her passion. Asking her to put her life on hold wouldn't have been fair.

"You helped me save the house," Mom murmured. "For which there are never enough words to thank you."

"I was never going to let anything happen to this house," Bailey said.

"Felicity Potter," Hannah grumbled. "Trying to con our grieving mother into selling the house."

Irritated memories prickled the back of Bailey's neck. "Trying to con everyone at George Family Homes to sell out to her."

"That was part of what kept your dad going," Mom said. "Even when times were tough. He wanted to make sure people weren't at the mercy of Potter. That there was another option in town."

"That's why I stayed on," Bailey said. "Why I still stay on."

Hannah patted the couch for Lulu to join her, which Lulu did eagerly. "I don't know how you did it. You were, what, eighteen, and took on the responsibility of Dad's business and its employees."

"Something I couldn't do," Mom chimed in. "We needed my steady income and benefits from the elementary school. Besides, I was an art teacher. I loved your dad's mind for numbers because I *so* don't have one."

Bailey had to admit, "If I ever stopped to think about those first few years keeping the agency afloat, my brain might explode. It was intense."

It was also a lot to dump on a young person who'd suddenly lost her father. *Run your dad's business or profit-hungry Felicity Potter will swoop in and take over.*

"Though if I do say so myself . . ." she added to take the sting out of her words. "I was young and inexperienced, but I fought old Felicity with a conviction she never saw coming."

"Right on," Mom cheered.

"How many times have you refused her offers to buy you out so she can rule the local market?" Hannah asked.

"Too many to count," Bailey said.

"Well, I appreciate every one of them. I would've never been able to stand up to her the way you do."

"Your heart wouldn't have been in it."

"True. My dreams were never in residential real estate. I would've caved in a long time ago."

They shared an understanding smile. It was all true. So Bailey had stayed on to run the agency. To take the reins on what Dad had stood for while taking care of her family.

And then, *boom*. She'd woken up one day and was thirty-five. Where had the time gone? What did she have to show for it other than a few improvements to the town?

She had Lulu. Even if the monster was lying on Hannah's lap, begging for treats that did not exist.

"Is Maria living with her parents?" Mom asked.

"No. Ooh, Han." Bailey waved both hands at her sister. "She's renting the old Grant place over on Sycamore."

Hannah's lips curled in dismay. "That creepy place? Eww."

"The little stone cottage?" Mom said. "It's a bit outdated, but—"

"Mom, Mrs. Grant scared us when we were kids. She had a pet possum she let roam in and out. And she gave us old pennies for trick-or-treating. The whole house has a weird vibe."

No kid had ever liked that house. Bailey and Hannah had run past it more than once, not wanting to be caught in some kind of odd energy vortex.

"Oh no," Bailey gasped in mock concern. "What if Maria gets affected by the house and starts allowing squirrels inside or something?"

Hannah giggled and said, "Rosie would have some new playmates."

"I'm sure you can help her find something more permanent," Mom said.

Bailey opened her mouth to say she'd already offered, but Hannah said, "If you're not too *busy*."

"I get busy after New Year's," Bailey defended. "People come to the Wonderfest and fall in love with the town and want to know about moving here."

"Then you'd better come back from New York." Hannah gave her a cheesy grin.

"Again, my dog will be here. And my wonderful mother."

"Who'll be holding your dog as insurance," Mom said, not entirely joking.

They shared a laugh. This was a nice send-off before going out of town. A reminder of why she'd stayed. Of their strong family bond. Of what truly mattered. Bailey would always come back. Then again, did she really have a choice?

Well, maybe now. Everything was in order. Maybe she *could* entertain thoughts about her future more seriously. A future filled with what she wanted to do, where she wanted to do it. More travel, more excitement.

She held in a private smile. This vacation could be the start of all sorts of wonderful things.

*   *   *

Tuesday right before lunch was the perfect, not crowded time to make a quick run to Gruber's General Store. Bailey cradled a shopping basket in the crook of her arm and hummed loudly to "Jingle Bells" playing overhead. She snagged a bag of caramel corn, then shrugged and tossed another one in her basket. Vacation snacks didn't have calories.

The sky hung heavy and post-snow gray outside the large picture windows. No matter. It was all clear blue skies in her mind. Her oxfords tapped in time to the music on the well-worn hardwood floor. She turned the corner to head for the cookies and stopped short.

Felicity Potter seemed to block the entire narrow aisle. Her tall, thin body loomed large and imposing with a severe dark coat and hat over her silver hair. People who didn't know her might've thought she was a striking older white woman. Those who did knew her insides were filled with lumps of coal.

"Ms. Potter," Bailey said, her words terse and clipped.

"Ms. George." Felicity stood still, waiting for Bailey to make a move.

Did she really need cookies that badly? Yeah. They were essential vacation snacks. Maybe she could loop around the store, chat with Mr. Gruber, then circle back.

"Happy holidays," Bailey drawled, and began to turn around.

"It seems as though yours will be very merry this year." Felicity's matching tone made the hair on Bailey's neck stand up. "You're finally free of Winter Wonderfest."

"It's in good hands."

"Of course you'd ensure everything was in order. You always put everyone's needs *so high* on your priority list. Higher than your own."

Whoa, Felicity was in a mood today. "My current priority is buying snacks for the trip I'm taking."

"And you're going on vacation." That amused her to no end. "I do hope it's everything you want it to be."

"I hope so too."

"I can't imagine you missing our charming little festival for anything."

"Not to worry," Bailey said. "I'll be back to handle all the inquiries from prospective buyers wanting to live in this charming little town."

The older woman held her ground, smirking like she enjoyed these snarky exchanges. "As will I."

"You mean developers looking to tear down older houses and buildings."

"Improvements to the town benefit all."

"Not when those improvements are cookie-cutter structures and corporate-owned businesses."

"An excellent way to maximize profits."

"Maximizing your commission," Bailey pointed out.

"Something you could have if you thought bigger." Felicity gestured to the wooden shelving. "Not so quaint."

"Quaint is what people want when they come to a place like Lanford Falls."

"Yes, but is it what *you* want?"

A flicker of annoyance flared in Bailey's chest. Felicity never missed an opportunity to poke her with that verbal jab.

"From a business standpoint, I don't want things to change around here," Bailey said. She shifted the basket from one hand to the other. "No one does. They're just too intimidated to say anything to you."

"You certainly are not." Felicity chortled. "Neither was your father."

"Then you should know better than to mess with a George."

"Indeed."

This was going nowhere, as most of their conversations went. Bailey gave her a jaunty salute and said, "Indeed."

She turned and walked away. Irritating though it was, keeping Felicity in check was crucial. Not many people relished the chance to knock her down a few pegs. It almost felt like Bailey's destiny had been passed down from her father, sworn to protect the citizens of Lanford Falls. Much grander to think of it that way.

Dad hadn't set the world on fire, but he'd kept the lights on at home. She and Hannah had wanted for nothing. Sure, they hadn't taken fancy vacations, but they'd had a father who ate dinner with them every night. Went to all of Bailey's choir concerts and softball games. Always found a little extra money to foster a dog and then adopt them so they could be spoiled rotten. To say nothing of the love he gave to Lanford Falls.

Felicity would never understand any of that.

Bailey shook those thoughts away. Her competitor was just trying to get under her skin. No one was going to ruin her day. By this time tomorrow, she'd be stepping off the bus and into the energy and excitement of Manhattan.

Mr. Gruber smiled behind the counter when he spotted her. "My dear Bailey," he said. "Come to get your goodies for your trip?"

"You know I need my snacks," Bailey laughed. She set the overflowing basket next to the cash register.

"I recall a certain young woman who said she wouldn't mind being paid in candy bars."

He went on with one of his usual stories about when she'd helped out at the store. His slicked-back hairstyle was exactly the same, though the color had changed over the years from brown to salt-and-pepper to gray. Bailey leaned against the counter, not in a hurry for anything. Well, maybe for today to be over so tomorrow could come that much sooner.

The bell on the door jingled, followed by Ellis rushing in. The belt around her red coat was tied in a messy knot. "Bailey!" she cried. Her box braids swung over one shoulder from her hasty movement. "I'm so glad I found you. I stopped by your office, and they said to check here."

"Morning, Mayor Thompson," Mr. Gruber said.

"Come to see me off?" Bailey joked. She picked one of the candy canes out of a glass jar. "Candy cane?"

"We have a crisis of epic proportions," Ellis said.

She was not prone to hyperbole, so Bailey asked, "What's wrong?"

"Susan's in the hospital. She had to have an emergency appendectomy."

"I'm sorry to hear that."

"The surgery went fine. She's in recovery. But she'll need to stay for a few days for observation."

"Poor Susan," Bailey said. What a crappy time of year to be stuck in the hospital. Especially since Susan was the head of the Winter Wonderfest committee . . .

Ellis nodded gravely.

Stuck in the hospital.

Oh no.

The town mayor nodded more emphatically. "Bailey, I know you have plans, and I absolutely hate to ask you . . ."

Oh nooo.

"But you're the only one who could step in so late in the game."

Bailey's heart hammered in her chest. "What about the rest of the committee? They're fully capable of running the festival."

"Normally, yes. But, well . . ." Ellis gave a helpless shrug of her hands. "There's no committee."

"What do you mean there's no committee?" Bailey's mouth hung open in disbelief.

"Susan took on everything herself. She wasn't as good at delegating as you were."

OH NO.

This was a nightmare. But it wasn't her nightmare. It was the mayor's problem. The town's problem. Not Bailey's problem.

"I'm very sorry about Susan," she said, fighting to keep her voice even. "But I'm confident you all can get it done. Just follow the detailed timeline. Everything's laid out for you."

"It's just that . . ." Ellis sighed, rubbing her forehead. "We need someone to *do* all those things. Everyone at the park district is stretched thin with their duties. I can see if anyone from past festival committees is available, but it's such a busy time of year, and some things need to get done ASAP."

Bailey's resolve slipped a tiny bit. Her sense of duty hopped up and down, reminding her she had a responsibility to do what was right for this town, for her family and friends.

Damn it, Susan. Why didn't you delegate like I told you to?

She shook her head and said, "I'll do what I can to help today, but I'm leaving early tomorrow."

"Isn't the installation set to begin tomorrow?" Mr. Gruber said.

"It is," said Ellis. "Everything for the performance stage is being delivered, and the frames for the activity booths are being moved from storage onto the village green."

"That's Vince's department," Bailey said. The park district's director did a great job with the setup and takedown of the festival.

"I guess there's a scheduling conflict. He can't be there when the stage stuff gets delivered."

The door jingled again. Arnie chugged in, on duty in his olive green deputy sheriff's uniform. He was a big, curly-haired guy with an even bigger heart. "Hey, Bails," he said. "Kurt said you could help with the toy drive."

"He did?" Bailey crossed her arms.

"We need an extra set of hands to collect the goods from the donation boxes. If you have an hour or two to spare . . ." He smiled. "I'll make you taco dip with extra olives. I know how you love black olives."

Ellis held up a hand. "Sorry, Deputy Hernandez. I need Bailey desperately."

"Oh no." Arnie stuck his hands on his hips. "Is everything okay?"

The mayor relayed the Susan situation while Bailey's pulse thudded in her ears. Did they not get the memo? Not see the basket full of vacation treats?

"You know I love the toy drive," Bailey said. "I'd be happy to help if there wasn't this emergency."

Ellis's phone rang in her coat pocket. She took it out and grimaced at the screen. "Yes, Vince?" she answered. "Please don't tell me there's a problem. We don't need another problem."

She listened for a few moments, her dark eyebrows drawing closer and closer together. Clearly, there was another problem.

"Now? They're being delivered *now*?" Ellis closed her eyes. "Yes, she's right here. I'm trying to. Thank you, Vince." She ended the call.

"Now what?" Bailey almost didn't want to know.

"The portable restrooms came two days early. Vince is on his way to deal with that." She gave Bailey a tired, pleading look. "Is there *any* way you can push your trip back even one day? If you could be around tomorrow, it would be *so much* help."

Bailey sighed. How could she leave with a clear conscience knowing they needed help? How could she relax and enjoy her vacation with a nagging sense of guilt plaguing her thoughts? She could give them one day to get everything back on track.

"Tomorrow," she stated. "But then I'm gone on Thursday."

Relief noticeably washed over Ellis. She grasped Bailey's hand and squeezed. "Thank you."

"I'll send an SOS to last year's committee. See who's around."

"You're a lifesaver." Ellis's phone rang again. "Sorry, I have to take this. I owe you one."

She rushed out as quickly as she'd come in. Arnie chucked Bailey's shoulder and said, "Thanks, Bails. I have to run too, but double the taco dip for you."

He shared a wave with Mr. Gruber and headed out. The cold blast of air hit like a rude awakening.

Just one day. It's only one day.

Mr. Gruber gave her a small smile. "That was very kind of you."

Frustration spiked like lightning through her bloodstream. Just one day, but then what? Were they really going to let her go? Who was going to make sure the vendor booths were in order? Who was going to make sure all the food and beverage carts had proper power supplies? Who was going to handle the eight thousand last-minute questions she always got inundated with in the days and hours leading up to the festival?

You, Bailey. It always falls on you.

Felicity Potter appeared, making Bailey jump. She'd completely forgotten about the woman.

"Problem?" Felicity said.

"Slight delay," Bailey said through gritted teeth.

"It sounds like they're not capable of running the festival without you."

"They'll be fine. They just need a little help."

Felicity set the money for her loaf of plain white bread on the counter. "If I were you, I'd go ahead and cancel that trip now. You know as well as I do the situation will not improve."

Bailey dug her fingernails into her palms and didn't give her the satisfaction of a reply. Because Felicity was right. Mean and awful to say so, but she was right. There was no way Bailey was getting out of Winter Wonderfest this year.

As Felicity moved toward the exit, she smirked over her shoulder. "Happy holidays," she said, her voice oozing with sarcasm.

Bailey slumped onto the counter. *Another dream taken away.*

Mr. Gruber patted her arm. "I can put these away for you," he said, reaching for the shopping basket.

She set a protective hand on it. "I'm keeping the snacks," she grumbled. She needed them now more than ever.

THE ANGELS

The trio of Angels peered around the magazine rack inside the general store. Clara was certain it was Felicity Potter who needed their help. Only that woman had left the store, and Gabi had made no indication for them to follow. Her drag mother focused on the brunette white girl in the long wool coat. The one lamenting having to postpone her vacation.

"Who is that?" Clara whispered.

Gabriella consulted universal wisdom in her mind. "Bailey George. Resident of Lanford Falls."

Bailey George paid for her groceries and thanked the man behind the counter. A deep scowl marred her otherwise lovely face. Clara would die for those high cheekbones and that lustrous mane of hair. It put her wavy chestnut wig to shame.

"Look on the bright side," the man said. "You get to spend another day in Lanford Falls during the most wonderful time of the year."

Bailey barely managed a smile in response before exiting the store. Gabriella motioned for Clara and Jovanna to follow her out the side entrance. Jovi moaned in protest and tossed a celebrity gossip magazine back on the shelf.

"I want to see where this goes," Gabriella said.

They crept out the side door, trying to keep a low profile by staying off Main Street. Though keeping a low profile in full drag was easier said than done. But their power came from the magic of drag. They had the ability to snap their fingers and become invisible, but Gabi didn't like them using their gifts unless absolutely necessary.

Besides, being invisible would deprive people of seeing Clara's delightful burgundy frock coat.

Bailey rounded the corner. The queens jumped behind a large wooden cutout of Santa Claus and a reindeer. Gabi poked her head through the circle in the middle, while Clara looked through the hole in the reindeer's face. Jovi peeked around the opposite side.

Bailey paused at a wrought-iron bench and set her paper bag down. She pulled her phone out of her coat pocket, angrily jabbing at the screen. Such a despondent face around so many joyful decorations.

A familiar man approached her. Kurt Driver. They'd previously interacted with him. He had an abundance of holiday cheer.

"Hey," he said. "Arnie said he just talked to you."

"He did."

Kurt noticed Bailey poking intently at her phone. "What are you doing?"

"Canceling my trip."

"What? Why?"

Bailey looked up and visibly drew in a long breath. "Because otherwise, Lanford Falls can't put on Winter Wonderfest."

"Because Susan's in the hospital?"

"Because I foolishly thought I could do what *I* want to do."

"Aw, Bails, that's . . ." Kurt rubbed at the back of his hair. "Sorry. I know they appreciate it."

"Yup." Bailey swiped at her phone screen.

Her friend was quiet for several moments. Clara readjusted her crouching stance in her nude six-inch heels.

Kurt tilted his head and said, "You okay?"

Bailey pressed on her phone a few more times, then shoved it in her pocket. "I'm so frustrated. Every time I try to make plans, something comes up and I get stuck here."

"It's a good thing you always use that website that gives refunds for cancellations."

She groaned and tossed her hands. "*That's* what I did wrong. I gave the universe permission to stop me from leaving town. I should've been more confident and done no refunds."

"You know better than that," Kurt laughed.

"I just wanted one December where I could go somewhere and enjoy myself without having to worry about anything. Just *one*."

"Maybe you can go for New Year's," he said. "Or right after Christmas."

"What's the point of trying? Something always derails my plans." Bailey gestured around them, which made the queens duck behind the cutout. "Uuggghh. This town. This ridiculous festival."

Kurt shrugged. "'Tis the season."

"The season for stress, and gross snow and cold." She scuffed the toe of her wingtip oxford against the sidewalk. "Damn Winter Wonderfest. If it didn't bring in so much revenue, I wouldn't care if it never happened again. It's ruined the holidays for me."

"You can still go to New York."

"No, I mean it's ruined the whole idea of the holiday season. Every year, I can't wait for it to be over."

"You don't mean that," Kurt said.

Bailey gave him a dead-serious look. "Yes, I do. If I could leave town November first and come back after New Year's, I'd be one jolly elf. I'm so over it."

The queens gasped in unison. Clara set a hand on her chest. How could Bailey George not want to spend the holiday season in this delightful place?

"Ebenezer Scroogette," Jovanna muttered.

Kurt patted Bailey's shoulder. "I know it sucks, but we're all here to help. Let me know what you need."

"I just . . ." Bailey shook her head. "I need to scrape together a committee. And I guess I have to let my mom know she doesn't have to dog-sit Lulu."

She picked up her grocery bag. Kurt stepped to the side and said, "Well, hey, you'll be here for trivia night." He gave a thin smile and mimed raising a cocktail glass. "It's not Manhattan, but I could make you a Manhattan."

"We'll see."

Kurt watched her walk away. "You're the best, Bailey George," he called after her.

Bailey kept on walking.

Gabriella moved back, and they joined in a huddle. "That's her," Jovanna said. "The one we're here for."

"Most definitely," Gabi said.

Clara still wasn't fully convinced. "That Ms. Potter also needs a good dose of holiday cheer. Why not her instead of Bailey George?"

"Felicity Potter doesn't care about the holidays," Gabi said. "Bailey George once loved Christmastime. That love's been dimmed. She can find it again with the right encouragement."

"Ahh." Clara nodded in understanding.

Gabi tapped her chin with one holly berry red fingernail. "We need to remind her of that joy. Show her she belongs in this place. Lanford Falls is her home."

"It sounds like she's done a lot of good," Clara mused. "That good needs to be returned to her."

"Yes, Daughter."

"Should we step in?" She was jazzed to get started.

"Girl, chill." Jovanna rested her arm on the wooden Santa.

Gabriella held up a finger. "Let's observe a bit longer. See where you can nudge her in the right direction."

Clara clucked her tongue and crossed her arms. "If all she needs is a nudge, I won't get my wings."

"Oh, she's gonna need more than a nudge," Jovanna chortled. "That woman is *not* happy."

"It's a life transformation," Gabi reminded Clara. "It won't happen overnight. I'll let you know when it's time."

She *so* wanted to pout, but her mother was right. Transformations took time, and it looked as though Bailey was going to be there for the foreseeable future. Which meant they'd be on the job for the foreseeable future.

A tiny old woman who looked like Sophia on *The Golden Girls* shuffled toward them. She paused, boxy black handbag swinging on her arm. "Don't you look lovely," she said. "I wish more people dressed up like we did back in the day."

"Thank you, sweetheart," Jovanna said, tossing her bright orange curls.

"We had some wild times. Artists know how to live life to the fullest." The woman nodded once, then continued on her way.

"I love this town," Gabriella said.

Clara quietly agreed. Lanford Falls was easy to love for someone filled with Christmas spirit. How was she going to make Bailey George see that?

CHAPTER THREE

Since the day already sucked, it might as well snow. Big, fluffy flakes
fell on Bailey's eyelashes. She batted them away as she mounted the
wide stone steps leading to the library's main entrance. It was after
five o'clock and dark, and she'd been going nonstop and hadn't eaten
anything other than handfuls of caramel corn.

She pulled on one of the heavy glass doors. Good thing Susan
had been on top of everything. The timeline was mostly on schedule.
Still, so many tasks could've been delegated. Then Bailey wouldn't
have been put in this situation.

At least she had a committee somewhat available. Her three
cohorts from last year would be pitching in where they could.

She paused near the circulation desk and looked around for Jane.
Displays of holiday-themed books and movies mocked her. *Get in the
holiday spirit! Let your Chanukah nights shine bright! Celebrate a joyous
Kwanzaa!*

Her gaze skimmed past a woman holding a large notepad. She
blinked. *Maria.*

A big smile spread across Maria's face. "Bailey. Hi."

She made her way over. Her high ponytail, off-white sweater, and black pencil skirt made her look like an old Hollywood movie star. There hadn't been a spare moment to consider that Maria would be at the library.

"Picking up some reading material for the road?" Maria asked, tucking her pen behind an ear.

"I wish."

Her eyebrows met in concern. "Is everything okay?"

"Not really." Bailey glanced around again for Jane. "There was a situation, and I'm in charge of Winter Wonderfest again."

"Oh no. What happened?"

Thankfully, Jane came bustling past the rows of bookshelves. Her brightly patterned dress hugged her generous curves. She waved a file folder at Bailey. "Here you go," she said. "All the permits and important paperwork."

"Thank you," Bailey said, the weight of her gratitude hanging on the words.

"This should be what you need for now." Jane handed the folder over. "Any problems getting into the shared online files?"

"No, I've got full access again."

"I'll do whatever I can, depending on how Susan's doing."

"Of course," Bailey said. "That's your priority."

Maria watched them talk back and forth like a tennis match. "What's going on?" she asked.

Adjusting her glasses, Jane said, "My sister-in-law had an emergency appendectomy. I was able to go to her house to get this for Bailey, but I really should check in with my brother. See what he needs."

"Wait, your sister-in-law Susan?" Maria hugged her notepad. "As in Winter Wonderfest Susan?"

Jane nodded. Realization dawned in Maria's eyes.

"Thanks for giving me access to everything," Bailey said. "I was able to get up to speed."

"That's great. Sorry, but I've got to get to the hospital," Jane said, already retreating.

"Of course."

"Of course," Maria echoed. "Please give Susan my best."

"Mine too," Bailey said. *And maybe ask her why she thought this was a one-person job.*

Maria gave Jane a small wave, then focused on Bailey. "So Susan's out, and you're in."

"Yup." She flipped through the file folder to get a quick visual on the necessary permits.

"You had to cancel your trip, I'm guessing."

"Uh-huh."

"That's awful," Maria murmured. "I'm so sorry."

"It happens."

"You really seemed to be looking forward to it. Not that that's a helpful thing to say."

Bailey stepped aside to let a young mom and two kids pass. She opened her mouth to say goodbye, but Maria touched her arm.

"Do you need help? Let me help you."

"You don't have to do that," Bailey said.

"I want to."

"I'm sure you have tons of work to do here."

"I can manage both." Maria held up her notepad. "I'm mostly training and in meetings this week. The timing is perfect."

"I mean, if you really want to . . ." The committee could use more help. Any help.

"I really want to," Maria said with a smile. "It'd be my pleasure."

"Well, then, thanks." Bailey gave a firm nod. "You're hired."

"Excellent. I'll be done with work in an hour. Where can I meet you? Can I bring Rosie? She's with my parents, but I'm sure she'd love to see Lulu."

"I'm meeting two former committee members at Martin's. You're welcome to join us. My mom came and got Lulu from the office."

Maria gazed up at her with those big brown eyes. "Then our girls will have to wait until tomorrow morning at the dog park."

"That's kind of the last thing on my mind," Bailey couldn't help saying.

"Oh, right. Priorities. Yes." Maria pulled the pen from behind her ear. "Let me finish up so I can be with you. Join you, I mean."

Was she blushing? No matter. She was a much-needed extra pair of hands. "I'll see you soon," Bailey said, then added, "Thanks."

"No problem. Can't wait. Hey, Bailey?"

She turned back. "Yes?"

"Thank *you* for saving the festival."

"Sure." Yup, that was her: Bailey George, patron saint of civic duties.

She walked toward the exit. It was pretty nice of Maria to offer to help. She had way more important things to do—unpacking, settling into her new job, acclimating Rosie to her new home.

A fresh dusting of snow coated the sidewalk. A brief memory flitted in and out. Maria and a couple of friends from school shoveling the Georges' driveway after the first big snowstorm the year Dad died. Bailey had been so busy with work and helping Mom and Hannah that she hadn't thought to check and see if they had gas for the snowblower.

Maria had done a lot of considerate things to help ease that time of profound grief. She'd dropped off countless casseroles and easy-to-reheat meals from her mother. Then again, she could've done those things out of guilt. For rejecting Bailey's prom invitation. For disappearing and being unable to hang out, or at least not hanging around when Bailey was doing things with Dan.

No time to think about that now. She wasn't just busy—more like one step below panic. She didn't have time to eat, let alone get distracted by Maria's adorable wrinkly-nosed smile. Even though it was an adorable smile.

She pulled her scarf to the side and tucked the folder in her coat to protect it from the snow. The only smiles that mattered were the ones on Saturday at Winter Wonderfest.

*   *   *

A couple of hours later, Bailey was feeling much more in control. Her stomach was full of real food, which had helped stabilize her mood. The plates had been cleared from their corner table at Martin's, allowing for more work space. Multicolored lights blinked all over the diner. The sixties holiday tune coming from a nearby speaker matched the retro décor.

Pete and Tom flanked her sides, the three of them tapping on their tablets. What the middle-aged brothers lacked in detail orientation, they more than made up for in creativity. They'd both turned to writing novels after careers in print media. Pete, older and grayer, had leaped into thrillers, while baby-faced Tom had dug into mysteries.

"I think we've addressed everything," Bailey said.

She caught Maria's eye. Her mouth tugged into a small smile. Maria had been taking handwritten notes, albeit very thorough ones. No worries about *her* being detail-oriented.

"Jane will handle the social media and email. You guys"—Bailey nodded at Tom and Pete—"will decorate, and make sure the snowman competition and wreath stations are set up on Friday. Maria, you're going to help when you can."

"As much as I can," Maria said. "Whatever I can do to lighten the load."

"You might be needed when the vendor booths start setting up. That's always a bit of chaos."

The food and beverage setup was its own special headache Bailey wouldn't foist upon anyone else. There was always a problem with at least one vendor not having proper power supply.

Maria flipped her pages of notes back to the beginning. "I can spend my lunch hour at the village green tomorrow. Or if there's an errand you need me to run, just say the word."

"Thanks, I will." Bailey nodded slowly at the trio. "Thank you all again."

"We love helping with the fest," Pete said, and Tom agreed. "I was sad Susan never reached out. It's almost like we're righting a wrong."

I wouldn't go that far.

"At least we know it'll go off without a hitch," Tom said. "If there are any problems, Bailey always fixes them."

"Nobody sees the madness behind the scenes because of you." Pete grinned at her appreciatively.

"That's the idea," Bailey said. "Like a duck treading water. Calm on the surface."

The brothers noticed the time and said they needed to get home to help their elderly mother with her bedtime routine. Bailey scooted across the vinyl booth to let Tom out.

Maria checked her phone. When Bailey sat, she told her, "My mom's texted three times asking when I plan on picking up Rosie."

"That doesn't sound good," Bailey said.

"Rosie's a vocal girl. She whines and moans when she's not sure about what's going on. It's been a long day for all of them."

"Lulu cried a fair amount when I first brought her home. Give it time. Rosie's been through a lot lately."

"She has. I feel like a bad dog mom." Maria's face pinched with worry.

"You brave the weather to let her run at the dog park," Bailey said. "And I'm assuming part of your renting that house is because of its fenced-in yard."

"That was one of my requirements."

"Plus, she gets to hang out with your parents while you're at work. You're a great dog mom."

That eased the concern off Maria's face. "I hope so. Rosie's my first dog that's, like, mine alone. I want to do everything right for her."

Bailey smiled at Maria's sincere desire to give Rosie the best possible life. Kind of how she made sure Lulu never lacked for anything: coats, treats, hanging out at Mom's house whenever Bailey was too busy.

Hmm. Rosie was Maria's first dog by herself. Did she have pets with her ex? It kind of sounded like it.

She really did have a lot on her plate, starting over so completely. It'd be best to only bother her with Wonderfest tasks as a last resort.

"Is there anything else you need help with tonight?" Maria asked.

"For you and Rosie to get a good night's sleep."

A cute grin lit up her face. "That I can guarantee."

As they gathered their things, Maria asked, "Will we see you in the morning at the park?"

Bailey looped her messenger bag across her torso. "Lulu's spending the night at my mom's. I have a lot to do."

"Sure."

Maria looked so sad. She must've really wanted Rosie to make new friends.

"My mom might bring her," Bailey said, trying to make things better. "She sometimes takes Lulu to the park."

This time, Maria's smile didn't reach her eyes. "Rosie would like that."

"So would Lulu."

They passed the counter, where a few late-night diners were finishing up their meals. Bailey shared a wave with Nick, the evening manager. He'd probably made her more dinners over the years than Bailey had cooked for herself.

"Who's your friend?" he asked, nodding at Maria.

"Maria Hatcher," Bailey said.

"Hi there, Maria Hatcher."

"Hi, person whose name I don't know," Maria said.

"I'm Nick." He glanced up at an old-timey paper Santa Claus taped to the wall. "Like Saint Nick."

"Minus the beard, white hair, belly . . ." Bailey said. "Not to mention that Bronx accent."

"Sometimes Santa likes to keep it on the down-low," Nick said. His Italian heritage was unmistakable.

They all laughed and said goodbye. If things had gone as planned, she'd be hearing a whole lot of that accent tomorrow. And the day after.

She gave herself a mental shake. No sense going down that road.

She held the door open for Maria so her companion could pull on her big mittens. Her canvas tote was from the independent bookstore in town.

"I'm that way," Bailey said, gesturing across Main Street.

"My car's still in the library lot," Maria said. "I drive to work, since I drop off Rosie at my parents' house."

Bailey nodded. The Hatchers resided on the rural edge of town near Lanford Creek. A lot of high school bonfires had been made at the back of their property. "Well, thanks again," she said. "Good night."

"Good night," Maria said.

She walked down the sidewalk in black loafers. Improper footwear for a snowy night. What if she slipped in the empty parking lot and nobody was there to help?

"Let me walk you to your car," Bailey said, and took several long strides to catch up.

"You don't have to . . . Well, if you don't mind . . ." Maria gave a little smile. "Thanks. I'd like that."

They fell in step together. Bailey shoved her cold hands in her coat pockets. She felt one of the extra dog treats Kurt had given Lulu that morning. Had it really only been twelve hours since she'd all but skipped to Caffeinated Corner, thinking she was a day away from New York?

Maria turned to her. "Dan said to say hi. He's sorry his family's not coming here this year for the holidays. They alternate visiting our parents and his in-laws."

"Don't his in-laws live in San Diego?" Bailey vaguely recalled.

"Yes."

"And he's sorry he's not coming *here*?" She kicked at the light accumulation of snow.

Maria giggled. "My two nephews love the snow. They almost never get to experience it."

Bailey shook her head. "I can't get over that Dan has kids. Dan *is* a kid."

"That hasn't changed at all."

"He treated me like a sister our whole lives. He'd sit on me and fart. When we were seventeen."

"You should see him with his sons." Maria wrinkled her nose. "It's honestly embarrassing sometimes. But he's a great dad."

"I'm sure he is."

"I forgot about the farting torture. He was so annoying when we were kids."

"Yeah, but I loved to hang out at your house with him. Watching *Die Hard* every December because—"

"*Die Hard* is absolutely a Christmas movie," Maria finished.

"Exactly."

They shared a smile, then looked away. After a few kisses at Winter Wonderfest, Bailey had found herself wanting to hang out at their house for an entirely different reason.

No one knew about those stolen kisses under the arbor at Mistletoe Grove. It'd been a private moment between two girls discovering themselves. And up until that night, Maria had simply been Dan's upbeat, chatty little sister.

"I'm kind of surprised *Die Hard*'s on your list of Christmas classics," Bailey teased.

"Why? You think nerdy librarians can't enjoy something that's not snooty literature?"

"No, it doesn't seem like it'd be your thing."

Maria's lips curved up in amusement. "You'd be surprised at what's my thing."

Surprised? More like intrigued.

They passed Town Hall and the large evergreen glowing to the top with multicolored lights. A twenty-something man and woman bundled against the evening chill took a selfie in front of it.

"I'm really sorry you had to cancel your trip," Maria said quietly.

"It was my choice," Bailey said. "I could've said no."

"You wouldn't do that. It's not in your nature to leave people in the lurch."

She raised an eyebrow at Maria. How did she know what was in Bailey's nature? They barely knew each other as adults. Sure, Maria seemed caring and thoughtful and charming, like when she was younger. That didn't mean Bailey was anything like who she'd been as a teen. Actually, she was a lot more cynical than that girl with the big dreams.

"Do you know how I know you're thinking about something?" Maria pinched two fingers together inside her mitten. "You get this deep indent between your eyebrows. It's your thinky face."

"My thinky face?" Bailey laughed.

"Yes," Maria giggled. "It's very cute. But it also makes me wonder what's going on inside your head."

"I was thinking how people change. How life changes us."

She studied Bailey's "thinky face" for several long moments. "Your life went a lot differently than you thought it would."

Bailey nodded. *That's an understatement.*

"Mine did too. I thought I was going to fall in love, settle down, work at a great library."

"Isn't that what happened?" She pointed to the library as they approached it.

53

"Well, two out of three," Maria said.

"I wouldn't tell Rosie she's not the love of your life. She seems like a sensitive girl."

Maria's laugh echoed in the cold night air. "You're ridiculous," she said, batting Bailey with a floppy mitten. "Of course I love Rosie. But I thought my life was settled in Concord. I had a good job and a nice home and . . ."

"And someone special?" Bailey ventured carefully.

"Well . . . I was in a long-term relationship that ended a few months ago. It was fairly mutual. We finally accepted we were never going to be right for each other, no matter how hard we tried."

"She didn't think *Die Hard* was a Christmas movie?"

Maria's eyes widened. "You know what? She didn't. I should've known we were doomed."

They chuckled together. Bailey felt obliged to give the customary, "I'm sorry. Breakups are rough."

"Thanks, but it's okay. We were raised pretty differently. Nancy isn't super close with her family, and . . ."

"You Hatchers are very close," Bailey said.

"Very. She never fully understood why I wanted to move back here, to this small town life. To be closer to my family. It sounds funny, but she was really supportive when I applied for the job here. She knew this was what I truly wanted."

"It wasn't what she wanted."

"Nope." Maria gave a little shrug.

It probably wouldn't win any brownie points admitting she could see Nancy's point of view. "Your path brought you to what you wanted eventually," Bailey said.

"Eventually." Maria glanced up at her with a Mona Lisa smile. "What about you? Is Lulu the only love of your life?"

"She is."

"Any two-legged romantic prospects?"

She was fishing for information. It'd be easy enough to tell her no and leave it at that. Only Maria had just been open and honest. Bailey could be honest too. "Not really. Dating's been kind of low on my priority list for a while."

Maria nodded. Did her smile get bigger? "Any particular reason?" she asked with fake nonchalance. It was actually rather charming.

"Uh . . ." Bailey shrugged. "Slim pickings around here? I don't know. I get busy with work and town committees and hanging out with Lulu."

"I'd rather hang out with Rosie than be set up on a bad blind date. Or who knows? Maybe I'll run into a woman at the dog park. One who loves her rescue dog as much as I love mine."

Wait, was Maria flirting? How long had it been since anyone had flirted with Bailey? Hard to say. She was oblivious to things like that.

The Mona Lisa smile was back. Yeah, Maria was definitely flirting.

A warm curl of longing unfurled in her stomach. Bailey pursed her lips like she was thinking hard and said, "I'll keep my eyes open for you."

"Would you?"

"Sure. There has to be someone who fits the bill."

Maria gazed up through her long lashes. "I'm pretty sure there is."

Bailey opened her mouth to make a joke, only there was something in Maria's expression that lodged the words in her throat.

The longing in her belly settled to a dull ache. An empty space that had sat vacant and neglected far too long.

They approached the lone car in the lot, a forest green hatchback with New Hampshire plates. "Why don't you get in and warm up," Bailey said. "I'll wipe off the snow."

"I can do it," Maria said, but Bailey held up a hand.

"I owe you a snow removal from when you did it for me a long time ago."

Maria just looked at her. "That's what we do for each other in Lanford Falls. We help one another."

"Then let me help you. Your feet must be freezing."

She glanced down at her shoes and thick black tights. Then she wiped at her windshield. The powdery snow came off easily. "My wipers can handle this. Get in. I'll drive you home."

"I'm fine," Bailey said. "I could use a little fresh air to clear my head." *And this weird pit in my gut.*

"Are you sure?"

"Yeah. I'll see you tomorrow."

She was a few steps away when Maria called, "Hey, Bailey?"

She turned.

"I know this isn't what you wanted, but I'm glad to be working on Winter Wonderfest with you. Excited, if you want the truth. It's going to be a lot of fun."

Bailey mustered up a tired smile. Fun would've been taking the bus to the city, ordering room service, not having a care in the world. But Maria looked so hopeful. Why squash her optimism?

"At least I'll be able to get some of that hot cocoa Mr. Gruber's son makes every year," Bailey said.

"Oh my gosh, that is *the best* hot cocoa I've ever tasted." Maria clenched her fists in glee. She really was a Christmas elf.

"I'll buy you an extra-large one as thanks for helping out."

"I'll hold you to it." She gave Bailey a smile, waved a floppy mitten, then got in her car.

Bailey turned up the collar on her tan wool coat. Adjusted the messenger bag strap on her shoulder. Sucked a deep breath in and out to settle her stomach. Once the car rumbled to life, she headed toward home.

At least Maria appeared to be genuinely enthusiastic about working on the festival. Though, admittedly, trusting her to follow through was something that had to be seen to be believed. She'd also been enthusiastic about going to prom together, only to make up excuses about not being allowed to go. Then showing up with Ted Anderson.

Most memories from senior year were a bit fuzzy. They were too tied to her plans for the future, and then Dad's sudden heart attack in June. But Bailey could very clearly recall feeling like crap when Maria had evaded her the rest of the school year.

Time and age had brought clarity. They'd been young, and neither had been out. Even telling people they were going as friends might have been a lot. Still, Maria could've been honest. Not gotten Bailey's hopes up only to dash them. Especially after what they'd shared a few months prior at Winter Wonderfest.

Well, the fact that they'd had a few sweet teenage kisses something like eighteen years ago was not reason enough to be excited for the festival. Hopefully, Maria's enthusiasm would be contagious. It might even be fun to lightly flirt with her and find out what other surprising holiday movies she liked. Bailey could use some Christmas magic to lighten her mood.

CHAPTER FOUR

Warmth and sugary scents assaulted Bailey as she stepped inside Caffeinated Corner. *Wednesday.* The day that had been circled in red ink on her calendar for weeks was now just another day. She trudged up to the counter, where Kurt was already holding out her café au lait.

"That's a mighty big cup," she noted.

"I figured you needed a boost." Kurt gave her a sympathetic smile. "How are things going?"

"They're going. We're still on track."

"That's good."

"Anyway . . ." Bailey raised the cup to him. "Thanks."

"Hang on." He bent behind the counter, then emerged with a couple of small dog treats. "For my girl."

"She greatly appreciates them."

"I've got a treat for you too. Don't worry about dinner. Come to trivia night."

Bailey started to protest, but Kurt continued, "Relax, unwind, have a good time. You deserve it."

"It depends on how my day goes," she said. "I'll let you know."

"Since you're not able to do what you really want this week . . ." He shrugged. "Have some fun. You're not working. You can stay out late on a school night."

She couldn't help but laugh a little. "I could be swayed by a certain taco dip."

"Extra black olives?" Kurt snapped his fingers. "You got it."

Bailey moved out of the way for him to wait on the next customer. It always felt a bit strange heading to the office without Lulu. But she might as well check in before the trucks began to arrive at the village green.

Bright sunlight glistened off the small piles of snow on the sidewalk. Water dripped from the garland hugging the lampposts. At least the weather should cooperate for the rest of the week. Setting up for the festival in rain or sleet or snow was a real bite.

The lush wreath on the glass door of George Family Homes hung a bit crooked. She readjusted it, fluffing the shiny blue bow before heading inside. It was quiet and empty. Most of the small staff worked shortened days this time of year. The Christmas tree in the quaint reception area glimmered in front of the window.

Familiar rustling of paper came from Uncle Bill's office. She moved past the four desks arranged comfortably in the main area to peer inside his cluttered workspace. His balding, sandy blonde head was bent over the documents strewn about his desk. He squinted up at his monitor, then noticed Bailey in the doorway.

"Working on the Oak Avenue closing?" she guessed.

Uncle Bill grunted in agreement. He wasn't really her uncle, but Dad's best friend. Even though she was technically his boss, he'd always be her Uncle Bill.

"Aren't you supposed to be on a bus?" he said.

"Not anymore, because of the situation with Winter Wonderfest."

He looked at her blankly.

"Because someone had to step up to run it."

He blinked, still not comprehending.

"Because Susan's in the hospital." Bailey scrunched her face in disbelief. "How do you never know any of the town gossip?"

"I don't care what's going on," he groused.

"Well, I'm working on the festival again. Not going out of town. I just wanted to see if anything needed attention before I got started on today's tasks."

"Everything's fine," he said, then went back to his paperwork.

Bailey crossed to her office and flicked the overhead light on. Once again, Uncle Bill had proven why he'd been ill-equipped to take over. He was brilliant with numbers and mortgage rates and predicting market trends. The people-ing side of residential real estate, not so much. His motto never wavered: *Give me a stack of papers and an office, and that's all I'll ever need.*

That and a few pets, since animals loved him. Even squirrels ran up to him in the village green.

She set her messenger bag on her tidy desk. Her in-bin was as empty as it'd been yesterday. Cleared out in preparation for a relaxing vacation. She turned on her computer, then sank into her ergonomic office chair.

Lulu's dog bed sat sad and lonely in the back corner. Above it on the window ledge were the same framed photographs that had been there forever. A picture of Dad in front of the office the day he and Uncle Bill opened George Family Homes. One from Hannah's wedding of her and Bailey and their mother. An adorable photo of young Lulu, face covered in dirt from digging up a no longer existing flower patch in Bailey's backyard.

Was it sad to only have these photos? Her coworkers had spouses and children adorning their desks. Yes, Lulu was her four-legged kid, and yes, she loved her family and wanted to honor Dad's memory. What was she going to do, anyway—photoshop herself onto a picture with some random gorgeous woman? That was more depressing than being single.

A dull ache wound through her stomach, not unlike the one she'd kept getting last night. Maybe Hannah was right. Bailey had been "too busy to date" for far too long. Although she *was* legitimately too busy right now.

Her phone jingled in her coat pocket, as if to prove her point. Great. Not a crisis so early in the day.

Thankfully, it was her old pal Sammie video calling from New York. Bailey answered and was greeted by a rush of city noise.

"Hey, George," Sammie said, her sweetheart-shaped and suntanned face filling the screen. Tall buildings towered in the background.

"Hey, Wright," Bailey said.

"What's with the text you sent last night? You can't make it after all?"

"No. Lanford Falls strikes again."

"Can't they do one thing without you?"

"Apparently not."

"George," Sammie groaned. "That place is sucking you dry. You need to escape."

"Every time I try, something comes up."

"Maybe you're cursed. Do you think you might be cursed?"

Bailey leaned back in her chair, smirking at the suggestion. "I wouldn't put it past Felicity Potter to do whatever it takes to make me fail."

"Is that old crone still giving you trouble?"

"It's fine. She's like a low-grade irritant."

"Listen, I'm just about to the office," Sammie said. "But I wanted you to know I did want to see you on Friday."

"I really wanted to too."

"I was hoping to have more to tell you then, but since you're not coming, I'll tell you now. My firm's opening three more offices next year. Business is booming, and they're looking to hire top-notch realtors. I tossed your name into the mix to head up the new office in Brooklyn."

The air stilled inside Bailey's lungs.

"There's nothing definite, and I was obviously going to talk to you about it in person. The partners are impressed with your credentials. You've run your own office your entire adult life. You have a neighborhood mindset. They're looking for someone like you who can find homes for families."

"Wow" was all she could say.

Sammie beamed a gleaming white smile. "I'll touch base when I have more info. But if you're interested, I'll let them know."

"Yeah," Bailey said, pulse pounding in her ears. "Yes. That would be amazing."

"No guarantees, but I'll see what I can do. Your sales numbers and everything are up to date on your website?"

"They should be."

"You sell yourself, George." Sammie looked away for a moment before saying, "I'd love to have you here. Imagine how you'd thrive in an environment where you can shine."

A big grin pulled at Bailey's mouth. *An environment where you can shine.* "It sounds like there's a lot of growth potential."

"The sky's the limit, and the market is hot. Get down here."

"I'll see what I can do," Bailey said. "After the holidays."

"The new year could be a big one." Sammie held her phone out. "Ooh, a client's calling. Gotta go. Talk soon, George."

Bailey ended the call. She stared at her lock screen photo of Lulu tilting her head. The silence was more pronounced in her office. No energy, no excitement.

Brooklyn. Homes in a bustling borough of the city. A market that wasn't limited to a small population.

Unlimited growth potential.

Her pulse thudded throughout her body. She was almost afraid to be excited about the possibilities. This could be a wonderful challenge. A fresh start. A . . .

She shook her head. It was just talk. Professional courtesy extended by an old friend. A lovely thought to tuck away with all the others. Plus, with her luck, Mom would break her leg just before Bailey moved down there.

"Not that I want that to happen, universe," she said to the ceiling. "Don't drag my mom into this."

Uncle Bill released a thunderous sneeze in his office.

"Seriously. Mess with me, but leave my loved ones alone."

She shined here for all the wrong reasons. The woman who put aside what she wanted so other people could thrive. Whose job was literally making other people's dreams come true. Who couldn't make plans, couldn't build a future, because her choices had been taken away at a young age.

Incredibly limited growth potential.

*　*　*

The village green bustled with various projects. To the left of the paved walking path, the stage crew had just finished unloading the large platforms and supports onto the snow-covered grass. Farther down, several park district employees were setting up the wooden activity booth frames.

Bailey floated between the two until Vince could get there. Things were going well, which had lowered her shoulders from her ears a notch. This was a well-oiled machine after so many years.

Her phone bleeped in her coat pocket, then bleeped again. She tucked her clipboard in her armpit to get it. Jane had sent two texts.

Susan can't thank you enough! She's so relieved the festival is in good hands.

I'm monitoring the email. If you want to send pics for social media, I'll post them.

Sure, why not? Bailey could send her a few snaps of the early progress. Build the excitement. She squinted at her screen in the midday sunlight as she sent them to Jane.

Someone behind her hummed "Sleigh Ride" joyfully. She turned to find Maria stepping off the path, fortunately in snow-appropriate boots. Well, well. She'd shown up when she said she was going to. It was nice to see her and her big smile.

"Hi," Bailey said.

"Happy Wednesday," Maria sang.

A pang vibrated through Bailey's stomach. *Not so happy Wednesday.*

"I came to see what you need. And also . . ." She held up an insulated bag. "It's lunchtime. I wasn't sure what you might want, so I packed a couple of options."

"Thanks," Bailey said. "That was nice of you."

Maria pulled out a wrapped sandwich. "I have turkey on whole-grain." She pulled out a second sandwich. "And chicken salad on whole-grain." She propped the bag in the crook of one arm to pull out a third sandwich. "And veggies with provolone cheese on whole-grain. Basically, they're all on whole-grain, so I hope you like—"

"You made a bunch of sandwiches?" Bailey said.

"I'll eat anything, so whatever you don't want, I'll have." Maria's eyes twinkled. "It's my lunch break too."

"It wasn't necessary for you to—"

"You mentioned last night you barely ate anything yesterday. I want to be sure that doesn't happen again." She maneuvered the bag so she could look inside it. "There's also chips and sliced carrots and hummus."

"Here," Bailey said, and took the bag before it toppled into the snow. "You really didn't have to go through all this trouble."

"It's no trouble." Maria cradled the sandwiches against her emerald green coat. "I woke up early and couldn't fall back asleep. Meal prep is my way of relaxing."

There were a hundred other more relaxing things, but Bailey simply nodded.

"Can we sit? Or do you need to be in on the action?"

She peered down the path at the crew assembling the station for decorating wreaths. Then she gestured with her chin to a nearby bench. "I can sit for a minute."

"Good, because you have to try this hummus. It's a new recipe I'm psyched about."

The sun had fortunately melted the snow off the metal bench. Bailey set the lunch bag and clipboard between them.

Maria displayed the three sandwiches like they were playing cards. "Which one do you want?"

"Whatever one you don't," Bailey said.

Maria considered them. "Hmm. Take the chicken salad. It's really good."

"Don't give me the best one."

"What good is tasty food if you can't share it?" She handed Bailey the sandwich. "Besides, I ate a bunch of it when I made it."

She couldn't help chuckling at Maria's charming honesty. This was unexpectedly thoughtful.

"How's it going today?" Maria asked as they unwrapped their sandwiches.

"So far, so good. How's the library?"

"Still full of books."

"Glad to hear that."

Maria glanced up at her. "Do you need any errands run or anything? I could do something quick if you can't get away."

"No, I think I'm okay. Having food delivered helps."

"Ah, I see my *real* committee task is making sure you eat," she teased.

"My mom will be most grateful," Bailey said.

They smiled over their sandwiches. She took a bite. The delicious tang of flavors danced in her mouth. She chewed on a juicy cranberry. "This is fantastic chicken salad," she told Maria.

"I wouldn't bring you a crappy sandwich," Maria laughed.

They savored their lunches. If making food this delicious brought her calm, Bailey was fully on board with Maria being the committee head of lunchtime.

"Why do you think you couldn't sleep?" she asked. "Too much on your mind?"

Maria nodded as she swallowed. "I was mostly mulling over a presentation I'm going to give to the library board of trustees. One of the things I mentioned during my job interview was wanting to coordinate more events and displays with the historical society. Lanford Falls has such a rich history as an artists' colony. There's so much the library could do to expand on that."

"That sounds interesting," Bailey said.

"It is. Our town was a haven for painters in the summer during the 1920s. They came here to capture the landscape. And then writers would come in the winter for the quiet solitude. Many of them were queer. I'd love to highlight those authors and their work. And also the artists who . . ." Maria wrinkled her nose. "Listen to me. I'm giving you the pitch."

"No, it's nice to hear about something other than Winter Wonderfest."

"I'm just really passionate about it, and once I get started . . ."

Bailey gestured at her with her sandwich. "They definitely hired the right person."

"I think so too." Maria's good humor dimmed a bit. "I'm nervous. I really want to do well. Part of me won't let go of the fact that I have my dream job, so I'd better not screw it up."

"That's a lot of pressure to put on yourself."

"Yeah, but I'm sure you understand. You probably have big goals and sales levels to reach."

"Business goals," Bailey said, then admitted, "But not dreams. I don't fantasize about . . ."

Maria leaned forward. "About what?"

Right now, I'm fantasizing about sitting in Central Park instead of here. But Maria didn't want to hear about how Bailey didn't have the luxury of following her dreams. "I just hope each year, we do better than the last. You're going to do great. Your enthusiasm alone will sell your ideas to the board."

"That's my plan," Maria said. "Dazzle them with my charm."

"It'll work."

Their gazes locked for a long moment. Bailey's heart gave a big thump. Then she looked down to further unwrap her sandwich.

What if she started over in the city, with a new job and fresh vision for the future? Would she find more enthusiasm for selling homes? It was the only thing she'd ever done, and while she enjoyed it, she wasn't sure if it was her passion.

Maria gave her a sideways glance. "Thinky face," she murmured.

"Nosy face." It was meant as a joke, but it didn't land. Not by how Maria quietly turned her attention to her sandwich. So Bailey said, "Did you ever want to do anything other than work at a library?"

Maria took her time chewing and swallowing. "I had a brief phase where I thought I could be on Broadway. But liking to sing and being really good at it are two different things."

Bailey chuckled in agreement. "I feel that. I loved being in choir, but a career in a four-part harmony group . . ."

"The world needs more professional choirs tearing up the charts. I'm just saying."

"Totally."

"I saw the madrigals the other day," Maria said. "I love how they still go caroling around town, like we did."

"That was a lot of fun." Bailey stared at the paved path where generations of high school carolers had sung the same rotation of classical tunes. "One of my favorite memories."

"Mine too. Except when there were those below-average temperatures my senior year. Brr." She shivered rather adorably.

"I vaguely recall being glad to be inside that year, watching through my office windows."

"Do you remember any of the songs? I'll bust one of them out every once in a while."

Bailey smiled and said, "Yeah. I can't remember what I ate for breakfast, but I can still sing the alto line to 'Carol of the Bells.'"

"Want to give it a go?" Maria wiggled her eyebrows. "Give the workers some quality entertainment?"

"I think they'd appreciate it more if we didn't," Bailey said, which made Maria laugh.

Her phone chimed with an incoming text. It was a photo from Arnie of his red-and-green taco dip, with two big arrows drawn on it. *Extra olives just for you!*

Bailey breathed out a small laugh and shook her head.

"Good news or bad news?" Maria asked.

"Taco dip." Bailey showed her the picture.

"Yum. Who made that?"

"Arnie Hernandez."

"Kurt's husband?"

"Yes."

"Is it for trivia night?" Maria's face lit up like a Christmas tree. "Are you going?"

"I'm not sure. Why? Are you?"

"I am. Kurt invited me. We survived chemistry class together. And when I say survived, I mean that quite literally."

"That does not surprise me," Bailey said. Kurt was infamous for being the only kid at Lanford Falls High to almost blow up the science lab not once, but twice.

Maria tilted her head in thought. "Y'know, I just realized he mixes hot liquids for a living. I guess he's learned a few things since he nearly exploded a rack of test tubes."

"He was a bartender for years and knows how to pour drinks. But that first year at Caffeinated Corner *was* pretty messy. Especially when we painted it together." Memories of errant brushes and Kurt stepping in the paint tray made Bailey smile. "He eventually got the hang of everything."

"I'm kind of sorry I missed that."

"Feel free to bring up those embarrassing stories. Arnie gets a kick out of them."

"I can't wait to meet him. He's obviously a fellow home chef." Maria pointed at Bailey's phone.

"He is. And he also likes to make sure everyone's eating."

"With promises of taco dip?"

"He knows I can't resist that taco dip."

Maria laughed. "Boy, the way to your heart really is through your stomach."

She was teasing again, but Bailey had to admit, "You are not wrong."

"Noted." Maria mimed checking a box. It sent a swizzle of delight through Bailey's midsection.

She spotted Vince's tall frame near the snowman building station. They shared a brief wave of acknowledgment.

Maria noticed and said, "Reinforcements?"

"Yup. That means I can focus on the stage." Bailey wrapped what was left of her sandwich. "I'll finish this later. Thanks again."

She lifted the papers on her clipboard to make sure the envelope was still there. The check for the stage rental was *not* something she could afford to lose. Literally. It would of course be more efficient for Ellis to authorize electronic payments for festival expenses, but . . . Lanford Falls. Business was still done with a handshake and a check.

Maria rooted around in her lunch bag. "Take the chips."

Bailey waved them off. "I'm good."

"Then take the other sandwich. I can't eat all this." Maria set the veggie sandwich on top of the clipboard, making an offer Bailey couldn't refuse.

"If you insist," she said.

"I do." Gathering her things, Maria said, "I hope you come to trivia. Spoiler alert: there's going to be more chicken salad."

She was pretty darn cute. "That alone is reason enough to go."

"Good." Maria nodded several times. "Then I'll make sure you eat dinner too. Lulu's coming, right? Kurt said I was welcome to bring Rosie."

"He adores Lulu, so yes." Bailey quickly added, "If I end up going, I mean."

"Right." Knowing shined in Maria's brown eyes. As far as she was concerned, Bailey's attendance was already guaranteed.

The way her pink-tinted lips curled up in delight was another reason to go. They looked so soft. Inviting. It'd been so long since their first kiss. Would they feel familiar? Different? Better in the years since—

Bailey's phone rang. It was Vince, so she answered, "What's up?"

"I've got a logistical question," he said. "Are you almost done?"

"Be right there." She ended the call, then turned to Maria. "Duty calls."

"Are you sure you don't need me to do anything?"

Bailey shook her head and stood. "Go focus on your cool new job."

Maria joined her on the path. "I'll check in when I'm done with work."

"You really don't have to. Get Rosie and have fun at Kurt's."

"But I'm on the committee."

Raising her half-sandwich, Bailey said, "You did your part admirably today."

"Well, then, have a good afternoon."

"You too."

Bailey couldn't make her legs move. Neither could Maria, from the looks of it. They smiled at one another, easy and comfortable, like they didn't have a hundred other things to do.

She really did have a beautiful mouth. The kind of lips that begged to be kissed, an expression that had never made sense until now.

"Enjoy your sandwiches," Maria said.

"Thanks. I will."

What *would* it be like to kiss her again? If there wasn't a mile-long Wonderfest to-do list, it might be nice to find out.

But there *was* a mile-long to-do list. The whole reason Bailey was standing out in the cold, staring at Maria's tempting mouth. Her own lips were probably chapped and dry from the elements. Not sexy.

She forced her feet to work and said, "Bye."

"Until tonight," Maria said, humor playing about her impish face.

Bailey headed across the snowy grass. Maybe having Maria there would make it worth stopping by trivia night. It *was* really tasty chicken salad. And she did have to eat dinner. And there would be super special taco dip.

So she'd go for the food, and for Lulu and Rosie to play. And the company. It'd be nice to hang out with friends.

She glanced over her shoulder and caught Maria doing the same. Maria's grin widened. So did her own.

It might be nice to reconnect. So far, Maria had backed up her words with action. Maybe they could get to know one another as adults. Start fresh. Or at least make peace with the past. Or at the very least, get through this week.

It might also be nice to watch Maria's expressive mouth smile and laugh and talk excitedly about the things she was passionate about.

Maria might be reason enough to go.

CHAPTER FIVE

Kurt opened his front door, looking mildly surprised. "You made it," he said to Bailey. "All right. We were just about to start."

Lulu danced on her back legs to reach him. He leaned down to give her kisses.

Holding out a bag of Twizzlers, Bailey said, "I didn't have time to go shopping, so I brought what was supposed to be a vacation snack."

"It's all good. Come on in." Kurt moved aside for her and Lulu to enter. "It's a small group due to the holidays, and Jane helping with family stuff. But our numbers are even."

"You mean I don't have to be the third wheel on someone else's team?"

"Not tonight. Maria Hatcher's here. But I guess you know that."

She chose to ignore the amusement twinkling in his eyes and handed him the candy. Lulu headed straight for the kitchen, of course. Bailey listened to Arnie greet her as she hung her coat and scarf beside the door. Her pulse picked up at the sight of Maria's familiar green coat.

"Look who Santa dropped off," Kurt said as they entered the living room.

Bailey waved at Ellis and Yvette and their husbands on the large sectional couch. Then she locked eyes with Maria bending next to Rosie. Her pulse kicked up another notch.

Rosie trotted over, more cautious than their previous meeting. The wrinkles on her face telegraphed uncertainty in the new surroundings.

"Hey, buddy," Bailey said, holding her palm out to be sniffed.

The dog hopped up and wrapped her front legs around her.

"Nice to see you too," Bailey wheezed, leaning into the overzealous hug so she didn't fall backward.

"Rosie!" Maria pulled her off. "Sorry. She really likes you."

"Apparently."

Lulu followed Arnie into the room. She and Rosie spotted one another and ran to greet each other. Bailey smoothed out her thin purple V-neck sweater as Maria wiped little white dog hairs off her fuzzy pale pink sweater.

A shade of pink similar to her lipstick.

"I'm glad to see you," Ellis said, holding a couple of chocolate chip cookies on a festive napkin. "Hopefully, that means everything went well today with the festival setup."

"It went fine." Bailey was there to enjoy herself, so she added, "Let's not talk about it, if that's okay."

"Fine with me." Ellis nodded at her husband, Carter. They wore matching green-patterned sweaters that said *Happy Kwanzaa* beneath a kinara. "I'm pretending for the next two hours everything is totally normal and I don't have the town's biggest event in three days and haven't wrapped a single present and the kids get out of school early on Friday. And my parents are coming in tomorrow." She actually reeled a bit.

"Working moms are amazing," Arnie said as he set a bowl of guacamole next to the chips and salsa on the table against the wall. Umm, where was the taco dip?

"You're doing great, Madam Mayor." Kurt smiled at her.

"Mayor who?" Ellis looked around. "I don't see any mayor here."

They all laughed. The dogs flopped onto the beige carpet to wrestle.

"Super quick question," Kurt said. "Did they hire drag queens for the festival?"

Bailey shook her head. "Not to my knowledge. Why?"

"I saw a couple the other day. I thought they might be here for Winter Wonderfest."

"Maybe as visitors. Our town's known for its welcoming atmosphere."

"Maybe they're filming one of those TV makeover shows," Maria suggested.

Kurt and Arnie gasped and stared at each other. "I'd be perfect for one of those shows," Kurt stated.

"Let us know if anyone sees a camera crew," Arnie added, to which Kurt nodded vehemently.

Yvette set her empty plate on the coffee table. She glanced at her husband, Paul, and said, "I really hate to be a party pooper, but I have to get up extra early tomorrow. Can we start the game soon?"

Paul and Ellis agreed.

"Sure," Kurt said. "As soon as Bails gets some food."

Bailey held her hands up and said, "Let me grab a plate, and then I'll be ready."

"Eat that dinner, Ms. George," Maria said.

"Oh, it's happening." She cast another sad glance at the array of snacks.

"Don't look so forlorn." Arnie waved her toward the kitchen. "I know what you're after."

Bailey turned to Maria and asked, "Can you keep an eye on the monsters?"

Lulu and Rosie were lying on their backs in front of the Christmas tree, legs tangled, chewing on each other's faces. "Sure," Maria laughed.

The kitchen shined with its stainless steel appliances. The beautiful silver menorah on the table had been passed down from Kurt's grandmother. His and Arnie's house was a cute little cottage—legitimately cute, rather than the old Grant hobbit house of mystery.

Arnie did a grand flourish with his arms and gestured at the counter by the fridge. "Your taco dip. Thanks again for sticking around for the festival."

"Yesss." Bailey rubbed her stomach eagerly. The dip was in a small glass bowl—a perfect serving for one. Well, for one very hungry person who was *not* going to share. The casserole dish next to it had been mostly wiped out, so the rest of them were not going without.

Arnie stuck a spoon in the bowl and handed it over. "All yours. What do you want to drink?"

"A beer's fine. Whatever you have."

"You are my least picky friend," he said, ducking into the fridge. "I love that about you."

Bailey hummed in anticipation and dug into the taco dip. The layers of flavors and extra black olives made her instantly glad she'd come over. "Sooo goooood," she garbled.

"You know what's really good? This chicken salad Maria brought. I like her. She's a little bundle of energy." He popped the cap off a bottle of imported beer with the same amused look Kurt had given her.

"Mm-hmm." Bailey shoveled in another mouthful of taco dip.

"Oh, you think so too?" Arnie nudged her with his elbow.

After swallowing, she said, "She's always been cute. And she has a lot of dirt on your husband."

"And she's shared a lot of it already. Had I known that man had such potential to blow stuff up, I might have reconsidered things."

"But he has such a nice butt."

His mouth twisted in thought. "He does. I guess I'll keep him."

They rejoined the party. Bailey stopped by the tortilla chips and stuck a handful in her bowl of deliciousness like the classy person she was. Arnie set her beer on the coffee table, conveniently next to Maria's glass of white wine.

Ellis readjusted on the couch. "Kurt was telling us your volunteerism goes way back to when you were a kid."

"It does," Bailey said, snagging a napkin. "My dad was a big believer in giving back to the community. We spent more than one Saturday picking up garbage along Lanford Creek."

"Do you still have that shirt I got you for your birthday that says *Stop me before I volunteer again*?" Kurt said.

Bailey nodded. "I do. I wear it to Beautification Committee meetings."

"She was student council president in high school. In fact . . ." Kurt raised his well-groomed eyebrows. "Our senior class was the one that raised the money to have the *Welcome to Lanford Falls* sign put up. It was all her doing."

"Really?" Maria said. "I didn't know that."

"Class of . . ." Bailey held the napkin in front of her mouth. ". . . grumble-grumble rules."

"You have a serious case of volunteeritis," Carter said.

Kurt bobbed his head in agreement. "Student council, the Prom Committee . . ."

A mischievous gleam lit his eyes. Yes, she'd participated in a lot of clubs in high school. What was so . . .

Oh no. *Prom Committee.*

"We don't have to talk about that," Bailey muttered.

"About what?" Kurt said. "*Prom?*"

"Nothing to talk about."

"The prom that abruptly ended due to the sprinklers going off?"

The non-locals-as-kids cried in surprise and demanded to know more.

Maria shook her head. "The prom night sprinkler incident. I remember that *very* well."

"Honestly, I kind of forgot about it." Bailey made her way past Kurt and Arnie on their side of the sectional couch. She'd had other things on her mind that night.

"How could you forget about that?" Kurt said. "The mad dash out of the gym . . ."

"The ruined dresses and rented tuxes," Maria added.

"And I looked good in my tux. You know, I didn't get my deposit back."

"I don't remember a lot from that year." Bailey tried keep her tone light. She sat uneasily, acutely aware of Maria's presence beside her.

Kurt still didn't get it, but Maria quickly sobered. "Oh gosh, of course," she murmured.

"I'm all set." Bailey held up her bowl of dip. "Let's get to trivia."

Raising a finger, Ellis said, "I'd like to hear more of this prom story."

Maria shifted on the couch. This was so awkward.

"So our prom used to be held at the high school," Kurt said. "It's not anymore, thanks to what happened this particular year. I would like to go on record as having *nothing* to do with this, by the way, other than being Bailey's date."

"Aww," Arnie cooed. "The two gay kids went to prom together?"

Bailey shared a nod with Kurt. "As friends," he said. "I was barely out. And you weren't at all, were you, Bails?"

Bailey shook her head. She hadn't told anyone until her early twenties. Saving Dad's business had taken precedence over everything.

Maria's gaze bored into the side of her head. Perhaps if things had been different, Bailey would've come out sooner. Although she'd suggested they could go to prom as friends too. Or they could tell people it was just as friends.

"Anyway," Kurt said. "A couple of the guys on the Prom Committee—"

"Maria's brother being one of them," Bailey said. "He was my co-chair."

"They wanted the lighting in the gym to be darker, to make out with their dates or whatever. Why someone gave them access to the gym's main controls is beyond me."

Maria nodded. "This all checks out."

"Whatever they did didn't affect the lighting, but somehow set off the sprinklers."

Those who hadn't been there moaned, "Oh no!"

Kurt laughed and continued. "You've never heard screaming like teenage girls with their hair and makeup ruined on the most important night of their lives."

Blips of memories played through Bailey's mind. "It was such a mess. The decorations, the refreshments, all got destroyed."

"That's terrible and hilarious," Ellis chuckled.

"It was enough for Lanford Falls High to never host prom again." Kurt turned to his husband. "I never did any actual damage to the building, unlike Danny Hatcher."

"So you say," Arnie joked.

Maria lightly touched Bailey's arm. "I wasn't supposed to go," she said quietly.

"That's . . ." *What you told me.*

"I went with Ted Anderson as a favor to Dan. Ted's date got mono and couldn't go. Dan begged me to go with him." She dipped her head, forcing Bailey to make eye contact. "He did my chores for a month."

"And thanked you by dumping water on you," Carter said.

"I wasn't supposed to go, Bailey," Maria said again, this time with conviction.

Bailey racked her brain to remember that night prior to the sprinklers. Lots of running around, making sure everything was going smoothly. Making things special for others, even in her youth. And then Maria had shown up with Ted and avoided her all evening.

It'd been the worst night of her life up to that point.

"Bails wore this fierce white suit," Kurt said. "But then white became the wrong thing to be wearing, hahaha!"

"Oh God, that's right," Bailey groaned. She'd found a chic white suit at a department store while half-heartedly shopping for a gown. One look and she'd known it was what she was meant to wear. Mom had been cool enough to be cool with it. She'd already suspected Bailey was never going to be an evening gown sort of woman.

"I love it when a woman rocks a power suit," Ellis said.

Bailey told her, "Thankfully, the jacket buttoned up enough so it didn't turn into a wet T-shirt contest."

"Wow." Yvette shook her head. "I thought the limo showing up late to my senior prom was bad. This takes the cake."

"Did anyone get in trouble for what happened?" Ellis asked.

"The committee got to clean up afterward," Bailey said. A brief memory of heavy wet crepe paper and lots of mopping sprang to mind. "That was punishment enough. Suffice it to say, I've surrounded myself with much better committees since then."

"I'll say," Maria said, and grinned.

Bailey shoved dairy and beans down her throat even though there was a ninety-nine percent chance it'd give her heartburn. Was Maria trying to make amends? Explain what had happened?

A conversation for another time, when they were alone. Because she had some questions.

Kurt pulled the lid off the small rectangular box housing holiday-themed trivia cards. "We can all agree Maria is going to be a fun addition to trivia night and whatever committees we rope her into being on."

"Hear, hear." Arnie raised his beer bottle in a toast.

Bailey turned to the pretty blonde on her left. "It looks like we're teammates," she said, overstating the obvious.

"Looks like it," Maria said.

"I'm not great at holiday trivia," Bailey admitted.

"Lucky for us, I am." She swayed her shoulders. "I have an endless supply of random knowledge."

"Then I'm glad you're my partner."

A bright smile blossomed across Maria's face. "I'm glad to be your partner."

Yeah, they definitely needed to talk. And soon.

"You all know the rules," Kurt said. "You ask your teammate a question. If they get it right, you get a point. If they get it wrong, someone else can answer to get a point. Then we pass the box, highest points wins, blah blah blah."

"What does the winning team get?" Maria asked.

"Bragging rights 'til the next trivia night," Ellis said.

"Kurt and Arnie usually win," Yvette added. "So you'll have to put up with them for a month."

Maria nodded at Bailey like she was up for the challenge. It would be nice to see the Driver-Hernandez trivia night monopoly come to an end, so she nodded back.

Kurt pulled a card from the front of the box. "And the first question is a multiple choice. In what year did the poem 'A Visit from St. Nicholas' first appear in the *Troy Sentinel*?"

As he read the options, Maria leaned in and murmured, "I know this one." A subtly floral perfume wafted off her hair.

Arnie wrinkled his nose. "I have no idea. C?"

His husband slumped into the couch. "Why do you always guess C?"

"D?"

"No second guesses," Ellis reminded them.

Looking at the other couples, Kurt asked, "Does anyone know the answer?"

Maria waved her hand like an eager student in the classroom. Kurt pointed at her. "It's B," she said. "The poem was first published in December 1823."

He consulted the card before saying, "That is correct."

Everyone cheered. Bailey high-fived her teammate. "Nice work."

"Being a giant nerd comes in handy sometimes," Maria laughed.

Arnie read from the next card. Some obscure movie question nobody got right. The box got passed to Bailey. She pulled out a card and knew at first glance Maria would get this one.

"Okay, partner. What is the name of the employer Ebenezer Scrooge visits with the Ghost of Christmas Past in *A Christmas Carol*?"

"Fezziwig," Maria said without hesitation. "He's mostly referred to as old Fezziwig or Mr. Fezziwig in the text, but the answer probably just says Fezziwig."

Bailey chuckled at the ultra-specific answer. "You are correct. The answer does just say Fezziwig."

"I figured."

The cheering was a bit more subdued this time. "I forgot you spend your days holed up inside a library," Kurt groused.

"Let's see how my partner fares." Maria took the game box from Bailey. She made a face at the card she drew. "What? Nobody knows this."

"Uh-oh," Paul said.

"Hope your meteorological knowledge is strong, partner. Multiple choice. What is the average annual snowfall in Santa Claus, Indiana?"

Bailey listened to the four options. "Well, it's Indiana," she mused aloud. "So it can't be a huge amount, but not a tiny amount. I'd say . . . A. Five inches."

"Nooo. Darn." Maria dropped her head back in defeat.

"That's okay," Bailey told her surprisingly competitive partner. A rather fun new layer to her.

Carter correctly guessed 7.6 inches. They continued passing the box and asking and answering questions about movies and animated holiday specials and song lyrics. The dogs alternately sat on each other, then chewed on one another. Maria was a good sport, but there was a definite glint of a strong desire to win shining in her big doe eyes.

Bailey set her empty bowl on the coffee table. She reached for the cookies on a crystal platter at the same time Maria did. Their hands brushed over a frosted sugar cookie. Tiny tingles danced through her fingers. She picked up the cookie and offered it to Maria.

"Thanks," Maria said. She quite possibly deliberately let her fingers graze Bailey's in the exchange. The tingles flared into sparks from her touch.

Arnie tallied the points. "Okay. Me and Kurt are in a tie with Bailey and holiday wunderkind Maria."

"Thanks to holiday wunderkind Maria," Bailey added, to which Maria grinned at her.

He pulled out a card, saying, "Let's wrap up another victory, hon. Oh, you can totally get this."

"Hit me." Kurt did the *Come at me* gesture with both hands.

"Complete the following lyrics to 'Rudolph the Red-Nosed Reindeer': *Rudolph with your nose so bright . . .*"

"*Won't you guide my sleigh tonight,*" Kurt sang in reply.

"That's how it's done." Arnie gave him a big high-five.

"It's okay," Maria said to Bailey. "We've got this."

Unfortunately, it was Bailey's turn to answer. "I'll do my best," she said.

"You'll do great." Maria patted her upper arm. She took the box from a smug Arnie. Pulled out a card. Her eyebrows wrinkled in concern. "Okay, partner. Put your thinking cap on. In *The Nutcracker*, who gives Clara a wooden toy nutcracker as a gift on Christmas Eve?"

"I actually know this." It was a Christmas miracle. "Herr Drosselmeyer."

Everyone was surprised. "How did you know that?" Ellis said.

"My sister was obsessed with *The Nutcracker* when we were kids. She made me watch every film adaptation of it."

"Thanks, Hannah," Maria said.

"Yeah, thanks, Hannah," Kurt drawled.

"The game is still tied." Maria presented the box of cards to him.

"Not for long. Come on, partner."

Arnie rubbed his hands together.

Kurt pulled out a card. He relaxed when he saw the question. "Easy-peasy. In what movie did the song 'White Christmas' first appear?"

"Why is that even a question?" Arnie said. "*White Christmas*."

Kurt's eyes ballooned, and his husband instantly knew it was wrong.

"No, wait, that's a trick question."

Maria jumped out of her seat. "It's *Holiday Inn*. Ha! Yes!" She raised her arms in victory.

Bailey jumped up too. "Holy cow, we did it!"

She high-fived Maria with both hands. Their fingers laced together, and they pulled one another close. Bailey's breath caught, her lips inches from Maria's forehead.

"Great job, partner," Maria said with one of her wrinkly-nosed smiles.

"You did the heavy lifting," Bailey breathed. She cleared the sudden frog from her throat and stepped back, untangling their hands.

Everyone was staring at them. Plus, she probably had major taco dip breath.

The dogs wagged over to see what the fuss was about. Rosie half leaped at Bailey, but Maria stopped her in time. Lulu gazed up like she would never dream of behaving so badly.

"Looks like we have a new trivia power couple," Ellis noted.

Yvette pointed at Kurt and Arnie. "Your reign of terror has ended."

Bailey caught Maria's eye, then just as quickly looked away. She scratched at Lulu's head. Her heart pounded like the Little Drummer Boy was tapping away at it. Trivia victory had never felt so good. She'd never gelled so well with a partner. An adorably competitive partner with beautiful eyes and a beautiful smile.

Everyone took a chocolate chip cookie and stood to toast one another merry holiday wishes. If they were all stuck in Lanford Falls, they might as well try to enjoy themselves.

She blinked that away. When had she gotten so bitter? These were her friends. The people who made her life full. She genuinely enjoyed trivia night and hanging out with them. And more than that, they were trying to dull the sting of her having to be there. They appreciated her sticking around. That made it bearable. Almost worthwhile.

"This was fun as always, but we need to head out," Yvette said. Paul nodded in agreement.

Ellis hung her head. "Sadly, I have to return to reality too."

"Go on," Arnie said. "Winners help clean up. Did we not tell you that, Maria?"

Maria crossed her arms. "You left that part out," she teased. "But I'm happy to help."

"I always stay and help," Bailey said.

"Because you have no life to get back to," Kurt said. He smiled down at Lulu, who noticed and trotted to him. "And I get more time with my Lulu Bear. Yes, I do, shmoopy-shmoo. If we didn't work such odd hours, I'd steal you away."

Rosie lumbered over and almost knocked him down with her enthusiasm. Maria covered her eyes and shook her head.

The host couple walked their guests toward the door. Bailey bade her friends good night, then started gathering plates and glasses from the coffee table. She cautioned the dogs away from snuffling at the crumbs.

Maria joined her. She smiled and said, "What's your trivia specialty? For future reference, partner." Did she emphasize *partner* a little? Like she liked referring to Bailey as her partner?

"Geography. And history."

"Really? You know a lot about history?"

"Yeah. I wanted to be an archaeologist when I was young. I was obsessed with ancient Egypt, medieval castles, Angkor Wat. All the things we don't have around here."

"I vaguely remember that," Maria said.

"I wanted to see the world and discover new, exciting things about ancient civilizations." She lightly nudged Maria with her elbow. "You want to talk nerdy? I used to read the encyclopedia for fun."

"I wish I'd known that." The teasing glint was back in her chocolate eyes. "We could have read it together."

"Eh, Dan would've sat on us and called us dorks."

"He absolutely would have," she laughed. "But it would've been worth it."

They shared a smile. Arnie and Kurt peeked around the corner, beaming at them. Bailey shot them a *Mind your own business* look as Maria focused on grabbing the cookie platter. Kurt shook his head while Arnie gave two big thumbs-up.

Maria straightened and followed Bailey toward the kitchen. Bailey ignored the broad grins from her friends.

"Should I set this on the counter?" Maria asked, cradling the fragile platter.

"Sure," Bailey said.

"So archaeology was your aspiration?"

"That had been the plan. It's why I got early admission to Stanford. Three years on campus, one year abroad in Europe. Then I'd join the hunt to learn about long-ago people and places."

"Hmm."

"Why hmm?" Bailey asked, bemused by the amusement playing across Maria's face.

Maria dusted cookie crumbs off her hands. "The study of really old things."

"To be honest, traveling across the globe was what most attracted me to it. We never vacationed farther than Canada when I was a kid."

They were quiet for a few moments. The air hung thick with the distinct sense Maria wanted to say something.

"Bailey, I've been meaning to—"

Arnie meandered in with bowls from the snack table. "So Maria," he drawled. "What's your story? Are you single? Seeing anyone?"

It took all of Bailey's strength not to shoo him out. What had Maria been meaning to do?

"I am very single," she said.

"How is that possible? You're the total package."

Kurt smirked at his husband as he entered the kitchen with more dishes, Lulu and Rosie at his heels.

"That's sweet of you to say." Maria gave a little shrug. "I'm starting a new chapter in my life. Focusing on the here and now, not the past."

"That's good." Arnie bobbed his head a few times. "Someone will see how awesome you are and snap you up."

"When you're ready," Kurt added. He flicked a glance at Bailey. "Or when that person realizes what a catch you are."

They were about as subtle as Lulu begging for a treat. Bailey ignored them again and pulled at the dishwasher door.

She caught Maria watching her as she reached for a pile of small plates. Not dwelling on the past was exactly the right attitude. The future was where the *real* excitement could be found. Maria got it. She had a solid game plan. She had goals to meet.

Well, Bailey had something brewing down in New York. Even if the job with Sammie's brokerage firm didn't pan out, it had lit a spark. Every fire needed that first flicker to get started.

This week proved Bailey had more than put in her time for everyone else. It was time to go after something different. Something more.

Something just for her.

THE ANGELS

Clara couldn't remember the last time she'd been inside a library. Her education had come from fashion magazines and online makeup tutorials.

The Angels had managed to stake out a good hiding spot among the shelves. The library had just opened for the day, and they didn't want to draw too much attention with their fabulocity.

That sweet little Maria Hatcher was setting up a craft project in the children's area. She'd neatly arranged art supplies on several small tables: popsicle sticks, pieces of felt, pipe cleaners, cotton balls, and of course, glitter.

Bailey came into view in the distance. The queens had been observing their reunion with great interest.

Clara smiled and said, "Right on time."

"I can't believe your wacky idea worked," Jovanna said.

"Swapping their phones in their coat pockets was a guarantee they'd see one another today. People can't function without their devices."

Gabriella simply raised her broad taupe eyebrows. She hadn't wanted Clara to interfere last night, but ultimately allowed it to be the younger Angel's call.

"She needed a nudge," Clara said.

Jovi waggled her tangerine-tipped nails. "Even a miracle needs a hand."

"Or a queen rocking a blue jumpsuit and wig Dolly Parton would covet." Clara patted her platinum blonde curls.

Bailey approached the kiddie table where Maria was straightening a pile of construction paper. Maria grinned when she saw her.

"Good morning," she said, reaching into the back pocket of her crisp slate gray pants.

"I still don't know how this happened." Bailey pulled a phone out of her coat pocket.

"I wonder if they fell out while we were getting ready to leave Kurt and Arnie's house, and we grabbed each other's. The dogs were being pretty rambunctious."

"Possibly."

As they traded smartphones, Clara murmured, "Sorry. It was the old switcheroo."

Maria pocketed her own phone. "Well, the good news is now we have one another's phone numbers."

"I should have yours, anyway," Bailey said. "For Winter Wonderfest stuff."

Jovi inhaled several sharp times, then stifled a sneeze. Then let out a loud *"Aaah-choo!"*

Both women looked in their direction. The Angels flattened themselves against the bookshelves. Slowly, cautiously, they peered over a row of tall books.

"Care to check out any titles from our history section?" Maria said. "Jump-start your love of old-timey things again?"

"Not today," Bailey said. She glanced at the art supplies. "What's going on here?"

"Ornament crafting."

"I used to love making those when I was a kid. My mom still has all of them."

"Who says you have to be a kid?"

Bailey nodded at one of the tot-sized table and chair sets. "It's being set up for Santa's little helpers."

"I have a few minutes until my training starts." Maria slid into a mini wooden chair. "Let's both make something to give our moms Christmas morning."

A flicker of amusement danced across Bailey's face. "Do I have to write *Bailey, Age 35* on the back?"

"Why not?" Maria giggled. She picked up a piece of red felt. Then a pair of rounded scissors. "I'm serious. Join me. I wanted to talk to you anyway."

Bailey glanced at her phone. Surely she didn't have any festival duties this early in the day.

Clara sent her a silent plea to have some holiday fun. This was exactly the sort of activity to bring Bailey Christmas cheer.

Silent pleas didn't usually work, though. Clara needed to be more direct. She focused her energy on the yellow chair next to Maria's. It bobbled and knocked into a table leg, causing a few pipe cleaners to roll off the tabletop.

"Shoot," she whispered.

Bailey picked them up, then considered them. Ooh—maybe the plan had worked. Clara made a victory fist, only her energy was still focused. Several shiny pompons skittered across the table. When Maria reached for them, she bumped a glitter container.

Clara flapped her hands to stop it from falling over. Which made the lid pop off and shower a poof of silver glitter into the air. Maria cried in surprise.

"Cut it out," Jovi hissed.

"I'm trying to," Clara moaned.

Gabi snapped her fingers to sever the connection. She side-eyed Clara. "This is why we don't interfere unless we have to."

"Sorry." Clara covered her mouth in embarrassment. She tried so hard. *Too* hard.

Bailey helped Maria scrape the rogue glitter onto a piece of construction paper. "Maybe the library should reconsider glitter in the future."

"Seriously," Maria said. "Good thing we covered the tables with plastic."

They cleaned the mess, chatting about the unique power of glitter to get inside every fiber and crevice. Clara really wanted to go invisible and get closer, only it wasn't worth risking another hiccup. Bailey wouldn't stick around simply to help Maria clean up craft supply messes.

Once they were done, Bailey set her coat over one chair. She sat in profile to the queens. Not the best sightline.

"We need a better view," Gabi murmured. She slid a picture book off a shelf and opened it in front of her face. Bright cartoon birds dotted the cover of *Birds! Birds! Birds!*

Jovi did the same with a *Where's Waldo?* book. Clara grabbed *Fun with Sock Puppets* from the opposite bookshelf and held it high. They crept to the edge of the shelving unit and peeked around their books.

"Rosie slept like a log last night," Maria said. "Lulu wore her out. She was too tired to go to the park this morning."

"Lulu zonked out too," Bailey said. "I had to wake her up to go to my mom's."

"It's nice for them to have an exercise buddy."

"Especially when it's cold outside."

Maria tilted her head. "Mm-hmm."

Jovanna hummed a bit of "Baby, It's Cold Outside." Clara and Gabi clucked their tongues at her because that was one creepy song.

"What are you making?" Maria asked.

"A snowflake." Bailey snagged a few popsicle sticks. "You?"

"Since it's for my mom, I'm going to shape some red and white felt into a heart and write Happy Holidays in Polish on it."

"Wesołych Świąt," Bailey said.

Maria grinned at her. "You remembered."

"Of course. Have you gone to Poland as an adult? I know you and Dan went a few times as kids."

"I went with my parents a few years ago at Christmastime. Before Nancy and I started dating."

"Ah." Bailey nodded as she colored a popsicle stick with an icy blue paint pen.

"It was nice to see my mother's family. They mostly live near Kraków, which is known for its szopki. Christmas cribs, like the one my parents have on their fireplace mantel. They can be huge, and look like churches or castles in a rainbow of colors. They're on display all over the city."

"That would be cool to see in person."

Maria cut into the red felt. "What's your bucket list place you'd like to visit?"

"Anywhere?" Bailey asked.

"Anywhere."

"I've always wanted to spend a month traveling across the British Isles. Fly into London and drive all around. Visit the old cities and the countryside. See if Nessie really exists at Loch Ness. End up in Ireland. Stop in tiny villages, have a pint at the local pub."

"That sounds great. Why haven't you done it?"

Bailey hesitated for a long moment. She set the blue stick aside and picked up a bare one. "I guess . . ." She shook her head. "Nah, it's too embarrassing."

"Tell me," Maria said, nudging her with an elbow. "It can't be that bad."

"I guess I don't want to take that trip alone. I've looked into group tours, but they feel too structured. I want to explore what I want, when I want, with someone who wants to do the same things."

Her subtext was so strong, Clara could feel it behind the sock puppet book.

I want to take that trip with someone special.

Maria breathed in to speak, only Bailey continued, "Though judging by my attempts to take a vacation this year, I'd be lucky to get a long weekend in Buffalo."

"You could enjoy the festivities in Lanford Falls. I hear it's really pretty this time of year."

"Mm-hmm." Bailey focused on coloring with a silver paint pen.

"No place I'd rather be," Maria said.

"Mm-hmm."

They hit a lull in their conversation. Clara shifted her weight, wanting to do something. Anything. Did these two not know what a cute couple they made, sitting there, crafting ornaments together?

Maria held up her pieces of red and white felt. "Don't they have archaeological vacations? Like you can visit a dig site or something? It might be fun to revisit an old passion."

With a shrug, Bailey said, "That's not really my jam anymore. I'm looking for a climate-controlled vacation with room service these days."

"You had such big dreams." Maria's eyes widened. "That came out weird. I meant I'd eavesdrop when you and Dan talked about what you wanted to do after college. You said you wanted to backpack across Europe."

A small smile tugged at one corner of Bailey's mouth. "That was something my dad and I used to fantasize about. He hiked part of the Appalachian Trail the summer after college graduation with my Uncle Bill. That's when they first started talking about opening a business together."

"Aww," Clara whispered.

"Mine was going to be a continental European backpacking trip. Possibly the summer after a year abroad. My dad knew I couldn't wait to get out of here."

Bailey's gaze fell to the paint pen. She capped it and set it aside, then grabbed a fresh stick and a white pen.

Maria offered her a kind smile. "I think everyone knew that. We talked about it one time. Over spring break, after . . ."

"After Mistletoe Grove."

They shared a long look. Jovi elbowed Clara and Gabriella, and Gabi nodded. The Angels physically felt the attraction simmering between the two women.

"I was always trying to be alone again with you," Maria said. "Which was hard, considering you were at the house to hang out with Dan."

Bailey refocused on her art project. "I kept trying to be alone with you too."

"Really?"

"Yeah. After school, outside the choir room, at your house . . ."

Maria leaned back in her chair. "I was doing the same thing! Too funny."

"I couldn't tell your brother why," Bailey said. "I think more than once, I pretended like I was looking for him." She darted a gaze at Maria. "But there *was* that one night, in your room. We sat on your bed. I was desperately trying to work up the courage to kiss you again."

"Me too." Maria wrinkled her nose. "But then my mom barged in to ask about homework or chores or something. I was so flustered."

"*You* were flustered?" Bailey laughed. "I almost got caught smooching one of my best friend's little sister. I think I ran out of your room."

"I think I did too."

They chuckled together. Clara set a hand on her chest. How adorably sweet and embarrassing in the best possible way.

"Hey, Bailey?" Maria's voice came quietly.

"Hmm?"

"I'm really sorry about prom." She glanced up through her lashes. "I wanted to go with you. I really did."

Clara leaned in, searching Bailey's face for a reaction. It appeared as though she was carefully choosing her words.

"It's okay," she finally said. "I mean, I was pretty hurt and confused. You said your parents told you you couldn't go. Money was tight, and you couldn't afford a dress and new shoes and everything. But then . . ."

"Then I ended up going," Maria finished. "Like I said, Dan bribed me. I felt so bad, but I didn't know how to tell you."

"Tell me what?"

"Money *was* tight at that time. That part was true. I borrowed a dress from my cousin. Only . . ." Her eyebrows bunched together. "I never asked them if I could go."

Bailey tilted her head. "You never told them I asked you? Even to go as friends?"

Maria shook hers. "No. I chickened out. I . . . I just wasn't ready. I wasn't sure how to explain it, and honestly, I wasn't even, like, *sure* . . ." Quirking her lips, she said, "I didn't want to go as friends. Especially after what happened at Mistletoe Grove, and what almost happened at my house. It freaked me out a little."

"Is that why you avoided me the rest of the school year?"

"I felt so bad about lying to you, I couldn't face you. I'm so sorry."

"It's okay," Bailey said again. "Deep down, I suspected it just wasn't your time. To be honest, I'm not sure why I asked you. Other than . . ."

Their eyes met, gazes locking. Clara sensed the growing attraction deep inside.

"Well, because I wanted to ask you."

That made Maria smile.

Clara smiled too. It was so good they were having this conversation.

"In retrospect, I don't know if I was ready, either." One corner of Bailey's mouth tugged upward. "I got swept up in the moment, like at Mistletoe Grove."

Maria leaned briefly into Bailey's side. "I really regretted not going with you. Especially after I saw you in that white suit."

"I want to see pictures of this suit," Clara muttered.

"I don't really remember what you wore," Bailey said. "That whole night's still kind of a blur."

"Don't you mean a washout?" Maria giggled. "Sorry. Couldn't resist."

"You might have been roped into cleaning up, so consider yourself lucky."

"I meant to tell you the truth. I was going to, but then your dad passed, and you were so busy. I didn't want to bother you with something so trivial compared to what you were going through."

Bailey nodded slowly.

"Can I make it up to you?" Maria asked.

"You don't have to."

"I am at your disposal for my lunch hour. Whatever you need help with." She set her hand on Bailey's arm. "I'm here for you. I'm not going anywhere."

A range of emotions played across Bailey's face. "Thanks," she said, though oddly strained.

They crafted for a minute in a comfortable silence. Perhaps it was a bit tenuous on Bailey's part. An old wound beginning to heal.

A young Black man wearing a library staff lanyard approached the table. "Getting a head start on the kids?" he asked.

Bailey and Maria laughed and agreed. Maria noticed the specks of glitter she'd left on Bailey's deep purple sleeve and brushed them off. "I really should start my day," she said. "I'll finish my ornament with the kids. Do you want to take your project with you?"

Bailey considered her popsicle sticks. "I think I'll glue mine together first."

Clara swayed her padded hips in excitement. That was a very good sign.

Gabriella motioned with her head behind her bird book for them to fall back. The queens slowly tiptoed backwards in their heels.

Clara peeked around her book to watch Maria and Bailey exchange goodbyes. Maria gave her a pointed look and said, "I'll see you soon."

"Okay," Bailey said.

She reached for a bottle of glue. She shook it upside down, studied the opening, then shook it again.

Slowly, delicately, Clara pinched her thumb and index finger together just a bit. Enough to get the glue to flow out in a gentle stream. She breathed deeply, willing everything to maintain its steadiness.

Mercifully, it worked. Bailey pressed on her popsicle sticks to form them into a snowflake. She shook her head at the basic ornament, but she was smiling.

The library employee walked past the Angels. He paused, causing them to stiffen behind their open books. "Are we having drag queen story time today?" he asked.

"Ooh, that sounds fun." Jovi lowered her book to grin at him.

"Reading *is* fundamental," Clara said.

Gabi glanced over the top of her book at Bailey walking away from the table. "I think we can swing it this morning."

"Cool," the young man said.

"Hope to see you there," Jovi said, and winked.

He laughed and said he'd try to make it.

The Angels moved to reshelve their books. They lived to help anyone in need through their abilities. Reading to tiny tots with their eyes all aglow was just another way to bring cheer and share joy.

Good things all around. And one step closer to Clara getting her wings.

CHAPTER SIX

Bailey glanced at Martin's main entrance from her seat at the counter. Then she checked the time on her tablet again. Only three minutes had passed. Maria was due to meet up for lunch at one o'clock and was late. Which was fine—she was coming from work.

Her heart did that pulsing thing it'd been doing since last night. Well, since Tuesday night. Reconnecting with Maria was the lone bright spot in this unfortunate week. Though as fun as it had been, it could've waited a week.

The glass door opened to three older women laden with shopping bags. Disappointment sank in her stomach like a stale bran muffin.

Maria had said she was here for her. She wouldn't stand her up, would she? Not after their conversation earlier. Not after they'd cleared the air and were moving forward.

"Rockin' Around the Christmas Tree" began to play overhead as an incoming text from Hannah popped onscreen.

Sending a Happy Thursday hug! Still sad for your vacay but happy I'll get to see you Saturday. ☺

Bailey went to type a reply when another text popped up.

Have you seen Maria at the dog park again?

She could honestly answer no. That would get Hannah off her back. She didn't want to encourage anyone to think there could be something brewing with Maria. Not her family, not her friends, not even their dogs. Once they caught a whiff of possibility, they'd be relentless in their *Go on a date!* nagging. That was so not something Bailey needed with this potential new job opportunity.

Still, she felt lighter inside. Maybe a bit wistful. She hadn't thought about her childhood aspirations in forever. The hours spent learning about wonders across the globe. Counting the years until she was old enough to go to college, to travel through Europe. It was nice to remember something she thought she'd lost. Like a piece of pottery buried under thousands of years of sand. Waiting for someone to come along and unearth it. Someone like Maria.

Wait, what? Maria?

Maria was great, but someone putting down roots in the Falls was not Bailey's ideal mate.

But that didn't mean she didn't want to see Maria while she was still here.

The prom explanation had been nice. Okay, it'd been *really* nice to hear Maria had wanted to say yes. That she hadn't ignored Bailey for any awful reason.

Talking to her was so easy. She made Bailey comfortable enough to open up about the past, about her dreams. Very few people could do that. Very few people had ever been able to do that.

The door swung open to Maria in her Christmassy green coat. Bailey's heart thumped a few times. Jeez, maybe it was stress-induced tachycardia.

Or relief. Maria hadn't let her down.

"I'm so sorry I'm a little late," she said, pulling off her mittens.

"No trouble at all." Bailey closed the cover on her tablet.

Maria slid onto the seat next to hers. "It's worth it, though. I mentioned I was helping with Winter Wonderfest to the outgoing director, who's been training me. He heard about everything that happened, and . . ." She twirled her mittens. "He told me to take the afternoon off. I can help you the whole rest of the day."

"That's good," Bailey said. "I could use a warm body."

Maria started to speak, then stopped. Oh, crap. *Warm body* was not the best choice of words.

"A capable set of hands," Bailey amended, but that sounded even worse. "Uh . . . Another committee member." There, that was way more neutral.

Maria blinked, then settled her mittens in her lap. "I'm all those things," she murmured.

Bailey cleared the thickness from her throat. *I'm sure you are.*

She waved at Martin to get his attention. "Hello, ladies," he said, heading over with his little pad and pen at the ready.

"What's good today?" Bailey asked.

"The tomato soup and grilled cheese combo." Martin leaned on the counter. "My wife calls it the Cozy Blanket Combo."

"That sounds perfect." Raising her eyebrows at Maria, Bailey said, "I'm buying, so get whatever you want."

"Ooh, in that case . . ." Maria tapped her fingertips together. "Make that two Cozy Blanket Combos and a hot tea."

"And then a nap," Martin said with a wink.

Bailey chuckled. "No naps today, I'm afraid."

"Taking it to go, as usual?"

"I'm okay eating here." She glanced at Maria. "Are you?"

"Sure," Maria said.

Martin pursed his lips in surprise. "Well now, this is a rare treat."

"It's been a strange week, Marty," Bailey said.

"That it has." He slid his pen behind an ear. "Lunch is on the house. I heard what you did for the festival. You're a heck of a kid, Bailey."

She gave him a small smile in gratitude. "That's not necessary, but thank you."

Martin gestured like it was nothing before turning to put the order in. Shaking her head, Maria said, "I've missed this town. Everyone helping each other out."

Bailey made a noise in agreement. That was one nice thing about the Falls.

"Thanks for the free lunch," Maria joked, shrugging out of her coat.

"It's the least I could do for the committee head of meals."

Her arm got stuck in her attempted coat removal while sitting on a swivel stool. Bailey tugged on the sleeve, gathering the coat as it gave way. A hint of floral perfume clung to the lining, along with Maria's warmth.

Maria thanked her and reached for her coat. Bailey fought the urge to hug the welcoming heat, to bury her nose in the wool blend, to breathe in Maria's scent.

She really could use a warm body and capable hands.

Maria pushed up the sleeves on her cream-colored knit sweater. Bailey gave her plum blouse and dark-wash jeans a quick inspection for glitter. She'd worn both today because she felt confident in them, and wanted to look nice. Because she'd be going all around town, interacting with lots of people.

Sure. Right.

"What's on the agenda for the rest of the day?" Maria asked.

"Right now, they're setting up the food tent. The frames for the vendor booths should be out of storage, so those will be put in place. The emails got a little out of hand for Jane. Susan was discharged from the hospital this morning." Bailey picked up her tablet and set it in her messenger bag. "I dealt with those so Jane could help her family."

"What can I do?"

"If you want to come with me to Town Hall, I need to pick up the signs. We stick them all over the place to direct people where to go. We discovered tourists start showing up a day early for Wonderfest. It's better to have the signs up before Friday."

"Aye, aye, Captain." Maria gave a military-style salute. "You won't have to go it alone."

Bailey sipped from her water glass. It would be nice to have the extra help from an enthusiastic aide. An aide with big eyes and an easy smile and boundless thoughtfulness.

A familiar figure stepped inside. Uncle Bill. She raised a hand in greeting, only he turned to scowl over his shoulder. A long arm caught the door, followed by the rest of Felicity Potter. She came in looking like a puff of stale air. Dull gray hair under a drab gray hat.

She and Uncle Bill had one of their usual staring contests. Then he grunted and made his way to the cashier. He probably disliked her more than anyone, which was really saying something.

Bailey focused on him and not the hawk-like eyes burning a hole in her back. "Chili Thursday?" she called down to him, then muttered to Maria, "Every Thursday."

"Chili Thursday," Uncle Bill said. He reached over the counter to accept his to-go container from one of the servers.

"Ms. George." Felicity's voice made the hair prickle on the back of Bailey's neck.

She half turned and gave a flat, "Ms. Potter."

"I must say I am not at all surprised to see you."

"I made the choice to stay and help my friends."

"Indeed." Felicity shot a pointed look at Maria before directing her disdain at Bailey. "What would they do without you?"

At least I have friends. "What would the town do without the boost of income from the festival?" Bailey reminded her.

"Of course. Charm alone does not keep the lights on." Felicity watched Uncle Bill pay for his chili. "You of all people know that, having to work with that man."

Uncle Bill grunted again.

Ignoring her slight, Bailey said, "At least I'm doing something to preserve the charm of the town. What was it you proposed we do with the oldest section of Main Street? Tear down the buildings and put up condos instead of making structural repairs?"

"The location was ideal. Smaller housing options are needed in town. Not everyone wants the upkeep of a house and yard."

They were still having this argument, years later? "We'd have lost the florist and a well-established art gallery and two other businesses that have been in their families for generations. And there are apartments above those spaces. The tenants pay much less in rent than what you'd sell the condos for."

"Neither of us sees a profit from old buildings with a low turnover rate," Felicity said.

"Not everything is about profit."

She stared at Bailey for several moments. "You are your father's daughter."

"Thank you."

"It's not meant to be a compliment," she chortled. "He made emotional decisions, not rational. It nearly cost him the business long before you took over."

Heat flashed across Bailey's cheeks. "My father believed in doing what was right, even if he didn't get a financial windfall from it."

"While that's admirable in spirit, it is not the way to run a business."

"Well, it's how George Family Homes has managed to stay afloat all these years." Her heartbeat pounded in anger.

Felicity took a step closer and leaned in. "Wouldn't it be nice not to have to stay afloat, but prosper? You don't have to eke out an existence."

"We're doing just fine. Now if you'll excuse me, I'd like to enjoy lunch with my friend."

Bailey purposely turned and focused her attention on Maria. Her friend's eyes were as round as the saucer beneath the mug Martin set in front of her.

"My offer to buy you out always stands, Ms. George," Felicity said.

"And it will always be rejected."

"You'd have the financial freedom to travel. To live where you like, do what you like."

"Never going to happen," Bailey stated.

Maria made a face like *Dang, that's impressive.* Felicity finally shuffled off to dampen someone else's day.

Uncle Bill kept his eyes trained on her as he walked over with his Styrofoam container. "She give you any trouble?"

"Never," Bailey said. "She's a glorious ray of light."

His mouth twisted and he turned to leave. Then he turned back. "I miss your dog. Can you bring her by the office?"

She couldn't help the laugh that bubbled up. "Maybe I'll bring her by later."

Maria looked between him as he left and Felicity as she sat in a booth against the windows. "So much drama," she murmured.

Bailey did a little shrug. "He never forgave her for trying to move in on my dad's business after he passed away. She's never forgiven him for . . . existing. Uncle Bill was the one who convinced the other employees not to cave in."

"I see."

"He didn't want everything my dad worked for to get torn down. Literally and figuratively." Her heart gave a slight pinch. Gruff Uncle

Bill was the most loyal person she knew. That must've been why animals loved him so much.

Her pulse thudded in her neck. Man oh man, could Felicity get under her skin. "She even tried to fight the Beautification Committee on having the affordable housing subdivision built," Bailey added. "Her vision of Lanford Falls is an exclusive community for the wealthy."

Maria cast the old woman one last glance before swiveling her seat to face front. "I think she's jealous of you."

"What?" Bailey laughed.

"You're young, and smart, and successful, and super gorgeous, and you have a big heart. And your dog adores you, and your friends and family do too. Yeah, she's totally jealous."

A slight blush crept across Maria's smooth cheeks. What was that part about being super gorgeous? Maria was the super gorgeous one. A person could spend an entire hour gazing into those big brown eyes, and then another hour appreciating her nose, and about four hours enjoying her lips. Soft, supple lips that had crept into Bailey's thoughts a lot lately.

"She's just a cranky, lonely person." Bailey wagged a finger. "She did it to herself, so no sympathy here. She values money more than relationships."

"And you value people over profit."

"I guess." Her mouth quirked into a half-smile. "Though profit's nice too. Lulu's grown accustomed to a certain kind of lifestyle."

Maria's joyous laugh was music to her ears. She rested her hand on Bailey's forearm and squeezed. "For Lulu, then."

Her hand looked so nice on the dark purple material. Felt so nice. The urge to take her hand, to slide their fingers together, coursed through Bailey's veins. She had to stop herself from capturing Maria's hand when she drew it back.

Talk about being lonely. Maria was . . .

Okay, Maria was kind of everything she liked in a woman. Smart, and witty, and funny, and driven, and a little quirky, and she had the biggest heart, and dogs loved her as much as people. And *super* gorgeous yet completely approachable.

Arnie was right. Maria Hatcher was the total package.

Well, the total package with one huge shortcoming: she had zero plans to leave Lanford Falls. She'd said there was no place she'd rather be. That she wasn't going anywhere. Plus, just because they'd had one conversation about what happened with prom didn't erase years of uncertainty. Sure, she'd shown up to help with the festival, but then what? And what if Bailey got a new job and moved?

Wait a second. What if she *did* move to the city? What would happen to George Family Homes? Could she trust someone to take it over? Everything Dad had built, everything she'd strived to carry on, could go away. But almost as bad, Felicity Potter would win. Lanford Falls would lose.

Crap.

Crap, crap, crap. Reality came crashing through her dreams again. It always did.

She *was* her father's daughter.

Maria smiled at her over her mug. "Thinky face."

"What's with you and thinky face?" Bailey wanted to know.

"You tell me. You're the one with all the thinky thoughts."

"I think . . ." She saw Martin snag their lunch plates. "It's time for a Cozy Blanket Combo."

Ah, food, the great distracter. Bailey busied herself with stirring the steaming bowl of tomato soup. Maria settled a paper napkin on her lap. It wasn't like Bailey could tell her about the lifelong push-pull of wanting to do right versus getting to live life on her own terms. How she thought Maria was impossibly adorable, but nothing could happen between them.

"Can I ask you for a favor?" Maria said quietly.

"Sure." *Everyone always does.*

Her gaze swept over Bailey beneath long eyelashes. "Will you tell me someday?"

When she didn't elaborate, Bailey said, "Tell you what?"

"What you aren't telling me." Maria focused on her grilled cheese. "I'm tempted to say what you don't tell anyone, but that's a tad presumptuous. Though I don't think you do tell anyone."

Whoa, she'd really hit the nail on the head. Bailey couldn't talk about her aching sense of duty without feeling guilty for complaining about it. She couldn't tell Mom or Hannah or Uncle Bill she wouldn't trade a moment of all they'd been through, but also wished she hadn't had to give up so much. It was delicate, and messy, and not something to dump on someone else.

It was her burden. Nobody else needed to be weighed down by it. Besides, if Maria really wanted to know something, she should ask directly.

"Do you have any specific questions, trivia partner?" Bailey asked.

"Hmm." Maria took a bite out of her sandwich. Took her time chewing and swallowing. "If you were one of Santa's reindeer, which one would you be?"

"*That's* your burning question?" Bailey laughed.

"I base all my opinions about a person on this answer." Her eyes twinkled mischievously.

"So there's a wrong answer?"

"There is absolutely a wrong answer."

"Oh *dear*." Bailey slid her a sidelong glance. "Get it?"

"I got it."

She had no clue which one to pick. Dasher sounded like a workaholic. Dancer and Prancer, no. Vixen, hard no. Comet? Cupid? Donner, or drunken Blitzen?

Maria burst into the giggles. "I'm a hundred percent kidding. I looked at that paper decoration."

Bailey followed her gaze above the prep station to the long cardboard cutout of Santa's sleigh being pulled by a team of trusty flying reindeer. "Sneaky, Hatcher. Very sneaky."

"I shouldn't have said anything. I want to know which one you'd pick."

"Rudolph," Bailey decided. "Kind of an oddball. Helps guide others to great things."

Maria's perceptive eyes studied her. "You *are* a Rudolph."

The truth of the answer hung low in Bailey's gut. Guiding others to greatness was so incredibly accurate. "What about you?" she countered. "I'd say . . . Cupid. Or Prancer."

"Really?" Maria smiled wide. "Why?"

"Because you're cute, and those are the cutest names. You kind of have a spring in your step, like a prance. Like . . ." Heat rose up her neck, and it wasn't from the soup. "You just prance around, and are nice and friendly to everyone, and . . . Prancer."

She felt like a rambling teenager. But Maria's smile kept on growing. "Right answer," she murmured, and took a big bite of her grilled cheese.

CHAPTER SEVEN

The atmosphere in the village green mixed and mingled with hard work and holiday cheer. Cloud cover had gradually filled the sky, hinting at potential snow flurries.

Bailey watched Maria press her entire body weight into a small laminated sign on a lamppost. A grin tugged at her mouth. Her hardworking committee member had been a rock star that afternoon. Downtown was now full of signs directing visitors toward the Wonderfest. She checked her messenger bag to see how many were left. A few more and they'd be done.

Maria stood back and admired her handiwork. "That's some industrial tape we're using."

"We don't mess around," Bailey said. "Lots of trial and error over the years. This stuff is great. Super sticky, but hardly leaves a residue when we take them down."

"I'm learning so much about all the behind-the-scenes stuff."

She nudged Maria with her elbow. "Then you can take over the committee next year."

"Maybe I will." She lightly bopped Bailey with the thick roll of tape. "Will you be my adviser?"

"If by adviser you mean give advice but don't actually get involved . . ."

"As long as I can pick your brain." With a teasing smile, Maria added, "And that you make sure I eat."

Bailey laughed at the thought. "I hope you like takeout. The only thing I can cook is a bowl of cereal."

"I like cereal." Something in her eyes suggested she'd very much like to have breakfast with Bailey.

Having breakfast together did sound nice. Particularly if that breakfast came after Maria spent the night. A low, throbbing rumble reminded her it'd been a long time since any such breakfasts had taken place at Bailey's house. Or anyone's house.

Movement to their right snagged her attention. The park district employees had gathered their tools and were walking away from the huge white food tent. Tomorrow, they'd set up the tables and folding chairs inside it for people to sit and enjoy their snacks.

Vince walked over. His long limbs gave him a loose, loping gait. "We're done for the day. Everything's good."

"Much appreciated." Bailey crossed her arms and considered the tent and its side walls. "Is it crooked? On that back side?"

Vince settled his hands on his hips. "Might be a little. The ground's uneven from the snow. It'll settle."

"Are you sure? I don't remember it ever looking so wonky."

"It's the same one we use every year."

She didn't doubt that. The rental center out near the highway had supplied this behemoth since forever. Still . . . "I swear, it's crooked."

"I assure you, it's secure," Vince said.

It did look off, but there were little piles of snow here and there. The tent would even out as they melted.

She thanked him and waved goodbye to the crew. Maria tilted her head, then said, "It is a little slanted in the back."

"If it looks bad tomorrow, they'll fix it."

"Next sign, please." She made a grabby hand.

Bailey pulled out one of the laminated sheets of paper. A big gold star hovered above bold red letters announcing *SHOP*. "This goes on the side of the first shopping vendor booth," she said.

They made their way down the paved path. On Saturday, the open space beside the tent would fill up with carts and portable food apparatuses. And always that one festival newbie who didn't come prepared and expected Bailey to perform some kind of miracle to get their hibachi on wheels to work.

Maria closed her eyes and breathed deep. "I'm imagining the smells. That Gruber hot cocoa . . ."

"The stench of burnt hibachi meat."

"Eww."

"You must've missed Wonderfest that year," Bailey said. "The guy turned it up way too hot."

Maria wrinkled her nose. "I'm glad I missed that one."

Large plastic tubs sat open, bursting with fake garland and wide rolls of red and blue velvety ribbon. Pete and Tom were busy outlining the wooden frames for the little vendor booths. Thank God they were able to help or the chore would've fallen on Bailey. And they actually enjoyed it, unlike Bailey.

"Looks great, guys," she said as she stepped off the path.

They thanked her from where Pete held a ladder for Tom to secure a high swag. "We're shaking up the design this year," Pete said. "Alternating one booth with ribbon, then the next with garland."

"Knock yourselves out," Bailey said, then quickly amended, "Not literally. Be careful up there, Tom."

"Always." Tom wobbled on the narrow step. "The snow will cushion me if I fall."

"You'll crash on top of me and *I'll* cushion your fall," his brother said.

"Please do neither." Bailey stayed close to Maria as they walked to the first station. They swung wide to avoid being toppled over by overzealous decorators.

She held the sign as Maria readied several pieces of very sticky tape while humming "Deck the Halls." She'd been humming Christmas carols all afternoon, like the secret elf she was.

As Maria hung the sign, Bailey checked her phone in case Jane had forwarded any particularly pesky emails. The only notification was a flash sale alert for cheap Broadway tickets.

Her stomach sank. That had been her vacation plan for tonight—treating herself to a fancy dinner before catching a splashy, big-budget musical. Nothing at all to do with the holidays.

Maria hummed with more gusto. It wasn't exactly big-budget, though she did have good pitch. Bailey blew out a sigh. Maybe she'd treat herself to a pizza with extra toppings for dinner. Maybe Maria would want to join her.

No. Well, yes, Maria would absolutely want to join her, but it would send the wrong message. Bailey had promised her a hot cocoa at the festival, and that would be it. That and being her trivia partner in the future. And occasional dog park friend.

Maria took a few steps back as Tom wavered on the ladder. "Please tell me the other signs don't go near here," she murmured.

Bailey snagged the last two signs. *Of course.* Both had red hearts on them and curly letters directing couples toward Mistletoe Grove. She held them out for Maria to see.

Her light eyebrows rose. "I know where that is."

"Me too," Bailey said.

They shared a long look. Her heart throbbed hard in her chest. Then skipped a beat when Tom jumped off the ladder. He was just getting down, but still. This week was going to give her a heart attack.

"Will you *please* be careful," she said. "It's cold, and those metal steps can be slippery."

"Sorry, boss," Tom called.

She stuck the signs in her messenger bag and trudged back to the path. Maria hustled to catch up. Bailey shoved her hands in her coat pockets, feeling Kurt's treats for Lulu.

They passed the booth for the snowman building competition on the left. Bailey stopped at the lamppost just before the path curved into the woods and ended. She wordlessly snagged one of the signs. Maria taped it up quietly.

They were nearly there. The scene of the kiss—*the* kiss—once again.

Maria faced her, turning the roll of tape over in her hands. "Where does the last one go?"

Bailey pointed to where the grouping of evergreens grew thicker. "In there."

Mistletoe Grove.

They walked side by side until the paved path ended. The archway was already set up thanks to Pete and Tom. For two guys who wrote some fairly gory books, they were pretty romantic.

The grove was just a wrought-iron bench and a little arbor decorated with greenery and twinkle lights and a big ball of mistletoe in the middle. It looked much the same as it had the one and only time Bailey had stood beneath it. In the dark, with the same woman standing beside her now.

She awkwardly shoved the sign at Maria. "It goes on the lamppost in case anyone has any question what this is."

Maria nodded, then went over to the metal post beside the bench. Bailey wandered in a circle, studying the arbor. She glanced over at Maria. Maria caught her gaze and smiled. That smile had grabbed Bailey's attention years ago, and had tightened its hold again.

Her teenage crush was back, bringing a giddy flutter and sharp desire to be right here, right now with Maria Hatcher.

Bailey's senior year, they'd run into one another at the festival, and hung out with a group of music department nerds. They'd watched the concert, and then the other kids drifted off in pairs or went home. She and Maria wandered down the path, ending up in Mistletoe Grove.

At first, they'd sat on the bench and talked. About what was lost to time. But then something shifted. Something pulled at Bailey to go over to the romantic archway. She'd never stood under it. Had never wanted to. And then Maria joined her, like she was also being drawn by some invisible force. The magic of Winter Wonderfest had swept them up.

It had been scary and exhilarating wanting to kiss Maria. Any girl, really, but especially Dan's little sister.

She'd kissed Maria so sweetly, so innocently. It was only a few minutes of soft, short kisses and a few self-conscious hand placements on shoulders and waists. But it opened a doorway wide inside. She left that night wanting to kiss Maria again, also knowing with complete certainty she only wanted to kiss pretty girls like Maria again.

Something rustled in the pine trees. Probably a squirrel, although . . . Bailey caught a flash of bright orange. She craned her neck, but it was gone. Whatever. Must've been a cardinal.

Once the sign was hung, Maria joined her. She handed Bailey the tape. "Job well done, partner," she said.

"One more thing off the list." Bailey tossed the tape in her bag.

Maria rocked back and forth on her boot heels. She seemed to make a decision, then stepped over to the archway. She touched the garland draped along one side. "If this thing could talk, huh?"

"Oh boy," Bailey half laughed. "I'm not sure all the stories would be suitable for work."

"I'm sure. But most are." She cast a glance back at Bailey. "Mine is."

"It is," she agreed.

Maria stood there, glowing from the soft lights like the angel on top of a Christmas tree. Like how Bailey had seen her that night—really *seen* her for the first time.

Bailey walked over and stared up at the dark green kissing ball dotted with plastic white flowers and red berries. "You were the first girl I kissed," she admitted.

"You were the first *girl* I kissed." Maria smiled. "But not the last."

That made Bailey laugh. "That was a special moment." She met Maria's smile. "I'm glad it was with you."

"Me too." She leaned against the arbor. "I never told anyone about that night."

"Me neither."

Her grin widened. "I like that we've had this little secret all these years."

Bailey regarded her for a moment, her pulse points thumping a strong and steady rhythm. "Yeah."

Maria looked down at her pale pink fingernails. "Can you keep another secret?"

"Sure."

"That kiss is my all-time favorite holiday memory. More than any toy I got as a kid."

Bailey opened her mouth to say something like *Really?* Except . . . it was her favorite holiday memory too. Winter Wonderfest used to mean a lot to her. Kissing Maria had been the cherry on top.

"It's . . ." Maria drew in the snow with the toe of her boot. "It's why I wanted to help you with the festival. To make sure it's a special memory for someone else too."

She wasn't sure if Maria meant making it special for Bailey, or a general someone. "I appreciate all your help," she said. "And I appreciate you bringing a little fun to this week. It would've sucked otherwise."

"Yeah?" Maria looked so hopeful.

"Yeah. I'd be a lot hungrier and grumpier."

She shook her head and pushed Bailey back. Their hands grazed in the process. Because she'd reflexively reached for Maria's fingers.

They shared a private smile. Maria's eyes slid down to Bailey's mouth. Time inched to a standstill.

What do you say, Maria? Want to give the old arbor a go? See if it still has any magic?

"You know . . ." Maria began, but giggling and shushing came from down the path. A teen girl and a boy in a Lanford Falls High School jacket crept around the bend.

"Still the most popular make-out spot in town," Bailey murmured. *Which I was hoping to rediscover, damn it. Thanks a lot, kids.*

Maria blinked. Their intimate bubble had dissolved, so Bailey took a step back. She gestured at the archway and said, "It's all yours, guys."

Maria looked up at the kissing ball. "Make some holiday memories. But responsibly."

The girl giggled harder. The boy rubbed at his reddening neck in embarrassment.

Bailey adjusted her messenger bag and fell in step with Maria. The look of disappointment on her face would've made the Grinch cry. Had she felt the magic again too?

She shook off the mental glitter and flutters. What was with Mistletoe Grove? And Maria at Mistletoe Grove? Nostalgia was a powerful drug.

Bailey nudged her as they made their way back into the village green. "Teenagers," she said. *Like we were.*

"They were so cute." Maria crossed her hands on her chest. "To be so young and carefree again."

"To actually care about Winter Wonderfest again," Bailey said without thinking.

"Of course you care."

She shook her head. "It's a chore."

"I refuse to believe that. Anyone who cancels a trip to stay and help cares a lot about it."

"I care that the town doesn't lose precious revenue."

Maria halted her steps and faced her. "When are you going to stop saying that? You care that it's special. I've seen it in how you're handling everything. It matters to you, Bailey. It matters more than you want to admit."

She *wanted* it to matter, but it couldn't. Not after what happened this year. "I care that it's special for people. I want attendees to have a good time. It just doesn't matter on a personal level. It's another chore on my Lanford Falls to-do list. It has been for years."

Maria planted her hands on her hips. "Do you know what you need?"

"A vacation," Bailey answered very seriously.

"You need music." Maria grabbed one of her hands and pulled her down the path.

"Music?" She stumbled to keep up with the determined woman. Maria's dainty hand gripped her own like there was zero room for discussion.

She dragged Bailey toward the Christmas tree near the entrance. The high school madrigal singers stood in a semicircle in matching blue-and-white knit scarves. Their four-part harmony of "Ding Dong Merrily on High" echoed in the late afternoon air.

"Christmas music is exactly what you need, Grumpy McGrumperton." Maria was so emphatic, it pulled a grin right out of Bailey.

They stopped when they reached the group of twelve singers. Maria kept a firm hold on Bailey's hand, but it was more of a command to stay put than anything tender. Still, it felt nice to be holding hands.

They listened to the bright, bouncy tune until its crescendo to the final note. Maria let go to applaud. The sudden absence of her touch left a cold spot on Bailey's palm. She clapped to get some feeling back, and also because the kids sounded good. The madrigals were a select group of standouts from the school choir. Some years, they were better than others. This was a particularly tight group.

"Do you take requests from alumni?" Maria asked.

The teens laughed. A tall white boy in the middle said, "Sure."

"Do you still do 'Bring a Torch, Jeanette, Isabella'? That was one of my favorites."

"Yeah." The boy readied his pitch pipe. "You can sing along if you remember it."

Maria giggled. "I'll see if I can." She elbowed Bailey. "My friend will too. Won't you, fellow choir alumna?"

"You didn't say I had to sing," Bailey muttered.

"Singing releases endorphins, Grumpy."

The a cappella group erupted into the waltzing rhythm. Maria fumbled through the words, but soon caught on. Sopranos, always with the melody. She raised her eyebrows at Bailey, wordlessly demanding she give it a shot.

Bailey listened for the alto line. It came rushing back to her, like muscle memory.

Her voice was raspy and weak, but she found the notes. Maria nodded in encouragement and sang louder. Bailey bopped her head in time and shared a smile with three girls standing nearby. One gave her a thumbs-up. Her fellow altos, holding the song together.

Maria started swaying, bumping Bailey each time she moved to the left. Bailey finally bumped her back and gently rocked side to side.

They reached the last few measures of the song. She caught Maria's gaze as they sang *"Beautiful is the mother."*

Her voice cracked on the last note, but the kids and Maria applauded the effort. So did a couple of bystanders. Hopefully not potential homebuyers or sellers.

"Thank you." Maria clasped her hands in utter delight. She asked the teens about a few other songs. Groans and rolled eyes mixed with their affirmative answers. "We sang the same songs," she said.

"It's always the same songs," the tall boy said.

"It's your mom's fault, dude," a husky boy beside him said.

"Who's your mom?" Maria asked.

"The choir director," the tall kid said.

"Wait, Mrs. Walsh? You're baby Zachary?"

The teens cracked up while he said, "I'm Zack Walsh, yeah."

"Your mom had you when I was in school." Maria shook her head. "Oh wow, does that make me feel old."

"Mrs. Walsh was a newlywed when I was in school, so doubly old for me," Bailey said.

They went through the "Tell your mom Maria Hatcher says hi" thing. Maria touched Bailey's arm and said, "And Bailey George says hi too."

"I run into her now and again," Bailey said. "So she sticks to the classics, huh?"

"These songs are *old*," a redheaded boy complained.

"We want to do some modern arrangements too," said a South Asian girl.

"We've been working on them," a petite girl piped up from the back. "We sing them in the lunchroom at school."

"I'm sure you sound amazing." Maria smiled at the group. Of course she was good with kids, being one of Santa's helpers and all. She glanced around, then said, "I didn't mean to interrupt. Carry on spreading tidings of comfort and joy."

The alto who'd given Bailey the thumbs-up said to her, "What do you want to hear?"

She considered the question. "I always liked 'I Saw Three Ships.' It's an oldie but goodie."

"And has a kick-butt alto line."

"That it does." Bailey gave her a high-five. Then high-fived the other two altos.

Zack Walsh blew the starting note on his pitch pipe. They launched into the song like a ship casting off. It was ridiculous how much of it Bailey remembered. She'd really loved choir. Really loved to sing. She never did it anymore, unless it was silly songs she made up for Lulu around the house.

The delight on the kids' faces showed how much they loved performing. The pure bliss radiating from Maria . . . She loved music. It probably fed her soul, the way it did Bailey's.

She'd really, really missed this.

When the song ended, she hopped a little. Maria full-on jumped up and down. Loud whistles and woo-hoos came from Pete and Tom.

"That was so much fun," Maria said. "Thanks for the trip down memory lane."

Bailey shared goodbyes with the madrigals. There was an admitted spring in her step as she walked out of the village green.

"Feel better?" Maria said.

"Yeah, actually, I do."

She simply nodded as though she expected nothing less. She turned toward Main Street, singing "I Saw Three Ships" under her breath. It had felt pretty nice holding hands too. Maria's positive energy was contagious.

"Do they still have that adult choir in town?" Maria asked.

"Not for a while," Bailey said. "The membership aged, and it fell by the wayside."

"That's too bad. Maybe we can resurrect it."

"That might be fun."

No no no. This was how she got into trouble. One simple suggestion and Bailey would be heading up yet another civic project.

"If that's something *you're* interested in doing," she amended. "We have a good community theater. Most musically inclined people do their shows."

"I'll look into that too." Maria waggled her eyebrows. "Options."

The teens started singing "Here We Come A-Wassailing" behind them. Another madrigals staple. No wonder they wanted to shake things up.

"Speaking of options . . ." Bailey pulled her clipboard out of her messenger bag.

"The clipboard," Maria said, amusement twinkling in her eyes.

"What about the clipboard?"

"I figured you'd do everything electronically for the festival."

Bailey drew lines through the two items regarding obtaining and hanging the signs. "I get satisfaction from physically crossing things off to-do lists."

"That's interesting, considering you think Lanford Falls is so old-fashioned." Maria sent her a sidelong look. "But you love things like history, and making ornaments, and paper lists. And singing traditional carols."

"So?"

"So maybe you're a little old-fashioned too."

Hmm. She kind of had a point.

"Maybe," Bailey said. "Anyway, the rest of the things I have to do tonight *are* on my computer. You are hereby released from committee detail."

"I haven't completed *my* duties for the day," Maria said.

"You hung signs and made me sing." Bailey's brows knit together. "What more could I ask for?"

Maria sang along with the second verse of "Here We Come A-Wassailing."

"Another song?"

Spreading her arms wide, she said, "Your final meal of the day has yet to be consumed."

"I'm not very hungry," Bailey said.

Maria sang the carol like she couldn't help herself. Bailey picked up on her old part and sang a few lines. Maria gave one of her Mona Lisa smiles and strolled to the corner. Bailey joined her so she wasn't singing all by herself, and also, where was she going?

"I was planning on picking up Lulu from my mom's and ordering a pizza later," she said as Maria crossed the street toward Caffeinated Corner.

"Pizza is not a good meal for you to eat tonight," Maria sang in rhythm.

"But I want to eat pizza 'cause it's fast and cheap, all right?" Bailey countered in song.

Her warbling companion burst into laughter, but kept singing. Maria knocked on one of the café's large picture windows to get Kurt's attention as he wiped down a table. When he looked up, she waved and sang louder. He grinned and waved his rag at them.

Bailey shrugged and joined in the wassailing. She was helpless against Maria's elfin powers.

They caroled down the sidewalk, melody and harmony, perfectly complementing one another. Bailey nodded at an older white couple who seemed delighted at their impromptu performance. She turned down one of the side streets that led toward Mom's house. She didn't want her coworkers to catch her. Plus, she was still holding her clipboard and probably looked like she was soliciting donations for the Retired Choir Nerds Society. So she stuck it in her bag.

Maria slowed her steps as they finished the final verse of the merry tune. Bailey leaned down so she was closer to Maria's level. She sang *"And God send you a happy New Year"* directly to the pretty blonde. Maria's smile said she was also sending happy New Year wishes.

On the same note as the last one of the song, Bailey sang-asked, "Where are you heading?"

"I don't know," Maria said, still staring intently up at her. "You turned the corner."

"To my mom's house. Don't you need to get your car and pick up Rosie?"

Maria gave a slight nod, then took a few steps away.

"Isn't this out of your way?" Bailey pointed out.

She started to sing "Here We Come A-Wassailing" again.

"Do you want to carol at my mom's front door?"

She kept walking and singing.

Bailey shook her head, then caught up to her. "Do you want me to drive you to your parents' house?"

"No, thanks."

"What do you want, then?"

Looking up at the sky, Maria said, "I want the sun to come out. It's too dreary."

"You want the sun?"

"Yes."

"All right. I'll get you the sun." Bailey planted her boots on the concrete and tossed her head back. "You heard the lady. Come on back out." The haze didn't clear. "This is Maria Hatcher. Surely, you'll come out for her."

Still nothing.

But then, a sliver of light peeked through the cloud cover. Maria cried in surprise.

"That's it," Bailey said. "More of that."

A single ray of pale light was all they got, but enough to make her smile. "There you go," she said, gesturing from Maria to the sky.

"Impressive," Maria said.

"What else do you want? I'm on a roll."

Maria reined in her excitement, turned, and began wassailing again. Okay, she'd said she had to make sure Bailey ate dinner. Which meant she most likely intended to be a part of that dinner. Which meant Bailey either had to be on board with that plan, or put the kibosh on it.

She joined Maria and ambled past beautiful homes original to the town. "I promise I'll eat later. Once I get done with festival work."

"You know what makes work more exciting?" Maria said.

"Music?" Bailey guessed.

"Music."

"I could ask my mom to dig out my high school choir recordings."

"Or you could keep singing." Maria glanced up at her. "It agrees with you."

"I'm not so grumpy?"

She gestured at the fading ray of sunlight. "It's like that. A sliver of brightness shining through the gray. It makes doing chores fun."

"How is anyone as impossibly chipper as you?" Bailey elbowed her playfully. "What's your secret, Prancer?"

"Oh, I think you know," Maria said.

"You're secretly a Christmas elf?"

She quirked her eyebrows and sang, *Here we come a-wassailing among the leaves so green.*

"I knew it. Secret elf."

"Singing makes me happy. It's one of the simple joys in life. Good music, good food, good company."

"It's that easy, huh?"

"It can be."

She made it sound so straightforward. Maybe it was for her. "I just want to get out of here once in a while," Bailey said. "See parts of the world I've never seen. Which is most of them."

Maria tilted her head. "There's not even a teensy little part of you that's enjoying working on the festival?"

"I told you. The only good thing is hanging out with you."

They took the corner at Elm Street. Strings of lights outlined most of the houses on both sides of the street. Maria hugged her arms around herself. "I understand why you're upset about missing your trip."

Bailey kicked at a tiny pile of snow on the sidewalk. "If you want the truth, I'm not that upset about the vacation. It's what it represents. Freedom. The ability to leave town and do what I want. My choices keep getting taken away."

"That must be frustrating," Maria said.

"It is. Especially in the past year or so. It's been one too many disappointments."

"You're overdue for something good to happen." Her smile said *she* was the good thing, which was cute, and somewhat true. But . . .

"I don't know if that'll happen here," Bailey said. "I've been thinking about that a lot lately. About . . ."

"About . . . ?" Maria prompted.

"Other opportunities. Other places I could live."

"Like where? Syracuse? Rochester?"

"Bigger. New York City big." Heck, Maria made her feel comfortable enough to open up. Bailey told her, "It's probably nothing, but do you remember Samantha Wright? She was in my grade."

Maria nodded.

"She's also in residential real estate, in the city. She might have a job for me down there in Brooklyn."

The good humor drained from her face. "Oh."

"I mean, I haven't interviewed for it or anything. But it's kind of exciting to think about. A whole new place to experience."

"You could just go there for a visit," Maria said.

"I have. That's one of the few places I've been to more than once. I like it there. The energy, and always feeling like I'm a part of something . . ." Bailey grasped at the air, searching for the right word. "Big. Bigger than anything around here by a mile."

Maria glanced up at her. "Is that why you were going there this week? To interview?"

"No, but Sammie was going to talk to me about it."

She grew quiet for several long moments. "So that's what's behind your thinky face," she murmured.

"Most of the time," Bailey said.

Maria nodded slowly, almost dejectedly, like she'd been better off not knowing.

She looked really sad. That was not a look Bailey ever wanted on her pretty face. "It's a shot in the dark," she said. "Knowing my luck, it won't work out. You'll be stuck with me and Lulu in the Falls."

"I like having you and Lulu in the Falls," Maria said.

"And you saw Felicity Potter. No way is she going to let up on her quest to rule the local market. I'd feel terrible allowing that to happen."

"It doesn't change the fact that you'd seriously consider a job offer in the city."

Shrugging, Bailey said, "I've never done anything else, anywhere else. You went to college, you lived in another state. You came back for an opportunity."

"I came back because I want to be here," Maria stated.

She wouldn't want to hear it, but Bailey had to be honest. "I don't want to be here. I just . . . *am* here."

They approached Mom's two-story Victorian. Twinkly lights outlined the eaves. Animated white deer leisurely bobbed their heads in the front yard. Bailey had fought hard to save this house. Fought harder to save George Family Homes. She really had put in her time. Nobody would fault her if she moved on. Moved forward.

"Do you want to do a carol?" she asked. "Maybe 'Away in a Manger'? I think I can manage that one without too much embarrassment."

Maria stared off into the distance. "I'm going to head home. I haven't seen much of Rosie this week, and still have a lot of unpacking to do."

"Oh." Bailey slowed her steps. "Yeah. Sure. I figured you'd be busy this week."

"I'll touch base with you tomorrow. If you need help with the festival."

"It's getting dark. Do you want me to—"

"No, I can walk two blocks by myself."

The mood between them had noticeably shifted. Whatever magic that had followed them from Mistletoe Grove had dissolved in the face of reality. Maria wanted to maintain the Lanford Falls status quo, while Bailey felt life passing her by.

"Hello," an older voice called from across the street. Miss Josephine waved at them with one hand, the other holding a canvas grocery bag and her purse.

"Hi, Miss Josephine," Bailey called back. "Do you need any help?"

"I'm fine, thank you. Is that Maria Hatcher with you?"

"Yes." Maria visibly forced a tight smile.

"Hello, my dear. How lovely to see you." Miss Josephine nodded at Mom's house. "Are you having dinner with your mother?"

"Just picking up little Lulu," Bailey said.

"I'm going to my parents' house," Maria said, taking a few steps back.

A wrinkled frown settled between Miss Josephine's eyebrows. "That's unfortunate. It's always nice to have dinner with a friend."

Maria gave Bailey a weak wave. "See you tomorrow," she said.

"Yeah. See you tomorrow." Bailey returned the feeble gesture.

Miss Josephine shook her head, then continued on her way home. "Youth is wasted on the wrong people," she grumbled.

THE ANGELS

Clara watched as Bailey walked up the driveway to her mother's home. Maria headed back toward town.

They'd been following Bailey and Maria all afternoon to track how things were going. Mostly invisible, as they'd discovered going about a small town in drag drew quite a crowd. Particularly after enthralling the kids and parents with a holiday-themed drag queen story time. Invisibility meant they were free to roam where they pleased.

"What just happened?" Clara asked Gabriella. Things had been going so well.

"Bailey flat-out told Maria she doesn't want to be here," her drag mother said. "She dashed that girl's dreams about them getting together."

"But I've been nudging them in the right direction. I've been sending all the positive energy I can." Clara bumped her hip to demonstrate she'd done a lot of nudging.

Jovanna tapped her platform heels in a jazz square on the sidewalk while humming "Here We Come A-Wassailing" loudly. Her short, fiery orange wig made her look like the Heat Miser.

Clara waved her hands at her sister, then at Bailey closing the front door. "The singing together. That moment they shared at Mistletoe Grove. Bailey's a different person when she's with Maria."

"Maria's our ace in the hole," Jovanna said.

"Having them reconnect has been a happy surprise," said Gabriella.

"Exactly." Clara couldn't fight her mounting frustration. She'd been working so hard. "Did you see what I did with the lights on the arbor? I made Maria glow. How did that not set the perfect mood for them to kiss?"

Jovi wigged her fingertips. "You could've done a gentle snowfall."

"I made the sun come out."

"Barely."

Clara crossed her arms and stated, "*I made the sun come out*, Sis. Which is pretty good, since I'm still learning how to manipulate the elements."

"We can nudge them together," Gabriella said, "but we can't make them fall in love. They have to do that themselves."

"Maria's already there." Jovanna batted her long false eyelashes.

"Why is Bailey being so stubborn?" Clara groaned. "Can't she see everything she wants is right in front of her? Maria's bursting with Christmas cheer. How is she not picking up on it?"

"She is, but she doesn't realize it," Gabi said.

"She's fighting it," Jovanna added. "She doesn't want to be tied down to this place."

Clara stared at the light-up reindeer in the snow. There *had* to be something more she could do. "What if I send her an anonymous Christmas card that says Maria really likes her and she should give her a chance?"

Gabriella held up a hand. "A life transformation is about the person recognizing they want to change. Right now, she doesn't want to."

"But if she doesn't, and ends up moving away . . ." *Then I don't get what I want.*

"Have patience, Daughter. These things take time."

"I know," Clara mumbled. She slouched deeper into her burgundy frock coat. "There has to be an easier way to get my wings. Like, I don't know . . ." She tossed a hand. "A bell rings or something, and shablam! A drag queen gets her wings."

Jovi cocked an exaggerated eyebrow. "Every time a bell rings?"

"Can we get a gig every time a bell rings?" Gabi said.

"Ooh, yeah, that's better."

Gabi draped an arm across Clara's shoulders. "Things are moving in the right direction. Keep it up."

"Yes, Mother," Clara sighed.

"I'm encouraged by the rekindled romance. They clearly like one another."

"Their dogs even like each other," Jovanna said as she worked on another dance pattern.

Gabriella glanced at the house. "They have the support of the people surrounding them. Bailey has a lot of love around her."

"Maria could be so good for her," Clara said. "If only she could see that."

"Then keep on nudging." Her mother bumped her with a bony unpadded hip.

Jovanna tilted her head back to gaze at the darkening sky. "Can we tap out for the night? I'm in desperate need of slipper socks, a face mask, and a holiday movie marathon."

"I could go for some hot cocoa," Gabriella said.

"I'll take a hot toddy." Jovi shrugged. "Or a hot Todd."

Their mother gave Clara a kind smile. Clara cast one last look at the house before moving down the sidewalk.

Determination welled up from deep inside. She still wanted her wings. But just as much, she wanted to help Bailey see all the good around her. Not only Maria, but all her friends. Her family. She was such a vital member of this community, and was loved and respected for who she was and what she'd done. It all culminated with Winter Wonderfest.

So Clara did have to be patient. Perhaps being swept up in the festival, with Maria by her side, would be enough for Bailey to believe in the magic of the season again.

But would that be enough for a queen to get her wings?

CHAPTER EIGHT

Lulu sniffed intently at Bailey's long coat. "Yes, I was with Rosie's mom," she said.

"Is that my daughter or the Wet Bandits?" Mom called from upstairs.

"The Wet Bandits. We've come to steal this cute dog."

"Please feed her dinner while she's in captivity."

"Will do."

Bailey wandered into the kitchen. Mom had baked a batch of sugar cookies for her book club tonight. Fortunately, the book club was unaware one rogue cookie *accidentally* fell out of the blue plastic tub sitting on the butcher-block island. And then a piece of said rogue cookie *accidentally* fell into Bailey's mouth.

Mmm. Rogue cookies were the most delicious cookies.

Mom came in wearing a poinsettia red sweater. "You are a cookie-tracking bloodhound."

"I'm finding *all* the sugar this week," Bailey garbled. She swallowed before adding, "The stress eating is very real."

"Have you been taking the time to eat decent meals? You're much more productive on a full stomach." Mom snapped the lid on the tub to punctuate this fact.

Maria's cheerful smile came to mind. Her insistence that Bailey eat. Her making three different sandwiches yesterday.

"Yes, I'm eating," she said. She popped more cookie in her mouth. Several crumbs fell on her fluffy blue scarf that she wiped off.

Lulu hopped up and shoved her nose in Bailey's coat pocket.

"What are you . . . Oh, that's right." She gently extracted Lulu so she could dig out the treats from Kurt. "Here you go. From your best pal."

"Like doggie mother, like doggie daughter," Mom laughed.

"It's no secret the way to both our hearts is through our stomachs." Hadn't Maria said something along those lines?

Her stomach lurched, and not from the sugar cookie. What had she done to make Maria all but run away? She'd been honest and shared something private and special. Apparently, it wasn't what Maria wanted to hear.

Mom not so subtly slid the cookies out of reach. "I heard you had some help today. I stopped by Gruber's, and he said you and Maria were out hanging signs."

Her mother's brown eyes twinkled with how much she wanted it to be more than just festival duties. It had been, though. The laughing together, the singing together, reliving the magic of Mistletoe Grove together . . .

"Having extra volunteers gets the job done faster," Bailey said.

"Will she be helping you tomorrow?"

"I don't know." The way they'd left things, she honestly didn't know if Maria would still want to help.

The house phone rang. Mom checked the display and said, "Oh shoot, I forgot to call Hannah back." She answered, "Sorry, time got away from me. Talk to your sister while I get that address for you."

She shoved the cordless phone into Bailey's hands. "What address do you need?" Bailey asked, moving around the island to get another cookie.

"Brett moved over the summer," Hannah said. "I'm trying to get my super late Christmas cards done. Just waiting on our cousin's new address."

"What are my canine nephews doing in this year's card?"

"You'll have to wait and see."

"No hints?" Bailey pulled out a cookie, then quickly replaced the lid.

"It involves matching sweaters," Hannah said.

It was probably the dogs and Hannah and Reuben all in the same pattern. They did the most hilarious four-legged family photos for their cards.

"Speaking of dog pictures . . ." Her little sister cleared her throat. "I just so happened to notice Maria hasn't posted any new photos from the dog park. Which either means she's too busy talking to you, or nothing interesting is going on there."

"Or she hasn't gone to the dog park," Bailey pointed out.

Hannah made some kind of snorting sound. "Have you seen her?"

"Not at the park. She helped me hang some signs today."

"*Reeeaaalllyyy?*"

"She's as obsessed with Winter Wonderfest as everyone else. She wanted to be on the committee."

"Then you've probably seen her more than once." Hannah was all too perceptive.

"To work on the festival," Bailey emphasized. Well, and to carol, and have lunch, and be trivia partners, and make ornaments, and . . .

"Has it been fun? Getting to know her again?"

Yes. A whole lot of fun. "I guess."

"Are you going to ask her out?"

"Oops, Mom's back." Bailey took a big bite of cookie.

"*Bailey*," Hannah groaned.

"Love talking to you," she garbled with her mouth full.

"Ask that cute girl out."

Mom actually did come back to the kitchen then with her little address book. It was almost comforting how old school she was. She reached to take the phone, then slapped Bailey's arm. "Stay out of the cookies."

She could hear Hannah whine "*Moooomm*" through the phone.

Their mother's gaze settled on Bailey. "She did? She has? I agree. She should ask Maria Hatcher on a date."

Bailey shoved the other half of the cookie in her mouth.

"Well, your sister is going to be in a sugar coma for a week from all the junk food she's been eating."

"I deserve this sugar," Bailey mumbled.

"But after she wakes up, that would be nice." Mom shot her a smile.

She gave Hannah Brett's address, then said she'd see her and Reuben on Saturday. Because of course Hannah wouldn't miss Winter Wonderfest. Bailey was the only one counting the hours until it was over.

Fifty-one.

Mom set her address book and the phone on the off-white Corian countertop. "Hannah mentioned you've been seeing a lot of Maria this week."

"Hannah needs to focus on her Christmas cards."

"She wants you to be happy." Mom tilted her head. "I do too."

"I am happy." Bailey crouched and snuggled up to Lulu. "Look at this face. How could I ever be sad with this face?"

Lulu grinned at her like *I know, right?*

"You know what I mean," Mom said.

"Of course I want to fall in love and be one of those people who sends out goofy family Christmas cards. It'll happen when it happens with the right, adventurous woman." Bailey kissed between Lulu's shaggy eyebrows, then stood. "Anyway, I'm not the only single lady in this kitchen."

Mom let out a laugh. "I've dated more than you have! Don't worry about me. I've had a great love in my life. If it never happens again, that's okay."

Bailey gave her a small smile. "That's true." Her mom had dated a few nice guys over the years and didn't feel the need to settle down again.

"Now, I'm not trying to be one of *those* mothers, but how long has it been since you've gone on a date? Even just meeting for coffee?"

Huh. How long had it been since that very boring dinner with a client's niece? Four years ago? Five?

Bailey wracked her brain. "Four years, I think."

Mom raised her brows dubiously.

Wait, no . . . "It was five," she admitted. No wonder this little crush on Maria had hit so hard.

"My reliable girl," Mom said. She rested her forearms on the island. "Taking care of everyone else. Let us take care of you."

"Trying to fix me up with Maria—"

"—is our way of repaying all the good you've done for us."

"Mom . . ." Bailey swallowed a sigh. "I appreciate it. I do. Just . . . not with Maria."

"Why? Is it weird because she's Dan's sister?"

No, it was weird because she'd made it weird. And because Maria wanted her to stick around while Bailey was feeling more and more confident she didn't have to. "We don't want the same things," she said.

"It's just one date. You don't have to spend the rest of your life with her." Mom quirked her eyebrows. "Unless you want to."

She was just being nice. But explaining that it wouldn't work with Maria because Bailey might be moving away was complicated, to say the least.

"I already have the great love of my life." She winked down at Lulu. "She's pretty hairy, and has poor table manners, but she's my everything."

"You're her mom. It's a different kind of love."

"Didn't you used to say Dad loved you *almost* as much as that collie mix you had when you first got married?"

"He loved that dog more than any living thing." A wistful smile tugged at Mom's lips. "I sometimes forget how much you're like him. I love seeing Jim live on in you."

Bailey's heart did that little pinch. "Me and my deep love for dogs."

Mom shook her head. "In so many things. His heart was as big as Lanford Falls. He gave everything to help other people."

Bailey nodded slowly. "Do you think he'd be proud of me? Keeping the business going, helping out around town?"

"Oh, honey." Mom's eyes glistened with tears. "I *know* he's proud of you. Of both his girls, but especially what you've done for me and Hannah. And your Uncle Bill. A less patient person would have fired him years ago."

Bailey breathed out a watery laugh. It warmed her to the core to hear Dad would be proud.

"But I will say . . ." Mom wiped beneath an eye. "He would be bugging you just as much as I do about taking time for yourself. Go on *one date* with a very nice woman who I'm pretty sure has had a crush on you for years."

"*What?*" A hot flush crept across Bailey's cheeks.

"Every time I've seen Maria over the years, it's been the same thing. 'How's Bailey? What's Bailey up to? Oh, and Hannah too, but mostly Bailey.' I thought she was being nice because of your friendship with Dan, but in retrospect . . ."

"It's not like we weren't friendly too," she answered weakly. "Everyone knows everyone when you grow up around here."

Mom glanced at the clock on the oven. "You're lucky I have to get going. Just think about it, okay? Meet her for coffee after the dog park one of these days. Maybe you and Maria *do* want the same things. You won't know if you don't try."

Bailey mustered up a smile in response. "I can have coffee with her."

That was, if Maria still wanted to spend time with her. Coffee after the dog park was more of a casual hanging out thing than a date thing, anyway. Much less pressure.

She wrapped her mother in a tight hug. "Thanks for telling me you like seeing Dad reflected in me. I don't always know if that makes you happy or sad."

"So happy," Mom said without hesitation. She pulled back and touched Bailey's cheek. "To see him in your smile, in your big heart, brings me more joy than I could ever put into words."

They shared a smile. "Have fun at book club," Bailey said.

"Get some rest tonight. And eat a good dinner."

"I will." A veggie supreme pizza would be chock full of vegetables.

She told Lulu to go get her leash. Then she waved goodbye to her mom and headed for the front door. The bright foyer light highlighted the small wall of family pictures. Mom and Dad's totally eighties wedding photo. That unfortunate family portrait when both she and Hannah had braces and bad bangs. Their last family picnic down by Lanford Creek.

It really was nice to think Dad was smiling down with pride. But it was also kind of . . . frustrating. He'd been her biggest cheerleader, always telling her to think big, to reach for the moon. Would he be okay with her doing that now? Or would he be disappointed if she left Lanford Falls behind? It was hard to say what their adult relationship might've been like.

Lulu dragged her leash over. Bailey picked it up and clicked it on her pup's collar.

A wave of irritation pulsed through her body. Why should she feel guilty? She'd done everything that had been asked of her and then some. Dad would understand. He'd known Bailey had dreams that were bigger than this town. Sure, he'd sometimes told her to slow down and not forget to enjoy the here and now. That didn't mean he hadn't been supportive.

Well, she still had those dreams. And she wasn't going to hide them anymore. If Maria wanted to hang out with her, Bailey needed to be upfront about her goals. Besides, Maria was helping stoke that fire to do more. To go after what *she* wanted.

Bailey stepped outside with Lulu and walked across the driveway. She looked down the sidewalk, half hoping to see Maria's off-white hat and evergreen coat bobbing toward them in the dark.

Ugh. For all these big dreams and bold thoughts, she really just wanted to get a pizza and hang out with Maria and their dogs.

Maria's brown doe eyes flitted through her mind. The way she laughed with her entire being. Sunshine on an overcast winter day.

A smile pulled at one corner of her mouth. Being with Maria was fun. Her lightness and optimism made Bailey feel lighter and more optimistic. She needed to be honest about that too, but with herself.

She did like Maria. And Maria knew the deal, so they could hang out without it being weird.

Lulu stopped to sniff some pee-mail in the snow. Hmm. They hadn't been to the dog park since Monday. It'd be nice for Lulu to see her canine pals, particularly Rosie. That would be a good start to what was going to be a very busy day tomorrow.

Maria's adorable grin and contagious laughter were an even better way to start the day.

* * *

The morning sun lit up the sky over James George Park. Lulu jumped and whined at the gate to be let in. Bailey hadn't been able to manage two coffee cups and the leash, so she'd erred on the side of not spilling hot liquid all over Lulu and relied on her good off-leash training.

"I'm working on it," she told her overzealous dog. She carefully cradled the cups to unlatch the gate. Lulu nosed it open and ran straight to where Rosie was romping with a black Lab-husky mix. Rosie's tail flailed with excitement.

Bailey scanned the humans for Maria. She stood near the picnic table, arms crossed, staring at Bailey curiously. Eager anticipation danced through Bailey, and her grin stretched a lot wider than it usually did so early in the day.

"Good morning," she said as she walked toward Maria.

"I wasn't expecting to see you," Maria said, her breath visible in the cold.

"Lulu missed her friends." Bailey held the extra cup out to her. "I brought you a coffee."

Maria eyed the cup warily. "How do you know what I'd like?"

"Kurt. He thinks you're a peppermint latte kind of person."

Maria's eyebrows quirked. "Kurt is right," she said, and took the offered cup. She sipped kind of loudly, which was very cute, then gave an approving hum.

"I had breakfast," Bailey told her. "You can check that off your committee list."

"Okay."

A distinct air of caution surrounded normally open Maria. Or was it nerves? She seemed distracted. The dogs were merrily racing around, so it wasn't about them.

"Is everything all right?" Bailey asked. Crap, had she ruined things between them?

"Yeah. Yes." Maria lightly shook her head. "Sorry, I'm preoccupied. I got word last night the board of trustees wants me to do my presentation today. They're all around for Winter Wonderfest and want to have an informal chat."

"That's a good thing. Informal means you don't have to do a big presentation."

"I wanted to do a big presentation," Maria said. "Instead, I had to scramble together my notes from my job interview. It sounds like they're on board with the idea, which is nice, but I wasn't anticipating doing it so soon."

"You'll do great." Bailey clunked her to-go cup to Maria's. "You've given it a lot of thought, and your passion for the project will shine through."

"I think it will, but still . . ." She cupped her coffee in both mittened hands. "I won't be able to help with the festival today. I have family plans tonight, but could cancel those if there's work to be done."

"No problem. Jane and Pete and Tom are available, and the whole park district. And since this sucker is a well-oiled machine, tonight is for rest before the big day."

Maria nodded glumly. Was she more disappointed about having to do the presentation, or not being able to help with the Wonderfest?

"Focus on what you need to do," Bailey said, stepping back as two golden retrievers cruised by carrying a long stick. "Then we'll both have something to celebrate. You rocking your presentation, and me being one day closer to . . ." *Being done with this damn festival.* "That legendary Gruber hot cocoa."

A small smile touched Maria's lips.

"Today's a lot of chaos and moving parts as vendors try to set up early. Some of them sell stuff, which is fine. It just gets confusing with non-locals thinking things are happening today when nothing is technically happening."

"So you're saying it's a good thing I won't be around."

"You won't miss anything." Bailey moved closer. "But I'll miss having an impromptu concert with you."

Actually, I'll miss you.

"No one's stopping you from a solo career," Maria laughed.

Relief snaked through her bloodstream at seeing Maria relax. "I haven't sung like that in years," Bailey said. "I definitely need a partner."

"Are you sure? You're not too big-thinking to carol with a small town girl?" Maria deliberately stared out at their dogs.

Ah, she *was* still upset about that. "What I said last night doesn't negate the fact that I like spending time with you," Bailey said. Her heartbeat drummed as she added, "I do like you, and want to get to know you better."

Maria's dark eyes darted up to meet her gaze. "I like you too. That's why . . ." A rueful grin played about her mouth. "Okay, I'm a little embarrassed by how I reacted last night. It just triggered something in me."

"It did?" Bailey turned to fully face her.

"Yeah." Maria swayed a bit. "When you said you didn't want to live here, it reminded me of the times Nancy and I argued about moving to Lanford Falls someday."

Nothing like reminding a woman of her ex.

"I mean, I get it. There's not as much to do here, and everyone's in everyone's business. And my mother texts me more now than she ever did, though it's usually about Rosie. But this has always felt like home. It's full of art and artists and literature. And there are people who care about me as much as I care for them."

Bailey nodded in understanding. That had always been one of the good things about the Falls. Particularly how everyone rallied around her family after Dad died.

Maria glanced at her. "So yes, Bailey George. I get why you don't want to be here. But *I* want to be here. And I'd like to have you in my life for as long as you *are* here."

Their timing was so terrible. If Maria had moved back a year ago, maybe things would've been different. But . . .

"I'm here now," Bailey said. She raised her cup. "And I can hook you up with free food and coffee."

"That's literally the reason I want to hang out with you," Maria teased.

She was so adorable. The kind of woman worth settling down for, if one was the settling-down-in-Lanford-Falls type.

The people you care about are here. And you understand why Maria wants to live here.

No no no. Thoughts like that were not conducive to moving forward and onward and out of here.

Maria put all sorts of thoughts in her head. Reminders of good times. Reminders that not everything in Lanford Falls was a chore.

"Thank you," Bailey said without thinking.

Maria cocked her head. "For what?"

"For reminding me about some things I'd forgotten. Things from high school, like choir and madrigals, and how I wanted to study archaeology in college."

"And prom night."

"Even prom night," Bailey laughed.

Maria giggled, then leaned in. "You want to know the *real* reason that night sticks out so clearly in my memory?"

"Other than the sprinkler incident and all our awkwardness?"

"Your suit. It was fitted and feminine, but totally commanding. You looked . . ." Her eyes clouded over. "You looked *fine*. I couldn't take my eyes off you. It started me on a lifelong love of women in suits."

An unexpected flush heated Bailey from the inside out. Should she say thanks? Ask why Maria hadn't dragged her to a dark corner to reenact their kiss at Mistletoe Grove? "I, uh . . ."

I still like wearing suits, Maria.

A glimmer of recollection flitted through her mind. *Red*. Maria had worn a red dress, and had her hair been piled in a fancy up-do?

Lulu trotted over to say hi, Rosie galumphing behind her. Rosie leaped to give Bailey a hug, but she'd grown wise to the dog's modus operandi and moved out of reach.

"Rosie," Maria groaned. "Nobody wants your hugs."

Undeterred, Rosie rammed her boxy head into Bailey's thighs. "Subtle," she said, and scratched at Rosie's short hair.

"Anyway, thank you for the thank-you. It's nice to share embarrassing stories from our youth."

"Especially ones that involve your brother," Bailey added.

"So many of those," Maria sighed.

"Some of my favorite memories involve members of the Hatcher family."

"Some of mine involve members of the George family."

Their eyes met, wordlessly sharing Mistletoe Grove memories.

Maria smiled at Lulu and Rosie wrestling on the packed-down snow. "And the next generation here is making new ones."

It really was too bad they hadn't reconnected sooner. Though Maria hadn't been single, and she didn't have Rosie, so they just had the here and now.

"I'm pro making new memories," Bailey said. "For the two- and four-legged members of our families."

"Well, if you're interested . . ." Maria took a sip of coffee. "My parents are bringing their old fake Christmas tree over to my place tonight."

Bailey gasped in mock horror and cried, "A *fake* Christmas tree?"

Maria playfully shoved her. "I haven't had the chance to get a real tree or a tree stand. We're going to make golabki and decorate the tree. You're more than welcome to join us."

"I haven't had your mom's golabki in years."

"I'm sure she'd love to see you and feed you cabbage rolls. And for Rosie to have a diversion if you bring Lulu, which is a requirement."

"Of course."

"That is, if you don't mind being in my creepy little house." A teasing glint lit Maria's eyes.

"I'll work on shrinking myself so I'll fit." Bailey scrunched her body tight.

Maria looked down at Lulu. "Do you know how silly your mommy is? She's ridiculous."

Lulu snorted and pawed at Rosie's face. Rosie flopped onto her back and kicked her front legs in the air.

"It sounds like fun," Bailey said. "We can talk about our wins of the day."

Maria glanced at her watch. "I need to get to work so today *is* a win. I'll check in when I can."

"Don't worry about it. Just think about local art and literary history."

"I can do that and check in." She gestured with her cup. "Thanks for the coffee."

"Thank Kurt for the coffee," Bailey said.

"You're my hook-up, so thank *you*."

"It's the least I can do for my committee head of food."

Maria patted her leg and said, "Come on, monster."

Rosie trotted alongside her. So did Lulu.

"Hey, buddy," Bailey called, but Lulu ignored her. She and Rosie walked and chest-bumped one another.

Bailey shrugged, then jogged to meet up with them. "You'll get to play again tonight," she said, but was ignored by the dogs.

Maria could barely separate them at the gate to get Rosie's leash on. Lulu stared up at her human, thinking they were leaving too. "We don't have to go," Bailey told her.

"I think we're breaking up a beautiful friendship," Maria laughed.

Lulu followed them out. Bailey quickly stepped outside the park and closed the gate so nobody else could escape. "Lulu," she stated. "We're not going with them."

The confused canine slowed her steps, looking between her master and her new best friend.

"We're going to Grandma's. You wanna see Grandma?"

Her ears perked, but she didn't get wiggly the way she usually did.

"Aww, Lulu," Maria cooed. "We'll see you tonight."

Bailey had to attach Lulu's leash so she didn't wander any farther into the small parking lot. She whined as Rosie hopped into the back seat of Maria's car. Rosie mashed her face against the window and whined back. Maria chuckled at the pathetic display.

"I'd say you could bring her to my mom's house . . ." Bailey started, but Maria waved off the suggestion.

"Rosie would be a crying mess without me there. At least for the first visit."

"For future playdates, then. My mom would love it."

Maria nodded in agreement. "Future playdates."

They shared a wave, and then Maria slid into the driver's seat. Lulu strained on her end of the leash. "I promise you'll see Rosie in a little while," Bailey said.

She had to pull her despondent dog in the opposite direction. They crossed into the neighboring subdivision. Bailey raised her cup to take a sip of coffee, then paused. Wait a minute. She hadn't made it a point to mention tonight would be a casual hangout. Well, she didn't have to. Maria knew the score.

Her pulse thrummed steady and strong from the pleasure of seeing Maria. Just thinking about hanging out later would energize her throughout the day.

Uh-oh. This was an entirely different kind of anticipation. It wasn't trivia night with her buddies or going to the movies with Hannah. It was . . . It was . . .

It was the same giddy excitement she got before a date. Which was silly, because decorating a Christmas tree with Maria and her parents was definitely *not* a date.

Her heart skipped a beat. *A date with Maria.*

Like a summertime picnic at the old wooden bridge. Maria would appreciate the town history and how the Beautification Committee had revitalized the park surrounding the structure. Or a warm chocolate fondue at the fudge shop on a cold winter's night. Basically, their dates would involve food.

Or they could snuggle on the couch beneath a fleece blanket and watch TV or talk or just enjoy each other's company while their dogs slept soundly in front of Bailey's gas fireplace. Whatever they did would be wonderful because Maria was pretty wonderful, and spending time with her was really wonderful. And getting to do more than kiss her under the mistletoe would be really, *really* wonderful.

The bleep of a new text brought her back to reality. Especially when she read the message from Jane.

Vendors already showing up. Need you and the list of who's registered.

Bailey suppressed a sigh. She couldn't even entertain nice thoughts and daydreams today. "Come on, Lulu Bear," she said, and picked up the pace.

Two more days of this crap.

CHAPTER NINE

Winter Wonderfest had grown in reach and popularity over the years, which was great. The fact that people thought it started on Friday, not so much.

Bailey moved from the mobile food vendors to the little booths where artists and craftspeople were setting up their wares. Back and forth. Back and forth.

Two middle-aged women wearing fuzzy reindeer antler head-bands stopped her on the path. One of them pointed to where lights were being hung on the right side of the stage. "What time is the concert this afternoon?" she asked.

"There's no concert this afternoon." Bailey used her kindest tone, though it had lost any shred of upbeat an hour ago. "The festival doesn't actually start until tomorrow."

The women looked half confused, half disappointed. *Ugh.* She pasted on a smile and added, "I believe school gets out early today. You'll hear our fantastic high school madrigal singers around town this afternoon."

That seemed to mildly appease them. Bailey wished them happy holidays and not so discreetly shoved her clipboard into her messenger bag. She didn't need a visual aid for people to think she was the answerer of all festival questions. This was by far her least favorite day of prep week.

She snagged her phone out of the front pocket. Shoot, it was almost noon. Maria was set to give her presentation any minute now. Which Bailey knew because they'd been texting off and on all morning. She'd kept giving Maria encouragement to distract her from being nervous. Plus, Maria was cute and funny in her texts.

Sending some last-minute support, Bailey texted:

You're going to knock their socks off, Hatcher! Go get 'em!

She stepped from the path to allow extra room for the crew setting up tables and chairs inside the food tent. Huh. That one side still looked crooked. The bright sunshine was melting the snow, so that was clearly no longer the problem.

Bailey waved at the nearest guy. "Can you tell Vince that back side doesn't look right? It's sitting crooked and funny near the corner."

The park district employee said he'd relay the message. Maria's reply text popped onscreen.

Eww would it stink if I knocked their socks off???

Bailey laughed quietly. Tom and Pete walked by, each toting a short ladder. "What are you doing?" she asked.

"We don't like how the booths look," Pete said.

"We're going to rehang the ribbons and garland," Tom said. "Make them so they're more like swags at the top so there's more room for the vendors along the sides."

"Whatever makes you happy," Bailey said. She literally did not care at this point if the booths were as naked as the day God made them.

Jane tiptoed over and snapped a photo of the brothers with her phone. Thank goodness she had a handle on all the social media and emails from now on.

Pete called a greeting to her. "How's Susan?" he asked.

"Home and on the road to recovery," Jane said.

"Give her our best," said Tom. "Our mother's dropping off a casserole for the family."

"That's so thoughtful. Thank you. Susan appreciates all the help." She gestured with her phone around them. "*All* the help. Truly."

Bailey gave her a tight smile, then went to check on the three guys setting lights up around the stage. Purely an excuse to hide for a few minutes. They were hired professionals who never needed help.

"There's water and hot coffee and snacks in the food tent," she told the techies. "Help yourselves. It's a little warmer in there."

They thanked her and continued working. Hooray for techies, though this was their job and they were getting paid. She'd be more than happy to hand over their check tomorrow morning once the sound equipment was set up.

The sound equipment. She grinned and texted Maria:

There will be a sound check at the stage tomorrow morning. Want to sing, Prancer? 🎵

Maria's reply came almost immediately.

Only if you do it with me! 😊

Bailey started to text that she would be too busy. No, that she didn't want to make a public fool out of herself. No . . .

An incoming video call took over the screen. It was Sammie. Ooh, was she calling with an update?

"Hey, Wright," Bailey answered, and ducked around the stage.

"Hey, George." Sammie was sitting in her work cubicle in a shiny yellow blouse. "I forgot to take our lunch off my calendar, and my phone pinged to remind me."

"Oh." Disappointment crashed through her excitement.

"But I needed to call you anyway." Sammie tucked a pen behind her ear. "The Powers That Be want to set up an interview."

Bailey's mood did an about face and swung back to hopeful. "Definitely," she said, pulse pounding in her ears.

"It's for the Brooklyn office. You'll do an initial virtual one-on-one with one of the partners. If it goes well, which I know it will, they'll call you for the in-person."

"I can do an in-person whenever," Bailey said, to which Sammie smirked.

"Yeah, about that . . ." She peeked over her shoulder, then leaned in. "They kind of thought you'd be here today and would be able to swing by to say hello. When I mentioned you were stuck working on the festival committee . . . That didn't do you any favors."

Her heart sank into her stomach. "This was a fluke. I would never miss an interview."

"I know you wouldn't. But I also know the partners want dedicated employees who don't get easily distracted."

Not that Sammie was sugarcoating it, but her subtext rang loud and clear. "It looks bad that I missed coming to the city because of Winter Wonderfest," Bailey said.

"You know how it is in the big city." Sammie wiggled her eyebrows. "All work and no play. I made it sound like you keep your commitments, and it's fine. They still really want to chat with you. It would've given you a leg up on the competition, that's all. Get you in before they start interviewing. They want to hit the ground running in the new year."

Damn it, this was what she'd been worried about. "I really wish I could've met them today," Bailey said.

"It's all good, George. Just don't miss the interview because Town Hall needs to be repainted or whatever."

"No way."

Sammie typed off-screen on a keyboard. "You'll get an email from one of our assistants to set it up. Let me know which partner you're interviewing with. I'll give you the inside scoop on them."

"Okay."

"I can't wait to get you out of there. You need this."

Was that ever the truth. "Thanks, Sammie. I really appreciate it."

"You can thank me with champagne after your first sale." Sammie focused on typing, then said, "Anyway, gotta go. Later, George."

She hung up before Bailey could say goodbye. A text from Maria sat on her screen.

Going in! Wish me luck!

Crap, it was too late to reply now. She didn't want Maria's phone going off during her presentation.

Crap, she would've had an advantage if she'd met with Sammie in the city. And worse, staying behind in Lanford Falls told her prospective employers this little town festival was more important than her career. Than her dreams.

Ugh, crap, there were people trying to talk to the techies, like they were missing some big concert. And more people milling about the village green with steaming cups of cider and apple donuts. And was that the hibachi grill guy? No way. He wasn't registered. She stalked toward the food vendors.

Crap, the tent really was crooked.

Crappity crap, she should be in New York right now, having lunch with Sammie and schmoozing potential bosses instead of here with the same old, same old.

Okay, that was not Hibachi Guy. But still, crap.

"Hey, Bailey?" Jane called at the same time Bailey's phone rang. *Uncle Bill.* He never called unless it was major and work-related.

She held up a *Wait a sec* finger to Jane, then answered, "What's wrong?"

"The Oak Avenue closing hit a snag," Uncle Bill said.

"Define *snag*."

"The buyers want the furnace replaced before they take possession."

"That's not my client, so I don't know what was discussed in negotiations."

"You know how to smooth these things over," Uncle Bill said. "Can you get here? I'm listening in. It sounds like they might walk if this doesn't get resolved."

Bailey closed her eyes and tried not to groan. "Are you serious?"

"Helping both parties find a resolution is your specialty."

"Fine," she snapped. "I'll be right there." She didn't mean to get snippy with him. Any other day, she'd be happy to intercede.

"Bailey?" Jane called again.

"Yes, Jane?" she exhaled.

"Is it too late for someone who wants to set up a food cart to register?" She nodded to Not Hibachi Guy.

Absolutely. "Not at all. Here." Bailey tugged the clipboard out of her messenger bag. "I have to put out a fire at work. You are now the keeper of the clipboard."

"But—"

"She who controls the clipboard controls the festival. I'll be back as soon as I can."

Her boots marched in time with her pulse. The weight of the week crashed in on her like never before. In previous years, she'd actively chosen to lead the festival committee. This year was under duress, plus she had confirmation it might wreck her chances at getting out.

Winter Wonderfest was ruining her life.

She trudged down Main Street, avoiding eye contact or shop windows. Someone gave her a "Happy holidays" she simply thumbs-upped in return.

She caught sight of the library across the street. Hopefully, Maria was having a better day. Maria deserved all the good things. She should get all the good things. She didn't need a grouchy, discontented grump bringing her down.

Only I'm not grouchy around her.

Maria had been her saving grace this week. She would do a great job on her presentation and should celebrate her amazing awesomeness tonight.

Bailey paused at George Family Homes and straightened, shifting into work mode. *Suck it up for Maria's sake.*

CHAPTER TEN

That evening, Bailey parked outside the old stone cottage at 320 Sycamore. The familiar sloping roof and circular windows had never changed, though new curtains and a shiny silver wreath on the door dressed it up a bit. The lights flanking the tiny garage highlighted the cracks and slow decay of the structure.

Lulu raised her head in the back seat of the SUV. Bailey breathed a deep sigh. She was *tired*, and crabby. Spending the day outside had chilled her to the bone, and she'd have to do it again tomorrow.

She checked her phone one last time to make sure everything was good with Oak Avenue. They'd worked out a compromise just in time for Bailey to get called back to the village green to help set up the activity stations.

Her screen was free and clear of notifications. She glanced at the rental house, then went into her email. The message from Sammie's brokerage firm sat on top, awaiting her response. They wanted to set up a virtual call the day after Christmas. Nine AM the day after Christmas.

An interview before the end of the year. That was a good thing. Just . . . the morning after Christmas?

Well, sure. It was a normal business day in the U.S. Why not? If she was considering this job, she'd have to adopt that mindset. She'd been spoiled all these years by having a flexible schedule. The pace around here was light years slower than what it would be in New York. Plus, she'd have to work hard to afford a decent place to live. An apartment near a dog park so Lulu could make new friends.

Sammie had been copied on the email, so she'd see Bailey's reply. The only trouble was . . .

She couldn't do it. Yes, she'd been too busy earlier, but right here, right now, she could type two simple sentences agreeing to the date and time. Yet her finger hovered over Reply All.

What was the hesitation? Why couldn't she pull the trigger? Guilt? Nerves? Apprehension? Worry about leaving Dad's legacy in someone else's hands? The fact that Maria had opened the door and looked adorable in a red-and-green plaid apron?

Maria. She couldn't respond because it meant being away from Maria.

Which was absurd. Maria was going to be here no matter what. That should have no bearing on what Bailey chose to do with her life.

And anyway, fending off Felicity Potter from taking over and changing the character of the town was a way worse concern.

It was only a preliminary interview. A quick virtual chat. Why couldn't she say yes and see what might come of it?

"Are you coming in?" Maria called from the doorway.

Lulu perked up and stood. Oh. Yeah. It probably looked strange with Bailey zoning out in the dark. She undid her seat belt and slid out of her midnight blue SUV. She opened the door for Lulu, who hopped down and promptly sniffed around the front yard.

Rosie shoved her way outside. The dogs raced to greet one another. Maria smiled at them, then turned her grin to Bailey. *Maria with her cute apron and wrinkly-nosed smile and thick blonde hair falling about her shoulders.*

"My mom will be so happy the monster has a playmate," she said. "We just started on the tree and Rosie is way too interested in it."

Bailey clomped up the three stone steps. "Sorry I didn't reply much to your texts this afternoon. It got busy."

"No worries."

"Glad to hear the board approved your pitch."

"Pending budget approval, it's a go," Maria said.

"I knew you could do it."

She tilted her head. "Thanks. I knew I could too."

They called the dogs inside. Bailey had never actually stepped foot in the old Grant house. It was quaint, and in need of updating, but it wasn't terrible. The front entrance led directly into the living room, which had a small couch, two end tables, and lots of boxes marked *BOOKS*.

Maria gestured to the left. "I don't have anything to put in the dining room at the moment, so we set up the tree in there."

Her parents stood on either side of a tall fake Christmas tree wrapped in white lights. They said hello to Bailey. Mrs. Hatcher walked over to give her a hug. Bailey bent slightly to embrace the petite woman, who very much resembled her daughter.

"It's nice to see Dan's old friend," Mrs. Hatcher said. A hint of an accent from her childhood in Poland colored her voice.

"Nice to see you too." Bailey then hugged Mr. Hatcher, who was a solid foot taller than his wife. There were a lot more streaks of gray in his dark hair than the last time she'd seen him.

The dogs romped into the small room and bumped the plastic tub of ornaments. "No no, bad dogs," Mrs. Hatcher said, shooing them into the kitchen.

Maria followed the dogs. "I'll let them in the backyard so they can burn off some energy."

Bailey entered the kitchen behind her. The scent of boiled cabbage filled the air. Maria's mom loved to cook her traditional family recipes during the holiday season.

"This brings back Christmastime at your parents' house," Bailey said, noting the golabki sitting on a stoneware platter on the faded countertop.

"Dan always got in the way when he tried to *help* by taste testing." Maria opened the back door for the dogs.

"Very helpful." Bailey set her coat and scarf over the back of a wooden chair at the small circular table. "He's told me how much he misses your mom's cooking when he doesn't come home for the holidays."

"He should be missing mine. I made these and they're fabulous." Maria scooped one of the cabbage rolls covered in tomato sauce and set it on a blue-patterned salad plate. "We're kind of noshing and decorating."

An exposed wire stuck out of the ceiling light fixture, which in and of itself looked like it might fall at any second.

"Hello?" Maria said, holding out the plate and a fork.

"Do you know if the utilities are up to code?" Bailey stared at the fixture. "I'd love to see an inspection report."

"Everything's fine."

She shook her head. "Occupational hazard. Sorry. Thanks."

Her fingers grazed Maria's as she took the plate, causing little pulses of awareness. *Maria and her yummy cooking and kindness and ease and welcoming nature.*

You're making it really hard to leave Lanford Falls, Maria.

Bailey took a huge forkful and chewed irritably on the hardy blend of meats, onions, and rice. Thirty-five years of wanting to get out and here Maria was, back for mere days, making Bailey question everything. Almost like fate was trying to keep her here.

It wasn't fair.

"That's a pretty color," Maria said, nodding at Bailey's emerald green cotton sweater. "Very festive."

She grunted in response and took another bite.

"Any unexpected problems this afternoon?"

"Nope," Bailey garbled.

"Everything's ready for tomorrow?"

"Yup."

Maria toyed with the hem of her apron. "Long day, huh?"

"Long day," Bailey agreed.

Maria studied her with a thinky face as Mrs. Hatcher came into the kitchen. "Is Maria telling you how good her new job is going?" she said.

"Mom," Maria said, ducking her head.

"She's doing so well. We're happy she's home and doing what she loves."

Bailey got the odd sense Mrs. Hatcher's too-direct glare meant something. She'd always suspected Maria's mom might have picked up on the vibe that one night in Maria's room and hadn't been too keen on Dan's pal vibe-ing on his younger sister.

"Are you here to decorate the tree?" Mrs. Hatcher asked.

"Mom." Maria shot her a look. "Let her eat first. She's been on her feet all day. Bailey, what can I get you to drink?"

"Water's fine. And I'm here to work." Bailey set her plate down to snag another cabbage roll. "Tell me about your presentation."

"Yes, tell her," Mrs. Hatcher urged.

Maria reached into a cabinet and pulled out a pint glass. "It was really low-key. I showed them the slides from my job interview. They seemed enthusiastic about it. We'll do a monthly theme featuring artists of all kinds who've passed through Lanford Falls. Winter landscapes, love and romance for Valentine's Day, patriotic themes around Independence Day. Tom and Pete already told me they'd love to give a talk for Halloween."

Bailey nodded as she ate.

"The main thing we have to work into the budget is expanding on the Art Walk. We want to integrate the library more with the historical society to showcase our rich history." Maria paused to fill the glass with water. "But it should be okay. It's pretty minimal cost on our end."

"Maria is working so hard," Mrs. Hatcher said. She cast a loaded glance in Bailey's direction. "She doesn't need any distractions."

Oh yeah. She'd definitely picked up on the vibe-ing.

"Winter Wonderfest is important, not a distraction." Maria handed over the water glass.

Bailey took it and said, "After tomorrow, you can focus completely on the library. It sounds like you'll be busy."

"It's exciting work. I can't wait to get started."

"I'm happy for you." She smiled, meaning it. She *was* happy for Maria.

How very Lanford Falls to do a casual chat before a holiday festival to further one's career goals. Nothing like a corporate interview scheduled bright and early on Boxing Day.

Not that either of them were bad. Just different.

Maria walked to the back door. "If you're not careful, I might coax you into helping with the Art Walk next summer."

Her eyes widened, as though realizing Bailey might not be there come summer. She focused on letting the dogs in and stopping them to dry off their wet legs and paws.

Summers were busy at George Family Homes, so the Art Walk had never been Bailey's thing. But lending Maria a hand, the way she had this week, could be fun.

Well, Bailey could always come home for a weekend visit. Bring Lulu to see her old friends.

"Is your dog terrible like Maria's dog?" Mrs. Hatcher asked, eyeing Lulu suspiciously.

"Lulu's older," Bailey said. "And I've had her most of her life. Rosie just needs to adjust."

The older woman harrumphed at that. Maria toweled off one of Rosie's front legs and said, "Rosie loves you. Give her a chance."

Rosie slopped her tongue across Maria's face in agreement. When Maria released her, she trotted over to Bailey with that *I'm gonna jump* gleam in her eyes.

"Rosie, sit," Bailey said.

The dog leaped up and hugged her.

Bailey held her glass out of the way and pushed the lovable dumbass down. "You're not doing yourself any favors."

Maria shook her head. "Rosie, can you please sit?"

Rosie plopped onto her rear, tongue lolling out the side of her mouth.

"Thank you." Maria finished drying Lulu, and the dogs scampered off.

"Let's decorate the tree." Mrs. Hatcher waved at the open doorway. "Your father will think we ran away."

She swiped a piece of toasted crusty bread out of a basket. Wait, there was crusty bread? Bailey grabbed two warm, buttery hunks and added them to her plate.

"Did you eat anything today?" Maria asked, then turned on the faucet to wash her hands.

"Yes."

"That wasn't comprised mainly of sugar?"

Bailey concentrated on the third hunk of bread making its way onto her plate. "I had a granola bar and two mini bags of pretzels."

"That's it?"

"And . . . two apple cider donuts. And a cup of cocoa. Sadly not Gruber cocoa."

Maria flicked the water off her hands. "What am I going to do with you?" she murmured.

"Dinner." Bailey picked up her plate and glass. "Thank you."

"I'm going to have to hook you to an IV bag filled with soup to get you to eat tomorrow."

"That's true. I'll be going all day."

"And I'll be there beside you, feeding you little mini sandwiches."

"And coffee, please."

"Of course coffee." Maria snapped her butt with a kitchen towel.

Bailey quirked her eyebrows. Maria did one of her secret smiles and rehung the towel on the oven door handle. Kind of surprising she'd be so flirty with her meddlesome mother nearby. They definitely weren't awkward teenagers anymore.

"I owe you, Hatcher," Bailey said.

"Happy to help," Maria said.

"No, really. I owe you for all these meals."

"It's my pleasure. You know I love to cook."

"I like you too much to cook for you," Bailey said, which garnered a laugh in response.

Maria untied her apron. Wait a sec. She'd been the one who dropped off all those meals after Dad died. It was assumed they were from her mom, but . . .

Bailey focused on her plate. "Were you the one who made the casseroles and things when my dad passed? The ones you brought by the house?"

"Some of them," Maria said. "My mom made a few."

"But you made most of them."

"I guess."

The realization squeezed and twinged Bailey's heart. Maria *did* care after prom.

She still cared. What an amazing person.

"Thank you," Bailey said, looking up to meet the softness in Maria's eyes. "I don't know if I ever thanked you. Like, *really* thanked you. They were very much appreciated."

"You're welcome."

"I *am* going to repay your kindness. All of it. I . . ."

Maria tilted her head, waiting.

I want to ask you on a date. A real date, at a restaurant with linen napkins and no dogs. The kind of date Mom and Hannah would be thrilled about.

Bailey opened her mouth, only Mrs. Hatcher yelled, "Maria, get this dog!" from the dining room.

Maria gritted her teeth and went to rescue Rosie. Bailey's stomach clenched in equal parts relief and disappointment. An official date would be a bad idea. But a fun bad idea. It'd probably be *too* good, and she did not need further complications.

She should probably check on Lulu, since her girl was not exempt from bad behavior. The doggie duo had found a rope toy and were each tugging on it and play-growling.

"They're just playing," Maria said.

"They're going to knock the tree over," her mom said.

"They're fine," Mr. Hatcher said. He sorted through the tub of ornaments. "Are all of these yours?"

"I have *a lot* of ornaments," Maria said. "Nancy took a few, but most of them were mine to begin with. You know I love decorating for the holidays." She touched a well-worn branch. "I can't wait to go all out next year with a big, fluffy real tree. I love how they smell."

Her dad rubbed her back. They shared a wistful smile. Right, this was her first single Christmas in however many years. No wonder her parents wanted to help ease the ache of decorating for one. And why her mom didn't want Bailey moving in on Maria.

Yeah, it was good she hadn't asked her out. It was time for Maria to focus on building a new life for herself, like she'd said on trivia night.

The petite blonde snapped her fingers. "I have the perfect music," she said, and walked over to a small boombox sitting in the corner. "This will definitely bring back Christmas memories."

She took a CD out of its jewel case. Bailey couldn't help but observe, "You unpacked an old radio and CDs of all things?"

"You'll see."

An a cappella version of "Here We Come A-Wassailing" sounded from the speakers. Young voices.

Mrs. Hatcher perked up. "Is this you in high school?"

"It is." Maria gave Bailey a broad smile. "Like yesterday, when you made the sun come out."

"What?" Bailey took a bite of crusty bread.

"When we were caroling."

She hummed in response. Sure, she'd made the sun come out, rather than a logical shift in cloud cover.

Maria blinked those doe eyes and seemed kind of hurt. Bailey chewed faster so she could swallow and say of course she remembered, and it was sweet of Maria to dig up that particular song. But Maria turned to the ornament tub.

"Let's get to it." Mrs. Hatcher clapped her hands and skirted around the dogs. "Your dad and I want to be in our pajamas and in bed by ten o'clock."

"Living that rock star lifestyle," Maria joked.

"That's my plan for the evening too," Bailey said. "Tomorrow's a big day."

Mr. Hatcher unwrapped a crystal snowflake. "Winter Wonderfest gets better every year. You've done a great job with it."

Bailey thanked him, then finished off her piece of bread. They took turns hanging ornaments and eating as Maria's high school choir recording played in the background. Her tree had a theme: musical and whimsical. The dogs worked on destroying the rope toy.

"What are your family's traditions?" Maria asked as she looped a glass candy cane over one branch.

"My mom usually hosts our extended family for Christmas Eve," Bailey said, dusting crumbs off her hands. "On Christmas Day, my sister and brother-in-law and I and our dogs go to my mom's house. We eat leftovers and watch a movie or play a game. It's very simple and easy."

"That sounds nice. Just being together."

"Do you still do that scavenger hunt around your property?" she asked Mr. Hatcher.

"Not really," he said. "We wanted to the last time Dan and his family were here, but the weather didn't cooperate."

"It's hard to plan anything outside this time of year," Bailey said. "We've been extremely lucky with the Wonderfest, overall."

Maria stepped back to check the progress on the tree. "But it's Christmas weather. I can't imagine being in a warm climate, where you have to wrap lights around a palm tree."

"I would love to spend Christmas at the beach."

"What about hot cocoa and warm cookies?"

"Frosty margaritas and key lime pie." Bailey shrugged. "They're greenish."

Mrs. Hatcher picked up a knotted ball of string lights. "What do you want to do with this?"

"Throw it away," her husband said.

"I can hang it somewhere." Maria took the ball. "It just needs a little detangling. Here."

She handed the plug to Bailey. Bailey held the few available inches with her fingertips. "A *little* detangling?"

"It's fine."

She raised a doubtful eyebrow, but Maria set to the task in her determined way.

"I went out to Phoenix one year for New Year's," she said. "It was nice to spend time with Dan, but . . . I don't know. It was weird sitting outside and barbecuing. It just felt odd being surrounded by the desert landscape."

"Nothing wrong with changing things up." Bailey shook the entwined wires to get them moving in the same direction. "You can create new traditions in any environment."

It's a Fabulous Life

Maria tugged on the strand. The thick knot didn't budge. "It's pretty hard to do a scavenger hunt with scraggly little bushes and the one tree in their front yard."

"You can enjoy the colorful blooms on the Christmas cactuses. Cacti? Is it cactuses or cacti?"

"It's nothing you can wrap a string of lights around. Ooh, that's what I should do with these. Hang them outside."

She wrestled with the uncooperative lights some more. Bailey found the source of the major snag and untangled it. The tiny lights tinkled as they cascaded to the floor.

"Thanks, partner," Maria said.

Her saying *partner* was so nice.

Too nice.

"Make sure they work before you go outside," Mr. Hatcher said.

"Don't put them up in the dark," Mrs. Hatcher said.

"How else will I know how they look?" Maria said, and took the plug out of Bailey's hand. The wires were twisted and very well-used.

"Maybe this isn't the best string of lights to hang outside," she suggested.

"It's fine. Everything's intact. You can help me."

Maria scooped up the lights and headed for the door. Her mom said something in Polish that made her clap back in kind. Boy, when she set her mind to something, it was *happening*.

Bailey followed her to slide into her tall boots. The dogs noticed and figured it was time for a walk.

"We'll be back in a second," Bailey told Lulu. Rosie didn't get the hint and had to be faked out by tossing the rope toy.

They took the steps down to the unkempt hedgerow beneath the dining room window. The Christmas tree glimmered through the sheer curtains. Maria set the coiled strand on the bushes and dusted off the outlet on the stone exterior. It looked as sketchy as the rest

167

of the electrical around the house. Coupled with the curly string of lights, this was an accident waiting to happen.

"Let me do it," Bailey said.

"I've got it," Maria said.

"That outlet looks unstable. I don't want you to get shocked."

"It's fine."

"Please let me do it."

"*I've got it*," Maria stated.

She jammed the plug into one of the outlets. The white lights blinked on and off several times. She wiggled the plug, and they went on. Then off.

She huffed and tried the other outlet. Nothing happened. So she went back to the original one. The lights blazed brightly.

"There you go," Bailey said.

Maria dragged the lights down the length of the bushes. The strand just reached the end. Not particularly fancy, but they illuminated the top of the greenery. She planted her hands on her hips, seemingly satisfied with the results.

The lights flickered off.

"Come on," Maria growled, and started for the outlet.

Bailey held up a hand. "Let me."

She wiggled the plug and got a similar flicker-on, flicker-off result until they went on again. "We probably should've tested them first," she said. "But I think it's the outlet rather than the lights."

"Hopefully they'll work now that I'm not messing with the cord."

They stood together and stared at the lights, watching, waiting. "It looks nice," Bailey said in an attempt to cheer Maria up.

"It'll do." Maria brushed a hard chunk of snow off the front of the bushes.

Bailey shivered against the cold night air. She rubbed her arms and said, "Think of how much nicer it is to do this around a palm tree."

"This looks magical."

"Then I guess you're sticking with a good old-fashioned Lanford Falls Christmas."

"The best kind of Christmas," Maria said.

"And New Year's, and Easter, and Memorial Day . . ."

She whipped around and crossed her arms. "What's that supposed to mean?"

"Nothing," Bailey said with a shrug. "Just that you love being here."

"Yes, but not all the time. I don't know where you got that I don't like to travel. I love to travel. Just because I moved back doesn't mean I don't like to visit other places."

She mirrored Maria's cross-armed stance. "What about not wanting to spend the holidays where it's warm?"

"That's just for the holidays." Her eyebrows rose, wrinkling her forehead. "I grew up here too, you know. I like seeing places beyond the Northeast. I'm curious about the world and love to explore it. Like that tour you want to do around Ireland and Great Britain. It sounds magnificent."

Irrational frustration bubbled up in Bailey's core. Why did Maria have to be so perfect?

She pointed between Bailey's brows. "What is it, thinky face?"

Thoughts and emotions raced through her body. Excitement and irritation and a deep longing for more. New York. Cuddling with Maria on the couch. A warm sandy beach with crystal blue water. Maria there with her.

The words flew from her mouth. "Why do you have to be so . . . so . . . *you?*"

Maria's face screwed up in disbelief. "Why are you being such a grump about everything?"

"Why are you being so stubborn?" Bailey countered.

"Why can't you see what you have here is really great? Your real estate agency, and your friends . . ."

"Why don't you focus on your job and leave me alone?"

"Because I don't want to." Maria took a step closer. "And you don't want me to."

Bailey stepped in too. "I have the chance to get out of here and start something new. And you . . . you . . ."

Maria stuck her chin up, defiant. Daring Bailey to keep going.

The mad energy coursing through her made her reach out and grasp Maria's shoulders. "You don't get it. I don't want to break sales records, and I don't want to keep fighting Felicity Potter, and I don't want to settle down here. I want to do what I want to do."

"And I want to do what *I* want to do." Maria lifted a hand and skimmed her fingers down Bailey's cheek.

The thing she wanted more than anything in the universe was to kiss Maria Hatcher again.

She leaned down and caught Maria's lips with her own. Maria rose to her tiptoes and wrapped her arms around Bailey's neck and kissed her harder. Bailey pulled her close, reveling in Maria's warmth like a fire crackling in the hearth. She was softness personified. Her mouth welcomed Bailey's with sweetness and a yearning for more. Familiar and new at the same time.

Her warm tongue grazed Bailey's, sending a jolt between her thighs. Making her dizzy and . . . and . . . Damn, did she taste good.

She ran her fingers through Maria's silky hair. Smoothed her other hand down Maria's back. This filled the void, the deep longing, the realization of what she truly wanted.

This was home.

"Oh, Bailey," Maria sighed against her cheek.

"Maria," Bailey murmured.

Maria could be everything I want.

She kissed Maria gently, then nestled their foreheads together. "You came back at the worst possible time."

"I'm here at exactly the right time," Maria said.

"I really like you, but . . . Damn it."

"Do you have to move? Is it that terrible living here?" She tightened her arms around Bailey. "Is this so completely awful that you want to leave?"

It was the polar opposite of awful. "I don't want to be anywhere else right this moment."

They could go on a few dates. See if this might lead somewhere. They could try a long-distance relationship if it did. It was nuts to think that, but . . .

Maria beamed her big smile up at her.

But there was no place she'd rather be than holding Maria in her arms.

Bailey cleared the desire from her throat. "Maybe we could, after Wonderfest is done—"

The front door opened to high-pitched barking and two bodies racing outside. *Noooooo!*

They both stepped back, their connection fizzling into the darkness. Rosie barked at Maria like *Why did you leave me, Mother?* Lulu grinned at them.

Mr. Hatcher poked his head out. "They were going to scratch through the door."

"That's okay," Maria said. "We were just about to come in."

Bailey raised an eyebrow at her. *I was just about to ask you on a date and then do a little passionate necking.* The heaviness in her underwear throbbed in angry protest.

Rosie leaped up and squeezed her legs around Bailey. She pried the dog off on autopilot.

Maria acknowledged her father. "We'll be right there."

He nodded and closed the door. Was there a hint of knowing on his face?

Lulu sniffed around the bushes while Rosie planted herself between the traitorous humans. Maria patted her head and said, "It's okay. We didn't go anywhere."

A knock sounded on the window. Mrs. Hatcher pointed at Maria, then toward the front entrance. "Get inside before you catch pneumonia," she said through the glass. She gave Bailey a look before releasing the thin curtain.

"Your mom really wants you to focus on . . ." *Not being distracted by me.* "Job success."

"She says it's the chance of a lifetime." Maria gazed at Bailey with such sincerity shining in her eyes. The library job wasn't the only chance of a lifetime that had popped up since her return.

Lulu shoved half her body into the bushes, jostling them. The lights flickered off.

Maria tossed her hands. "I give up."

"Let's unplug them and deal with them another time."

Bailey moved to do so. There was still a chance to ask Maria out. Even though Mrs. Hatcher's frame was visible behind the curtains. Sadly no more chances to steal a kiss, because that was a freakin' amazing kiss. Her lips still tingled with a thousand tiny snowflakes, and her knees wavered and wobbled as she bent to unplug the lights. Not to mention what was going on in her unmentionables.

Rosie barked at something in the yard next door. "What?" Maria said, looking in the same direction. "What is it?"

Rosie wagged her tail, then let out a yap.

"There's nothing there, silly. Come on." She took hold of Rosie's collar and gently tugged her toward the house.

Lulu noticed whatever had caught Rosie's attention. She wiggled with excitement. Bailey glanced at the empty sidewalk, the large oak tree, the snow-covered lawn. "Whatever it is, I don't see it."

"It's the Ghost of Christmas Present," Maria joked.

"I hope it's not here for me." Bailey patted her thigh for Lulu to follow. "I don't have time to be visited by three spirits tonight."

"You're less grouchy than you were before. I think your heart is growing, like the Grinch's."

Bailey smiled at her. "Well, kissing you always makes the holidays brighter."

Maria beamed a huge, wrinkly-nosed grin in return. "Noted."

They paused at the door, each holding their wayward dog in one hand. "To be continued," Bailey murmured. She ran her thumb across Maria's smooth cheek, to her slightly parted lips.

Maria pressed a lingering kiss to its pad. "To be continued."

THE ANGELS

Clara braced herself on the thick trunk of the oak tree where they'd had to hide from the too-perceptive dogs, even while invisible. Jovanna peered around it.

"Are they gone?" Gabriella whispered.

"Yep," Jovi said.

"Thank goodness."

"Why are you still whispering?"

"Because the dogs could hear us."

"They're inside now." Jovanna stepped onto the sidewalk. She brushed at her tangerine orange coat. "This hiding behind trees thing is for the birds. Literally. Can we agree on no more snooping around? It's starting to feel icky. We could just do remote viewing."

Gabriella stomped the snow off her thigh-high red boots. "I wasn't expecting them to come outside. Or kiss each other like that."

"That was some kiss," Clara sighed, leaning against the tree. That kiss had been a long time coming.

"Can we also agree . . ." Jovanna hugged her arms across her body. "This is pretty well wrapped up? Those ladies are loca for one another. Happily ever after is totally in the cards for them."

"Not just yet," Gabi said. "Bailey's still thinking about leaving."

Clara waved her purple-gloved hand at the house. "Did you hear what she said about not having time to deal with Christmas ghosts? And she's still irked about the festival."

"Tomorrow will be the real test," Gabriella said with a nod.

Jovanna dropped her head back with a loud groan. "Clara's trying to drag this out so she can get her wings."

"Not true," Clara defended.

"The festival will go fine, and Bailey and Maria will have a smooch-fest under the mistletoe, and it'll be sunshine and roses. And you won't have done enough to be wing-worthy."

Clara pointed to the dark bushes. "I could make the lights go on."

"Ooh, that'll seal the deal." Jovi rolled her eyes.

"Children." Gabriella leveled them with a sharp glare. "What do I keep telling you about life transformations?"

She waited patiently for a response.

Jovanna kicked at the concrete. "They take time," she mumbled.

Clara stared down at her black booties. "They can't be rushed," she grumbled.

"And the person has to want to fully and truly change." Gabriella raised her carefully painted-on eyebrows. "Bailey has to be all in. Right now, she's only in because of Maria. She has to believe in this town and its holiday magic or it doesn't work."

"Maria's a big part of it," Jovi said.

"Maria's a huge part of it," Clara agreed. "But Mother is right. She can't be the only reason."

"I have every confidence it'll happen." Their drag mother touched Clara on the shoulder. "You've nudged her where you could. There may be a few more chances tomorrow. Anything can happen while she's surrounded by so much festive joy."

Clara planted her hands on her hips. Bailey was going to have an amazing Winter Wonderfest. She'd personally see to it. Bailey deserved to be happy, and adorable Maria deserved to be happy. And, well, *she* deserved her own set of wings and was going to earn them this time.

She tiptoed through the snow to where the plug for the lights sat below the outlet. Then she focused her energy into the wires. "Let there be light," she said, and plugged it in.

The lights blazed ultra bright.

Jovanna shielded her eyes. "Whoa, Clark Griswold. Take it down a notch."

Ooh, they were glowing way too strong. Clara took some of the energy back until the lights shimmered at a more normal level.

"Clara's gonna get her wings," Jovi sang. "I'm gonna bring the house down with my split kicks and death drops."

"Mother's going to wish her daughters were polished pageant girls," Gabriella teased.

"You'd be so bored without us."

"Think about how big our hearts are," Clara said. "We love what we do. We help people and make their lives better. And look fabulous while doing so." She strutted down the driveway.

Gabi snapped her fingers several times. "Exactly."

"Werk," Jovanna said, and shimmied over to Clara.

They danced together, the excitement of the mission flowing through their movements. Everything was heading in the right direction. Bailey was starting to believe again. She'd had so much success with the festival in years past. That, coupled with her connection to Maria and a little help from the House of Angel, would make this a very happy holiday indeed.

Because really, what could go so terribly wrong tomorrow?

CHAPTER ELEVEN

Bailey squinted against the bright morning sun. At least the festival was going to have perfect weather. The only chance of snow was flurries, and late tonight.

She opened the door to Caffeinated Corner and was greeted by Maria presenting her with a to-go cup. Her smile instantly warmed Bailey from the inside out. She could definitely get used to being greeted by that smile every morning.

"For our fearless committee leader," Maria said. "Happy Winter Wonderfest."

"Thank you." Bailey accepted the cup.

In the background, Kurt grinned broadly at them. "Have fun today, Bails. You got this."

She nodded at him and turned to head out.

"Wait." Kurt trotted from behind the counter. "For my girl, for later."

He dropped a couple of small homemade dog treats into her gloved hand. Bailey slid them in her coat pocket and said, "Lulu appreciates it."

"I got a few for Rosie too," Maria said.

"Special treats for my special pals," Kurt said. He held the door for them. "I'll see you later, after we close. It'll be busy today."

"Enjoy," Bailey told him.

"I will."

When they hit the sidewalk, Maria cuddled her coffee close to her chest. "Where to first?"

"Martin's. Ellis always treats her staff to breakfast before they head over to the village green. I have to get the checks from her."

Cars and trucks were already turning into the small parking lot on the far side of the green. Vendors unloading their wares.

Bailey waved at two guys driving by in a park district van. "They're bringing in the supplies for the snowman and wreath stations," she said. "As soon as we get the checks, we can help Tom and Pete set them up."

"Sounds good," Maria said.

"Actually . . ." Bailey shifted her messenger bag. "I might have you help them while I start checking in the vendors."

They crossed Main Street to the diner. The chalkboard menu declared *Today's Specials: Winter Wonderfest Waffles, White Bean Soup & Wildly Hot Wings.*

Bailey paused at the entrance. She glanced down at Maria's open, excited face. "Good morning, Maria Hatcher," she said, trying to convey how much last night was still very much on her mind. If only she hadn't been too exhausted to stay later than Maria's parents . . .

"Good morning, Bailey George." The way her lips quirked said she was thinking about it too. Another stolen kiss on a winter's night, with the promise of more to come. "Thanks for fixing the lights on the bushes."

"I didn't. I unplugged them."

"Wait, you didn't plug them back in?"

Bailey shook her head. "No. Why?"

"They were on after you left last night. I thought you'd fixed them."

"Not me."

"Huh." Maria crossed her arms. "I wonder who did. Maybe my dad."

"Maybe." Bailey had been too distracted replaying the way Maria's soft lips had felt against hers to notice much of anything. "Or it was that Christmas spirit."

"That's who it was." Maria gently squeezed her arm, and they went inside.

The diner was packed with hungry locals and festival-goers fueling up for the day. Bailey spotted Ellis where several tables had been pushed together. As she passed the counter, she noticed Nick putting in an order. "What are you doing here so early?" she asked.

"Filling in for the old man so he can go to the festival." Nick gave Maria a chin nod. "Hey there, Maria Hatcher."

"Hi, Saint Nick." Maria gave him a little wave, hiding her coffee behind her back.

Ellis stood and held her arms out. "There she is. Our town savior."

She started a round of applause that the Town Hall employees loudly joined. Bailey dipped her head in acknowledgment.

"I owe my sanity to this woman. Thanks a million for everything."

"Glad I could help," Bailey said, because what else was there to say?

The mayor rummaged around the large purse hanging on the back of her chair. "Let me know if any issues come up today. Not that I anticipate any problems with you in charge."

She pulled out a white envelope and handed it over. All the checks to pay the remaining festival expenses. "It should be as smooth as it always is," Bailey said, and slid the envelope in the front pocket of her bag.

"Let's have lunch or dinner next week," Ellis said. "You name the time and place. My treat."

"Thanks, but that's not necessary."

"It's more than necessary." She laughed and added, "Plus, I like hanging out with you."

That made Bailey smile. "Okay."

She accepted thanks and well wishes from a few people at the table. A mom stepped out of a nearby booth to help one of her kids cut up his waffle, so she and Maria had to go the long way around toward the exit.

"Ms. George," a woman drawled behind her.

Bailey's hackles went up. She turned to find Felicity hogging a booth all to herself. Two different newspapers covered the table. "Ms. Potter. Come to join the festivities?"

Felicity made a face. "I'm having my breakfast before things get too crowded."

"You'd better hurry back to your castle. Town's about to get overrun."

"I do not enjoy the noise or children running every which way. I'm sure you can relate to wanting to skip the whole day."

"People have fun," Bailey said. "They enjoy themselves."

"Yes, but do *you* enjoy any of it?" Felicity raised one thin gray eyebrow.

"Sure. The food, the band . . ." *Mistletoe Grove.* She glanced at Maria, who gave her a small smile.

Felicity closed the newspaper in her hands. "I will never understand your stubborn loyalty to this town. Lanford Falls holds you hostage, and every year the hold grows tighter and tighter. You're trapped."

Nothing could refute that, so Bailey didn't say anything.

"You're never going to experience life the way you want to. It's . . . Well, to be frank, it's sad. Such wasted opportunity."

"I haven't wasted anything," Bailey said. "I don't need your pity."

"Of course not. You have friends." The older woman deliberately settled her gaze on Maria.

Anger flashed sharp and hot. Maria was *not* going to get dragged into this. "I do have friends. There are good people in this town. People who deserve to live here. To be able to afford their dream home."

"I see."

"And you know what?" Bailey leaned in for emphasis. "I'm tired of having this argument with a warped, frustrated woman like you. You know I am never going to let you take over George Family Homes, so let it go. Let Lanford Falls be the happy place it is."

With that, she marched across the diner. Maria hastened to catch up with her. Bailey shoved the door open, coffee sloshing out of her cup's lid. Had she really referred to the Falls as a happy place? On the least happy day of her year?

"You're amazing," Maria said, giving her a look that bordered on adoring.

"Someone has to stand up to her," Bailey said, heartbeat pounding in her ears.

Happy place. No, it wasn't the place. It was the people. People like Maria. Her positive influence had a lot to do with defending Lanford Falls.

They stood at the corner and waited for traffic to clear. Having it out with Felicity was not the best way to kick off the day. Though it could be used as a fire—a catalyst to get motivated. Bailey was here of her own volition and was going to make this the hap-hap-happiest Wonderfest since Bing Crosby tap danced with Danny freakin' Kaye.

She nodded to herself so emphatically, Maria's eyebrows met in confusion.

They hustled across the street and entered the village green. It teemed with day-of setup activity. Onstage, the sound tech checked one of the microphones nestled in a stand. Two park district vehicles were parked off the path. Boxes and plastic tubs littered the vendor stations.

Vince waved to her from near the food tent. Bailey raised her hand, then noticed the tent was *still* crooked. Maybe more crooked.

"Nobody fixed where it's slanting in the back," she said, pointing at the obvious slope.

He turned to see what she was talking about. "I thought my crew adjusted it."

"It looks worse. Can you get on that ASAP? People are going to think it's unstable."

"It's secure," Vince said.

"It doesn't look like it."

"All right." He called to two people on his crew.

Maria studied the tent and said, "They must've adjusted it in the wrong direction."

Bailey gestured with her coffee down to the activity stations. "If you can help set those up, I'll get started on my high-priority list."

"Okay." Maria gave her that smile that melted her insides. "Have fun today."

"Right," Bailey snorted.

"I'm serious. Have fun. That's what today is all about."

"That's what tomorrow is all about." She nudged Maria with her to-go cup.

"Maybe it's what tonight could be about," Maria murmured. "At Mistletoe Grove."

Bailey grinned at the thought of some canoodling under the mistletoe. "I like the way you think."

Someone cleared their throat loudly behind her. A twenty-something white guy in ripped jeans and a leather biker jacket. His hair was dyed Goth black. "I heard you're the one with our payment," he said.

"That depends," Bailey said. "Who are you?"

"Dustin. Of Dusty Dreams."

"Of course." That was the band she'd hired. "Thanks so much for—"

"We get paid before our gigs, so . . ." He held out a hand.

"Sure." The band had come highly recommended, so she wasn't too concerned about them taking the money and running. "You're welcome to start setting up around six o'clock. The concert is slated to begin at seven."

"We'll be ready," Dustin said. "Dusty Dreams is always ready."

Dusty Dustin is rather full of himself. Bailey slid her hand inside the pouch on her messenger bag. Huh. The envelope wasn't there.

She passed her coffee to Maria so she could use both hands to check the front pocket. It was empty other than a tube of lip balm and two pens.

"What's wrong?" Maria asked.

"I could've sworn I . . ." No matter. She searched the main compartment. The envelope wasn't immediately visible. She took out the clipboard. It wasn't stuck on there.

Bailey fished through the bag, but it just had the usual odds and ends. No envelope. What the hell?

"Is there a problem?" Dustin drawled.

"Just need to get your check," Bailey said, fighting to keep her tone even.

"I saw you put it in your bag," Maria said.

"I always put it in my bag." Ellis had handed her the envelope, and Bailey had placed it in the front pocket. Her memory wasn't so bad as to forget five minutes ago.

The sound techie approached them. Bailey recognized him, but couldn't place his face to his name. "Hey, good morning," he said in a deep baritone. "I just finished sound check. We're ready to rock and roll. Can I snag the checks for me and the lighting guy before it gets too hectic?"

"Of course," she said. "I'm getting the checks out now. Just having a bit of trouble finding them."

"If we don't get paid, we don't play," Dustin sneered.

"I have your check." Bailey looked to him, then Sound Tech Guy. "Both your checks. They're in here somewhere."

She looked through her entire messenger bag again. Flipped through every paper attached to the clipboard.

"I . . ." She checked one coat pocket. Just her phone. The other pocket only had Lulu's treats. Where the hell was the envelope?

"I didn't give it to you?" she said to Maria, then added, "Why would I give it to you?"

Maria set their coffee cups on the path and checked her coat pockets. She shook her head.

"I'm so sorry," Bailey said to the guys. "I know I have it. I'm not sure where it went."

"Maybe it fell out between Martin's and here," Maria said.

"It must have." Bailey searched all around them. Maria crouched and stared down the length of the paved path.

Sound Tech Guy waved a hand. "No biggie. We'll take ours whenever you find them."

Dustin gave him a look. "I have stuff to do before the gig. I can't wait around for you to find a check. Who still writes checks? Join the modern world."

"Settle down, Millennial." Sound Tech Guy glared at him.

Anxiety ramped up in Bailey's chest. This had never happened before. She was far too organized and reliable. "Give me a minute to retrace my steps. It's probably lying on the floor in the diner."

Dustin rolled his eyes so hard it was practically audible. Sound Tech Guy repeated it was no big deal for him.

Maria walked along one edge of the path as Bailey scoured the other. Snow, snow, snow, but no white envelope.

Nothing but brick sidewalk outside the village green entrance. The madrigal singers came from Caffeinated Corner with snacks and beverages. Bailey barely acknowledged their hellos.

"It has to be in the diner," she said. "I must've missed the pouch on my bag, and it's sitting by Ellis's chair."

"That makes sense," Maria said.

They stared down at Main Street, at the sidewalk, at the tiled floor inside Martin's. The Town Hall employees looked surprised to see them.

"Did you come back to join us?" Ellis asked. "We're all finished, but—"

"Did I accidentally drop the envelope of checks?" Bailey said. "I can't seem to find it."

Ellis glanced around her seat. "I don't see it."

The people near her scooted back and checked the floor. Nothing but a jelly packet and crumpled napkin. Maria searched the tabletops while panic bubbled inside Bailey.

"Let me check my purse," Ellis said, grabbing it off her chair.

"I know you gave it to me."

"It might've fallen into this bottomless pit."

She fished around her purse to no avail. Maria and Bailey squatted to see if it had skittered under a neighboring table. The Town Hall employees asked other diners if they'd seen it.

"It's not the end of the world," Ellis said. "Though I don't like to have a bunch of checks floating out there. If you don't find them, we'll cancel them."

The town treasurer waved from the opposite end of the tables. "I can cut you new ones before the end of the day," she said.

"Our band for the finale wants payment now," Bailey said. "The guy said he'll walk."

"I guess I can run to Town Hall and cut him another check." The treasurer checked her smartwatch. "That'll take some time, though."

Ellis held up a hand. "I don't want to write new checks until we know for sure. It couldn't have gone far."

Maria touched Bailey's arm. "Let's retrace our steps again. It's probably somewhere ridiculous outside."

"I am so sorry," Bailey told the mayor. "I don't know what could've happened."

"It's okay," Ellis said. "It'll turn up."

Bailey circled the diner one more time. Felicity was gone, and it wasn't around her table.

Maria met her at the entrance, shaking her head. "No dice."

They exited Martin's. Bailey looked beneath the chalkboard menu. When she straightened, Felicity was standing in front of her. "Problem?" she said.

"Not now," Bailey growled.

"You seem distraught, Ms. George. Did something happen?"

"It's none of your concern."

"My goodness, you're irritable." Felicity tucked her newspapers under one arm. "And you called *me* warped and frustrated."

"Oh, go away," Maria said. "Come on, Bailey." She tugged Bailey's hand to search the gutter running along Main Street.

"I hope it's nothing serious," Felicity called.

They ignored her, checking here and there and everywhere. No. Freaking. Envelope.

Worry snaked through her body. What if someone had found it and taken it? A bunch of checks written from municipal funds could be disastrous in the wrong hands.

The missing envelope was Immediate Problem Number One. Immediate Problem Number Two lurked inside the village green entrance. Dustin had his arms crossed, looking like A Very Emo Christmas. The last thing she needed was some dude acting like he was headlining Lollapalooza instead of a small town festival.

Bailey pasted on the smile she used when a homebuyer was being unreasonable. "Dustin, hi. Thanks so much for your patience. Our treasurer will cut you a new check if you can wait just a bit longer."

He blew a puff of air through his lips.

"If that doesn't work for your schedule, we can give it to you tonight."

"That's not how Dusty Dreams rolls." He shook his head. "I knew this was a bad gig. We got asked by a bunch of companies to do their holiday parties this weekend. They're willing to pay big."

"We *will* pay you," Bailey insisted. "I'm asking for a little patience."

"It is the holidays," Maria added.

Dustin pulled his phone from his back pocket. "Yeah. People are desperate. I don't need this hassle."

He started to walk away, but Bailey blocked his path. "Please. I'll pay you with my credit card."

He paused, eyebrows raised.

"If I had my wallet with me." *Shit.* All she had was a twenty she'd shoved in her jeans pocket for food. She couldn't ask Maria to cover the cost. "I could Venmo you."

"Forget it." He made a slicing motion across his throat. "Dusty Dreams out."

"Dustin . . ." Bailey watched his departure, helpless to stop him.

"Dustin's a dick," Maria said.

"A dick with a talented band. What are we going to do now? We don't have a finale."

"We'll think of something."

Bailey pulled out her clipboard and flipped through the papers. "The only other musical act is KidTunes, the kiddie music performers. That's all prerecorded tracks. The other stage acts are the guy who makes balloon animals and the local dance studio with little tap and ballet dancers. Not exactly showstoppers."

"Does it have to be music? Maybe there's a folksy storyteller who can read a Christmas classic? Or . . ." Maria glanced around at all the activity. "I don't know. A local band, or a singer-songwriter? An artist-in-residence somewhere? A church choir?"

"Didn't Kurt see some drag queens the other day?" Bailey said. "It'd be nice to have them now."

Jane practically skipped across the snow the greet them. Her head was covered with an oversized striped stocking cap that grazed the top of her glasses. "Merry Winter Wonderfest! How's it going? Have you checked in the vendors yet?"

"No. Something else came up." Bailey held out the clipboard. "Would you be able to do it? I'd appreciate it."

"Oh no." Jane quickly sobered. "Is everything okay?"

"We just lost our band for the finale."

"What? Dusty Dreams canceled? That's so unprofessional."

"Dustin thinks he's too good for us. We need to find a last-minute replacement."

Jane shook her head, her knit stocking wiggling back and forth. "This week has been a nightmare."

"No kidding," Bailey grumbled.

Vince joined them. "One of the tent's support poles is bent. My crew can't mess with it with everything set up. But the guylines are holding tight."

"So it looks bad, but it's secure," Bailey said.

"Completely secure. That sucker's not going anywhere."

She nodded, accepting security over appearance. "Honestly, that's the least important thing right now."

Jane took the clipboard from her. "I'll handle the vendors."

"Wait." Maria grabbed Bailey's arm. "I've got it." She pointed several times toward the tall Christmas tree.

"What?" Bailey said. "We have everyone stare at the tree for an hour?"

"The madrigals."

The teen singers had congregated in front of the tree, adjusting their matching scarves. "The madrigals," she murmured.

"They're not scheduled to perform, right?" Maria said.

"No. They just carol off and on during the day."

"Perfect."

Maria dragged her toward the group. "Hi, guys!" she called. "Are you in fine voice today?"

The kids said they were, both in words and in song.

"Great. That's so great. Weren't you telling us you wanted to perform some modern songs? And you've been working on them?"

"Yeah," Zack Walsh said. "We've got a tight Mariah Carey Christmas medley."

"That's amazing. Oh my gosh." Maria wrapped both her arms around one of Bailey's, hanging heavy with relief. "We have a gig for you. Tonight. Here. The grand finale."

"Doesn't a band usually play that?"

"We'd much rather have you," Maria said.

"They canceled this morning," Bailey added.

Maria squeezed tightly. "But we like you so much more and would be delighted to have you perform onstage, where your talent will shine."

The kids beamed with excitement. "Cool," Zack said.

"That would be lit," a short brunette boy said.

Two of the altos squealed and clasped hands and said, "'Last Christmas!'" in unison.

Bailey spoke above their enthusiastic din. "If you need to set up, you can start doing so at six o'clock. Performance is at seven. The band was slated for an hour, but really, whatever you have will work."

Zack pumped his fist. "I've got it. We'll put together a program."

The teens quickly volunteered to handle costumes and arrangements and a song list. At least they were psyched about this turn of events.

"I'll let the sound and lighting techs know about the change," Bailey said. "You can talk to them about your needs. They're nice guys."

Nice guys who may or may not get paid today.

The kids bounced ideas off one another. They were all in. "Thank you *so much*," Maria said.

They insisted they were happy for the opportunity. "You'll be paid," Bailey told them. "The band—"

The madrigals whooped and cheered about a paying gig. She'd figure that out later.

Okay. Immediate Problem Number Two was settled. Back to Immediate Problem Number One. She thanked the teens, then walked with Maria toward the small tent where the sound and light boards were set up.

"Thanks," Bailey said. "That was a good idea."

Maria looped her arm through Bailey's. "Hey, we're doing this together."

"I'm honestly mystified by what happened to the checks."

"They'll turn up. Have a little Christmas faith." She smiled, a secret elf spreading holiday cheer even when faced with challenges.

Bailey wrenched her lips upward. The madrigals would be an okay replacement. Hell, she'd rather pay them than dickish Dustin. Provided they could find the freaking checks.

CHAPTER TWELVE

The morning thankfully passed in more typical Wonderfest fashion. Attendees were in high spirits, and nothing else had gone wrong. Bailey stood from where she'd helped one of the jewelry vendors pick up a display that had gotten knocked over by a baby with flailing limbs.

"I think that's everything," she said, hanging a beaded necklace on a little hook.

The older Latina woman thanked her from behind the booth. Bailey checked the ground one last time to be sure she hadn't missed anything. She was triple-checking everything now.

She made her way to the food vendors. Competing odors clashed with the late lunch rush: popcorn and pizza and tacos and sugary-sweet pastries. She moved along the back side, asking folks if they needed anything.

So far, so good. The worst of the day had already happened. If only they could locate the checks.

Ellis had made the decision to cancel them when it became clear they were simply gone. She and the treasurer were working on issuing new ones (sans one for Dusty Dreams, plus one for the madrigals). It was so embarrassing.

Bailey's cheeks flamed just thinking about it. How could she lose the checks for the festival? They were her responsibility. And she'd given Ellis an unnecessary headache when the mayor had more important things to do.

She paused at the back edge of the food tent. Muted chatter came through the side walls. One of the support poles near the other end stuck out like an elbow. That must've been the bent one. She walked down to get a better look.

Jeez, no wonder the tent was so crooked. The pole wasn't just bent—it was at a good forty-five degree angle. She jiggled it. The guy-lines staked into the ground held taut. She jiggled it harder, and the metal groaned. Whoops.

She let go quickly. Then she pulled out her clipboard and jotted a note to ask Vince and his crew if the rental company had given them a bent pole, or had it happened during assembly?

Applause broke out near the stage. The KidTunes performers had just finished. Hopefully, Ellis would sign the new checks ASAP so Bailey wouldn't have to endure further embarrassment and could actually pay them.

Two young boys walked by wearing the wreaths they'd decorated around their necks. Pete and Tom did a great job coordinating the activity stations, but she should probably check in. Plus, it'd buy her time.

She strolled along the far side of the food tent. The crowd slowed her progress toward the path, so she checked her phone. Ellis was going to let her know when she got back from Town Hall.

An email notification from the hotel she was supposed to be at advertised a special January deal. *Why are you mocking me, email ad?*

Maybe things would be different in January. Maybe she could still take a vacation. Or maybe she had a reason to stay . . .

Or maybe you'll be making plans to move down there in January.

Shoot, she'd nearly forgotten about Sammie and that email still awaiting a reply.

"There you are."

Maria appeared beside her, blonde hair tousled and cheeks rosy from the breeze. She held two metal tumblers in her mittened hands. "It's been a while since you ate lunch," she said. "Time for a treat."

She'd been plying Bailey with food in regular intervals. Maria's unyielding optimism had kept her from spiraling into complete and utter grouchiness. She really was too good for this world.

Sunlight glinted off the familiar red mugs. "Is that Gruber hot cocoa?" Bailey said.

"It sure is." Maria held one of them out. "You more than deserve it."

"I was supposed to buy you one. That was our deal." Damn it, she couldn't even fulfill that task today.

"Oh, you will. I'm having two or three of these before the day is done." Maria danced the tumbler in front of Bailey. "That's why I got reusable mugs."

"You're amazing," she said, and took the offered tumbler.

"I know." Maria slurped loudly on her cocoa. She was amazing, but Bailey was royally sucking. "Is Ellis back yet?"

"Not yet," Bailey said. "I'm waiting for her text. I was about to check in with Pete and Tom."

"Have you seen the snowmen? People are bringing their A-games this year."

"They usually do."

The foot traffic along the path made it slow going, but Bailey had hot cocoa and Maria at her side and was not complaining. Maria continued to be true to her word and had been with Bailey every step of the way today. As she'd promised. Trusting her—counting on her—was easy to do now.

Bailey shared a wave with Jane and her girlfriend standing in line to buy giant pretzels. Yvette and Paul chatted with Carter and his and Ellis's three kids in another line. Bailey tried to hide inside her fluffy blue scarf so she wouldn't have to apologize for being the reason Ellis wasn't with them.

Maria elbowed her and said, "Ooh, look at the wreaths those guys made. They look professionally decorated."

Two snappily dressed men each carried a large grapevine wreath carefully dotted with faux white poinsettias, greenery, and baubles.

"Nice," Bailey agreed.

"You've probably made a dozen of those over the years."

"I haven't had time to."

"But you've done the snowman competition, right?"

"Not since I was a kid."

Maria regarded her as they stepped off the path. "You haven't had the chance to enjoy the festival."

"Not while being the official keeper of the clipboard," Bailey said, and took a sip of heavenly cocoa. The rich chocolate tasted like the holidays.

"No wonder you don't like it. You don't get to do any of the fun stuff."

"I'm too busy making sure everything runs smoothly." *Making sure everyone else is having a good time.*

"Well, this year you're doing something fun. I'm also the committee head of fun times for Bailey George."

"I didn't realize that was a committee," Bailey said.

"It's a newly formed one-person committee." Maria's face sobered. "For which I take my duties *very* seriously."

She was being her usual sweet self, but this wasn't the day to throw caution to the wind and whoop it up. Bailey had messed up and was literally hiding from people. "Maybe later," she said.

"Maybe now," Maria countered, and nodded to where four fake snowman forms were waiting to be dressed. Tubs full of hats and scarves and wacky accessories sat beside them. Three teams sorted through their tubs, laughing about the contents.

"I have to go tell the KidTunes actors their check is en route." Bailey swirled her hot chocolate. "I really hope this will be the push to do away with paying for everything by check. It's so outdated."

"That's one way to look on the bright side."

Maria shouldered her way to the folding table. Tom smiled at them from where he sat with the sign-up sheet.

"How's it going?" Bailey asked. "Any problems?"

"None at all," Tom said. "Everyone's having a great time. Do you two want to sign up? I can get you in in about an hour."

"No thanks," Bailey said as Maria said, "Absolutely!"

Bailey gave her a look. "I'm not sure what I'll be doing in an hour."

Tom's mouth twisted as he studied the sign-up sheet. "Actually..." He called over the crowd noise, "Are Bob and Lynn here? Last call for Bob and Lynn."

Nobody responded.

"People don't always come back. If you want, you can go now."

"Heck yeah, we want to go now." Maria took Bailey's tumbler before she could protest and set both mugs on the table.

She tried protesting anyway. "I really can't right now."

"It's ten minutes," Maria said as she de-mittened. "You can let your hair down for ten minutes. Come on, partner."

Maria captured her hand, which was starting to become a welcome regular occurrence. Their fingers laced together. A perfect fit. Two puzzle pieces made to join.

They went to the last snowman form in the line. Holes and little chunks dotted the three large stacked Styrofoam balls. The park district had to throw them out every year because they got demolished, but they couldn't count on having enough real snow to reuse all day.

"We're making a snow lady," Maria said. She rummaged through their tub, then held up a hot-pink feather boa. "A sassy snow lady."

Bailey nodded her agreement. It was hard to say no to a Christmas elf.

She slid her messenger bag off. She could do this for Maria, since Maria had done so much for her.

Tom clapped to get everyone's attention. "All right, contestants. You have ten minutes to dress your snowperson however you'd like. Have fun, and be creative." He stared at the stopwatch in his hand. "Starting . . . now!"

Maria pulled out two short but sturdy branches from the tub. Bailey looked for buttons or little things to decorate the face. "Are you as competitive about this as you are with trivia?" she asked.

"I like giving a hundred percent." Maria shoved a branch into one side of the middle ball. "Let's focus on big-picture items first, then the details."

The white mop head would make good hair. Bailey tucked it under her arm. She took the boa and draped it over Maria's shoulders. Synthetic pink feathers floated off it.

"Not on me," Maria said, brows furrowed in concentration. "On her."

"Hold on to it for her," Bailey laughed. She plopped the mop in place, adjusting it so it hung somewhat like hair.

Maria stepped back from pushing the other branch into place. "Ooh, good call on the hair."

They searched for an outfit, dismissing all the coats. Nothing about their assigned wardrobe was sassy enough to complement the boa around Maria's neck.

Bailey eyed a large Hawaiian shirt. "What if . . ." She snapped her fingers. "Got it."

She pulled it from the tub and wrapped it around the bottom fake snow ball. "This could be a sarong. I think there's a pair of plastic sunglasses in there. We just need to find something that looks like a bikini top."

"You'll do anything to pretend like you're at the beach," Maria teased.

"Let's be different. Sassy tropical snow lady."

As Bailey tied the short sleeves in a loose knot, her phone jingled in her coat pocket. She read the screen, relief washing over her. "Ellis is back with the new checks. She'll meet us by the stage."

"Five minutes," Tom announced. The young Black girl working next to them with her dad squealed.

Maria gestured at the tub. "We'll meet her in five minutes. Find those sunglasses."

"Maria—" Bailey began.

"The fate of Winter Wonderfest does not rest solely on your shoulders. They can wait. Let's finish what we started."

"But I have to—"

"You don't have to do anything." Maria rested her hands on her hips. "Everyone knows how hard you work. Nobody will mind if you actually enjoy the day you wanted no part of. They'll probably be thrilled for you to have fun. So enjoy yourself, damn it."

She nudged Bailey with an elbow. Amusement danced in her chocolate eyes. Mortals were powerless against her elfin powers of adorableness. And moreover, she had a point. Bailey was entitled to enjoy the festival. Especially this year, even with that morning's giant mistake.

"I'm telling Ellis to pay KidTunes," she said as she typed a reply text. "And that I'll—we'll—be there in a few minutes."

"We will," Maria said, then bent to search their tub.

Bailey watched her determined partner. Damn, she wanted to hug her, hold her, kiss her senseless at Mistletoe Grove. Then get warmed up in front of a crackling fire before getting really nice and warm—

"Don't just stand there." Maria waved her down. "Sunglasses. Bikini top. Beachy stuff."

"I love how bossy you are," Bailey murmured.

Her chest tightened. *Oh, crap.*

Maria didn't appear to have heard her. Saying *love* even while joking about her take-charge attitude was . . . whoa. Not something they needed right now.

The fluttering in her belly moved lower. She dug through the tub with numb fingers, and not from the cold. Loving Maria seemed so easy. Sounded so right. She could love a woman like Maria.

Who are you kidding? You could love a woman who IS Maria.

Bailey shook her head and found the comically large neon-green sunglasses. Maria held up two wool scarves. "We could tie these together for a bikini top."

"A very scratchy bikini top."

"Ugh, you're right." She dropped them, then pursed her lips.

They'd pushed all the gloves to one side. "Hear me out," Bailey said, and snagged a pair of knit red mittens. "It's tacky, but we could use these, and find a string or something to make them look connected."

"Oh my God, that's so perfect and tacky." Maria took them and propped them onto the Styrofoam form. They peeled off. "We have to get them to stay on."

"How about . . ." Bailey scanned the tub. She pulled a thick black belt from the bottom. "This?"

"A belt?"

"It'll be secure."

The minutes ticked by as they tried different ways to fashion a bra out of mittens and a leather belt. Maria burst into the giggles. "She's here to tell you you've been very naughty this year."

Bailey snorted at their tropical dominatrix. "Did you happen to spot a whip in our tub?"

"Sadly, no."

They laughed at the ridiculous faux bikini top. "All she needs is thigh-high black boots," Maria snickered.

"She needs something for a mouth," Bailey said.

"I've got lipstick."

"We can't use lipstick. It has to be something that can be removed."

"Shoot."

"One minute to go," Tom alerted the contestants. "Get those finishing touches on."

Exhilaration swirled through her bloodstream. "She needs lips!" Bailey cried.

"And cheeks!" Maria declared.

They checked their tub for anything red or pink. Bailey found two mismatched red buttons while Maria grabbed something for the mouth.

The buttons made okay uneven cheeks. Maria stuck a gnarly carrot sideways on the bottom of the top ball.

"Carrot mouth?" Bailey said.

"Desperate times." Maria stepped back, bright pink feathers against her green coat.

"The boa!" Bailey yelled, and reached for it.

"The boa!" Maria whipped it off and crossed it over Tropical Dominatrix's neck. It settled just as Tom called time.

Maria leaned against Bailey and twined their arms. They burst into laughter studying their creation. A stringy-haired, sunglass-wearing tropical dominatrix with a carrot for a mouth.

"We make much better trivia partners," Bailey said, which made Maria giggle harder.

Tom commented on each of the other snow people. The crowd cheered for their favorites. Everyone was so happy, regardless of how their design turned out. The festival attendees drank cocoa and cider and ate sweet treats. It was honestly something out of a Christmas movie.

How had she lost sight of that magic? Sure, the Wonderfest was a ton of work, but it was always worth it. And she was enjoying it with

Maria's arms nestled in her own. Maria smiling and laughing on a sunny, cool afternoon.

Maybe it was so enjoyable this year because she was sharing it with Maria.

"What do we have here?" Tom stopped in front of their snow lady, scratching his head. "A day at the beach?"

"Dreaming of a Caribbean Christmas," Bailey said.

"I see. Interesting use of mittens." He pointed at the makeshift bikini top to the delight of the crowd. "You defied convention by not using the carrot for a nose. Bold choice."

Bailey could only laugh. A gust of wind caught the feather boa. It waved like it was beckoning Tom over. Their tropical lady was terrible, but she loved it. Judging by Maria's wide smile, so did she.

"All right, folks," Tom said. "What do you think about a day at the beach here?"

People were very kind in their playful applause, but this was clearly not the winner. Tom walked back and did another cheer test for the second team and their Dickensian snowman. Then the father-daughter team with a colorful snow clown. Bailey hooted loudly for them both. When the father-daughter team got awarded the big blue ribbon, she and Maria shouted out with glee. The little girl was so happy, her joy could've melted Jack Frost.

"Sorry we didn't win," Bailey said.

"That's okay. It was fun."

"It *was* fun."

"See?" Maria teased. "It's nice to have fun once in a while."

"Okay, okay."

With you around, I'll always have fun.

They swiftly stripped Tropic Thunder so Bailey could get back to work. Her mind played through several lovely scenarios of sneaking off to Mistletoe Grove with Maria during the madrigals' performance.

As adults who knew exactly what they wanted. As two people who could have something really good here.

She liked who she was with Maria: lighthearted, relaxed, a bit silly. Hopefully, the same was true in reverse. Maria deserved someone who loved her with as much gusto as she had for . . . everything.

It would be an honor to be that person.

"Let me grab our drinks," Maria said, and rushed off toward the registration table.

Bailey picked up her messenger bag. Just a little while longer until darkness settled and they could revive their favorite Christmas memory. Everyone would be paid, and the volunteers would speed through the necessary post-concert cleanup, and then she and Maria could figure things out. And have a lot of fun figuring them out.

Maria returned with the tumblers clunking together as she read something on her phone. "My parents want to come, but don't want to leave Rosie alone." She held Bailey's mug out for her. "Do you think it'd be okay if I had her here with me?"

"How does she do in crowds? Is she a Nervous Nellie in new places?"

"She loves the attention. And she has this really cute, Christmassy coat I just got her that makes her look less like a big, scary dog and more like the love-bug she is."

After a sip of cocoa, Bailey said, "Then I'm sure it'd be fine. My mom's going to bring Lulu in her stylish green turtleneck."

"Ooh, yes. Rosie needs a role model to learn from."

They started in the direction of the stage, staying off the busy path in favor of the packed snow. Having their dogs tonight hadn't been part of the fantasy, but wasn't a deal breaker. Mistletoe and mutts could work.

"So." Bailey tilted her head downward. "There's some general takedown tomorrow. The tables and chairs, un-decorate, remove the signs. Purely voluntary. Just a few hours in the morning. I usually thank my committee by buying them lunch."

"Tomorrow?" Maria squinted like she was thinking hard. "I'll have to check my jam-packed social calendar."

"If you want, we could go to the dog park after. Let our monsters burn off some energy."

"Possibly." She made that mysterious Mona Lisa face. "And then what?"

"After the dog park?"

"Yes."

"Then . . . You could come over. We can watch a Christmas movie."

"Which one?"

"Whatever you want to watch," Bailey said. "Your choice."

"*Die Hard*?" Maria teased.

"If you want."

"What about dinner? You know Rosie will have to eat."

"Of course. Rosie can stay for dinner."

Maria blinked her lovely doe eyes. "Can I?"

"Hmm." Bailey pretended to consider it. "Do you like spaghetti?"

"I do like spaghetti."

"I can make us spaghetti. That's one of the few things I don't mess up too terribly."

A slow smile spread across Maria's face. "You'll cook for me?"

"Sure. Dine at your own risk, though."

"So you're asking me over for dinner."

Bailey's heartbeat drummed in her ears. "I guess I am."

Maria leaned into her side. "I can bring dessert."

"Dessert would be . . ." *The greatest thing in the history of things.* "Nice. Something that won't melt. I have a fireplace we can eat in front of."

"Mmm. A fireplace and a couple of comfy pillows and blankets?"

"I have some very comfortable pillows and throw blankets," Bailey assured her.

Someone bumped into her from behind. They'd stopped walking and were staring at each other again. The heat building in Maria's dark eyes was enough to abandon the festival and light that fire and grab every pillow and piece of linen at home and have themselves a *very* merry little Christmas.

Maria opened her mouth, but the sound of groaning metal filled the air.

They searched for the source. What the hell?

It groaned louder. Screams came from inside the food tent. The back side slumped like the *Titanic* going down. Shit.

Bailey raced toward it, watching the top partially collapse. *Shit.* That fricking bent pole must've given out.

A wall of people halted her progress. She shoved her way through, Maria on her heels.

Parents hustled their children through the exit. Voices blurred together in various states of alarm. A gaggle of tween girls walked out, filming the whole thing with their phones.

Bailey dashed inside the tent. Oh thank God, it hadn't caved in. The back side walls hung limp and the canopy sagged, but everything else appeared to be intact.

"Everyone please exit the tent," she called over the noise.

She and Maria politely but firmly ushered diners toward the opening. Calm on the outside, panic running through her body.

A female park district employee hurriedly turned off the two patio heaters. Bailey gave her a grateful thank-you.

"Never seen that happen," said an old-timer as he stared up at the top.

"I'm so sorry," Bailey said. "Please exit safely."

Ellis joined them to assist with the evacuation. "What happened?" she asked Bailey.

"A bent support pole, I think. I'll check as soon as—"

"We've got this. Find Vince. Get it fixed."

Bailey nodded and squeezed through the entrance. Vince was no doubt already there. Why the hell didn't anybody do something about that pole?

Vince and one of his crew were dragging two of the guylines from where they'd landed. All four in that corner had come unstaked from the ground. The asshole pole bent upward like it was giving them the finger.

Bailey grabbed one of the lines. "Is it going to fall?"

"No," said Vince. "We'll get these back in to hold the weight. That pole's shot, though."

Carter approached them, asking, "What can I do?"

"Grab that other support cable," Vince said.

Two burly bystanders offered to help stake the guylines. Once those were secure, they assessed the damage. The side walls were still slumping, and man, if the tent had been crooked before . . .

Bailey and Vince and the crew member walked down the back side. The other supports appeared to be holding tight. She couldn't help but say, "Completely secure, huh?"

Vince inspected the asshole pole. "I don't know what happened with this. It was just a little bent. It's like someone leaned on it or messed with it."

All the blood drained from her face.

She'd only wiggled it a little. Surely this wasn't because of *her*. Walking Lulu every day hadn't made her strong enough to bend steel.

Oh, shit. What if she'd jostled it enough to render it unstable?

Another male member of the park district crew came over. The trio discussed what they could do to bolster the tent. They had it under control, so Bailey said, "I'm going back in to see what they need."

This isn't your fault. It's a bizarre fluke. Someone inside the tent leaned on one of the side walls. Or the strain on the pole got to be too much.

By the time she reached the entrance, the tent had been cleared of festival-goers. The heaters had been pushed to one side. Maria, Ellis, and Carter dragged tables and chairs away from the slumping back wall.

"The tent is secure," Bailey told them. "But we shouldn't use it until they can do something about the support pole that's bent."

"You were right about it looking wonky," Maria said.

Bailey helped them get everything away from the sloping side. Ellis passed by with two folding chairs. "What a day, huh?"

"What a day," Bailey echoed.

The tent had never been anything but secure, even in years when the weather had been terrible. It figured it would happen this year. Just one more thing to—

"Look out!" a man shouted.

"Now what?" Bailey groaned.

She ran outside in time to see the Gruber hot cocoa cart crash into the base of the Christmas tree.

THE ANGELS

Clara stood with her face mashed against the door inside the RV. They'd claimed a parking spot (well, two) outside the village green, and she so wanted to get out to see what all the ruckus was about.

Jovanna and Gabriella sat at the small table, watching Bailey on the old TV. Jovi's nifty trick of remote viewing had come in handy with Bailey being here, there, and everywhere that day.

People yelled and screamed and ran away from the large Christmas tree. "I can't wait around any longer," Clara said.

"It's not time yet," said Gabi.

"When is it going to be time?" Clara planted her hands on her hips. "I've wanted to intervene all day, but you keep holding tight to your annoying wait-and-see approach."

"Because it's not time," Gabi repeated.

Clara shook her dark blonde curls. "I'm going in," she said, and pushed the door open.

"Hang on a minute," Gabi said behind her, but it was time for action.

She ran in her fuzzy slippers into the village green. Dodged a few people coming from the opposite direction.

The storeowner Mr. Gruber pulled his son back from a cheerful red cart buried in evergreen and lights. The park district employees grabbed at the swaying branches and tried to steady the tree. The impact had made it sway off kilter.

Clara hadn't been able to help when Bailey lost the checks and the band. She hadn't been able to stop the tent from caving in. But she could do this.

She rubbed her hands together to gather energy and focused on the tree. A natural breeze blew through the air. She piggybacked onto it and swirled the current around the tree. Using her left hand, she waved at the tree to get it to straighten in the stand. It wavered and wobbled. Not enough force.

She pushed her right hand at the tree. A big gust of wind kicked up. *Uh-oh.*

"Too much, too much," she said, grabbing at the air.

Clara watched helplessly as the wind caught the tree and sent it falling backwards. More screams came from frightened people.

Thankfully, it landed on a row of trees behind it. But oh, what a mistake. What a huge blunder.

She clasped her hands against her mouth. This was bad. Really bad.

Bailey pressed Maria back with a protective arm. The poor woman looked positively dumbfounded. This was not the way to make things easier for her.

"Clara Angel," Gabriella hissed from the sidewalk. "What did I tell you? Get over here *right now.*"

Clara clutched the lapels of her jade green blazer. She was in Trouble with a capital T. "It was just supposed to be a nudge," she said to her drag mother when she joined her.

Gabi gave her a long-suffering sigh. "Let's review how to properly gather energy," she said, and held out a hand toward the RV.

Clara glanced at Bailey staring at the once proud tree. "Sorry, sweetie," she said, and left the cleanup to the professionals.

CHAPTER THIRTEEN

Just . . . what? And how?

Bailey relaxed her arm now that Maria wasn't in imminent danger from a rogue Christmas tree. Thank God it'd been caught by neighboring maples. It rested in the branches like it needed to take a nap.

Then the lights went out on the tree. And outside the tent.

Fresh commotion came from the food vendors. Everything had gone suddenly quiet, and where were their lights?

"We lost power," someone said, and a bunch of others agreed.

Terrific.

Vince barked orders to his crew to get the bucket truck. Ellis held her palms up, looking around. "What happened to the power over here? The stage is still lit."

"One of the main generators is behind the tree," Bailey said. "I'm guessing it went out because of . . ." She waved at the reclining evergreen.

Jane rushed over with a wireless microphone. "Do you want to say anything?" she asked Ellis.

Ellis cleared her throat and pasted on a smile. "Hello, everyone," she said into the mic. "Boy, has today been full of adventure. We'll get everything back up and running just as soon as we can. In the meantime, please steer clear of the tree. And the food tent."

"That tree's gonna fall," a woman shielding her two young children said.

"What about the tent?" cried another mother.

"I hear your concerns, and we're working on them. Please head down to do some shopping, or create a special wreath to take home. This is certainly a day to remember." Ellis shared a look with Bailey.

The mayor continued assuaging attendees' concerns. Bailey couldn't stand there while the festival literally collapsed around them. She felt physically ill and a little dizzy.

She started toward the tree. Maria followed, but Bailey halted her. "Stay back in case something happens."

"I'm helping you," Maria said.

"I don't want you anywhere near that tree or the generator."

"I'll be fine."

Heat shot through her bloodstream. "I am not going to endanger you. Stay here. Help Ellis."

Maria protested, but Bailey turned and marched on. No way was she putting Maria in harm's way.

Mr. Gruber saw her coming. "We don't know what happened," he said. "The cart lost control and rolled away."

"I'm so sorry," his son said, wringing his hands.

"Whatever," Bailey said. It was par for the course today.

She joined Vince near the accident site. "Can we get the tree back up?" she asked.

"Yeah. It's still in the base."

"What about the generator?"

"The breaker tripped. It's a safety feature that gets triggered when it's jostled. We'll get it running once the tree's dealt with. I don't want anyone crawling beneath that." He held his arm in front of some dude snapping photos. "Stay back, man."

Bailey had to do the same to an overly curious young couple. It was beyond absurd. How did a cocoa cart knock over a tree? How did a slightly bent pole defy the laws of physics or chemistry or whatever? What was next—someone setting the wreath decorating station on fire with a too-hot glue gun?

An older white woman walked by and visibly sniffed to the man with her. "I heard great things about this festival. I guess they were wrong."

The man harrumphed in agreement. Bailey tried to dig deep to find her customer service skills, but they were gone.

Arnie rushed into the village green, fully dressed as Santa Claus. "Everyone step back," he commanded in his stern deputy voice. Which was slightly ridiculous, given his attire.

To Bailey, he said, "I got here as fast as I could. What happ—oh." He noticed the cocoa cart.

"Toy drive?" Bailey guessed, nodding at his padded belly.

"I was just finishing up when . . ." Arnie leaned his head way back to take in the tilted tree.

The Grubers approached him to tell their story. Bailey moved to stop a couple of teenagers dressed all in black, but they focused in on her.

A girl with flat-ironed green hair said, "Are you in charge?"

"Yes. I'm sorry for the—"

"What happened to Dusty Dreams? We came here for Dustin."

Her friends whined in agreement. "We want Dusty Dreams," a tall, thin boy said, pointing to his T-shirt bearing the band's name. Dusty Dreams had groupies?

"We had some creative differences with Dustin," Bailey said.

"Dustin is a *genius*," the girl declared. "He's just biding his time until they hit it big."

What? Bailey could only look around in the hopes this was one of those prank TV shows. Or had she been transported to the Twilight Zone?

"Umm . . ." She shrugged. "I don't know what to tell you. Dusty Dreams isn't playing tonight." She gestured over her shoulder. "A big tree fell. The tent almost collapsed. Today is full of disappointments."

The kids grumbled and groused and got on their phones. Great. This whole fiasco was going to be all over social media. It reflected so badly on the town. On its hardworking people. They didn't deserve to be raked over the coals when it was ultimately Bailey's fault.

This reflected badly on her too. Who would want to buy or sell a home from the woman who couldn't keep a simple festival running smoothly?

What if it got back to Sammie's bosses? What if it ruined any chance to . . .

Uncle Bill shouldered his way out of the crowd. "What are you doing here?" Bailey said. "You hate gatherings."

"They've got those hot dogs I like," he said, jutting a thumb toward the food vendors.

"Of course you're here." Uncontrollable laughter bubbled up in her throat. Naturally Uncle Bill, the man who hated people-ing, was there. Made total sense. "Next, Felicity Potter's gonna come running into your arms and you'll declare your decades-long love affair."

His face wrinkled with revulsion. "That's never happening."

Bailey plopped a hand on his shoulder. "That's the sanest thing I've heard all day. At least I know I'm not in an alternate universe."

"Are you okay?" he asked, genuinely concerned.

"Not even remotely," she laughed.

The park district truck pulled up to the entrance. Santa Arnie ordered everyone to clear a path. Bailey joined the crowd as Uncle Bill went to get his beloved hot dog. At some point, Ellis had started a sing-along of Christmas carols to keep the mood light. They were well into "Silent Night."

Maria sidled up to Bailey. "Will this work?"

"Now would be a good time to believe in Christmas miracles," Bailey said.

"I do." Maria crossed her fingers on both hands.

The bucket on the back of the pickup truck rose slowly beside the Christmas tree. It caught everyone's attention. Bailey crossed her fingers and hoped for the best.

Arnie and the Grubers dislodged the cart. They had to untangle it from the lights and branches. It was all dinged up and full of spilled cocoa.

"That's too bad," Maria said. "For them, of course. But I wanted more cocoa."

"It'd be pine flavored now," Bailey said, which garnered a slap on the arm in response.

The park district guy heaved the top of the tree while the crew at ground level guided it safely. They then worked on making sure it was secure in the base.

"All right," Ellis's voice echoed through the stage speakers. "Let's hear it for our terrific Lanford Falls Park District."

Applause broke out. The tree looked like it had just gotten home from a night of partying. The golden star sat crookedly on top.

Maria's eyebrows drew together. "What else needs to get done?"

"Huh?" Bailey shook the haze from her head. She just could not believe what was going on.

"What can I do to help?"

She reached for her messenger bag, then vaguely recalled setting it on a chair in the tent. There was so much to do. The tree had to get fixed. The power had to go back on. The tent had to be bolstered. The madrigals had to not suck tonight. And oh yeah, the festival still had all of its regularly scheduled activities.

"Bailey?" Maria said. "What can I do?"

She looked down at Maria's beautiful, sincere face. Sweet Maria wanted to have fun and be happy when all Bailey could bring her was disappointment. She was disappointing everyone. Maria didn't need to be on the receiving end of that.

Anger coursed through her body in sharp waves. She'd been distracted and hadn't paid attention to her duties. She'd never done that at past festivals, always focusing on the event, the schedule, what came next. Clearly, she was not meant to enjoy Winter Wonderfest or there would be dire consequences.

"I need to check with Vince," Bailey said, and walked away. Unsurprisingly, Maria followed.

They skirted the long way around the truck. Vince stood beside the generator, waiting for the all-clear. When his crew gave the okay, he flicked a switch.

The lights on the tree blazed once more. A section toward the top was out, but the crooked star glistened as the sun dipped behind the maple trees.

"And we have lights!" Ellis cheered through the microphone. "Sorry again for the disruption, folks. Thank you for your understanding. Let's do a verse of 'O Christmas Tree.'"

The carol floated across the village green, and the crew called up to the guy in the bucket. It all swirled in a dull roar in Bailey's ears.

Vince gave her two thumbs-up. "Crisis averted."

"For now," she grumbled.

"Bet you wish you didn't cancel your trip for this," he joked.

A sickening squish twisted her insides. "Can't wait to field all the complaints we'll get."

"It's one for the books, that's for sure." He pulled his phone from his jeans pocket. "I was on the phone with the tent place. They've got a replacement pole. I can run and get it."

"I'll get it," Bailey said. *Because I might be the reason we need one.* "You should be here for the next disaster."

"You sure? I can send one of my crew."

"I'm sure." She needed to get out of there. Escape the madness before she did even more damage.

"Use one of our trucks," Vince said. He slid a key off the carabineer attached to his belt loop. "The pickup truck parked at the far end of the lot."

Bailey took it and headed toward the maple trees. Maria fell in step with her. She wanted to help, so Bailey told her, "I need you to go to my bag. It's in the tent. Give Jane the clipboard. She'll know what to do. And ask Ellis to pay everyone. I'll be back as soon as I can."

They reached the sidewalk along Main Street. "Sure, but I was going to go with you," Maria said.

"I need you here."

"But—"

"You're not coming with me," Bailey snapped.

"What if you need help?"

"I won't need help."

"Bailey—"

"I don't want anybody's help. I just want to get out of here."

"Hey." Maria set a hand on her arm, gently forcing her to stop. "Talk to me. What's wrong?"

"What's *wrong*?"

"Other than the obvious."

Crossing her arms, Bailey said, "None of this was supposed to be my responsibility. I wanted out, and instead I'm here cleaning up the mess. As usual."

"This isn't your fault," Maria said. "None of this is your fault."

"I'm in charge. It falls on me when things go wrong."

"A couple of bad things happened, but you didn't—"

"I lost the checks. I lost our band for the finale."

"But you fixed that."

"I shouldn't have to be the one to fix it." Her voice rose as her frustration boiled over. "I'm always the one who fixes it. I'm so sick of it. Of this town. Of constantly feeling like I'm obligated to do everything for everyone else. When do I get to do what *I* want?"

"You can," Maria said, but Bailey's last shred of patience unraveled.

"You're right, Maria. I can. I can get out of here. I can take that job in the city. This town . . ." Her lips curled into a cynical smirk. "This town and its ridiculous obsession with the holidays. It's too much. It's all too much."

Maria took a step closer. "Please don't let today be the reason you leave," she murmured.

"It's not today. It's everything." Words that had been bottled up for years poured out. "I don't want to be here. I'm tired of feeling stuck. I don't want to settle for life in Lanford Falls and getting roped into fifty more Winter Wonderfests. You're all better off without me. *You're* better off without me."

"That's so not true." Hurt colored Maria's voice.

"It is," Bailey stated. "You don't want to hear it, but it is. You don't need me in your life. You deserve so much better than me. I'm only going to give you grief."

Maria gripped her arm. "Oh, Bailey, no . . ."

"And I deserve better than this damn town. I'm just . . ." She pulled away. "I'm just *done*."

"With everything?" Maria's eyes sparkled with tears. "With me?"

"Be done with *me*. You don't need me. I'm not this great person you've built up in your head. I'm pretty terrible."

She hated pushing her away, but it was the only way to rid Maria of her fantasies of them living happily ever after.

Maria dropped her gaze to the sidewalk. "You're being kind of terrible right now."

"It'll only get worse the longer I stay here."

"I don't want you to feel like you're settling for me."

"I don't want that, either," Bailey said, truly meaning it. "Nobody should ever settle for you."

"Agreed." Maria looked up with such sadness in her eyes. "Then you should go."

Bailey took a few steps. She paused, desperate to turn, to take back the pain she'd caused. But no. It was for Maria's own good. She needed to be free. They both needed to be free.

Her pace quickened until she was all but sprinting toward the parking lot. She was so tired of feeling responsible for everyone else's happiness.

She reached where the municipal vehicles were parked. Got into the cold pickup truck. It smelled like gas and oil and dirt.

"This is what you get," she muttered to herself. "You screw up, you deal with the consequences."

The engine sputtered to life. "It's the Most Wonderful Time of the Year" blared through the speakers. "No way, Andy Williams," she said, and turned the radio off.

Traffic had backed up along Main Street, so she crawled out of the lot. The sidewalk along the village green was crowded. Maria wasn't among them.

A wave of nausea crashed over her. Poor Maria. She only wanted to bring joy and happiness to Bailey's dreary existence.

"You don't deserve her. Adorable Christmas elf with a smile that lights up the whole town." She sat back in the worn driver's seat. "I'm gonna get out of here so she can find someone who treats her right. She deserves it."

Maria had broken her heart once. Now Bailey was doing it. Liking one another inevitably led to heartbreak.

She inched past the busy storefronts. The shoppers laden with bags. The excitement of the holidays bursting from every nook and cranny, every smile on every face. She wanted to block it all out.

Twinkle lights glistened outside George Family Homes. Crummy old George Family Homes. It was dark inside, since everyone was at the festival or doing something with loved ones. Hell, even Uncle Bill was enjoying the day.

"You've been my prison long enough," Bailey told her office.

Her heart pinched. That was so unfair. She'd made the choice to stay and honor Dad's legacy. Made the choice to stay and help with the Wonderfest this week.

"I'm making a new choice." She stopped at the last four-way intersection in town. "All sorts of new choices, just for me and Lulu."

The dog park was mostly empty. Dad's park. He would've loved it.

The car in front of her stopped short. She slammed on the brakes and pounded the steering wheel. "Come on, dude."

She craned her neck to see that outbound traffic was backed up. "Well, sure. Everyone's leaving Winter Wonderfest because it's a craptacular disaster."

There was almost no movement toward the main road that led to the highway. "Screw this."

She checked the oncoming lane before pulling out. She'd backroad it to the rental center.

She passed James George Park. Turned down the road that led to the old wooden bridge.

Did the heat work in this friggin' pickup? It was freezing. She fiddled with the controls. Seriously, was it broken?

A flash of movement caught her eye. She swerved to avoid a squirrel trotting across the road. The truck skidded and fishtailed and drove straight into a ditch.

The impact shook her hard.

She sat with her hands on the steering wheel for several long, slow moments.

"Jesus," she whispered, pulse hammering in her ears.

Hand shaking, she rolled down the window to inspect the damage. The ditch wasn't that deep, but it was packed with plowed snow on the far side.

She carefully put the truck in reverse. It rocked in place. She tried to ease it forward. The tires spun in the snow.

She tried to reverse-then-forward a couple more times. "I'm probably making it worse, because I make *everything* worse."

She got out of the truck. Not only was it stuck in the ditch, but the tires had created four deep mud ruts. "Great. Just great."

She stomped around the pickup, hands fisting in mounting anger. Yeah, she'd done a fantastic job lodging the tires in good.

"Nice work, Bailey. Way to make this day even worse. Ugh!"

She kicked the rear tire. Then set her foot straight into a mucky mush of muddy snow.

"Uugghh."

She tried to pull it out. Her other boot slipped, and she landed on her butt in the snow. The hem of her tan coat dropped into the muck.

"*Uuuggghhh.*"

Now both rubber boots were full of muck. She struggled out of the mud only to flop face-first into the tightly packed snow.

"*Uuuugggghhhh!*" she screamed into the snow.

Her palms chilled clear through as she pushed herself up. She trudged onto the street, brushing snow off her scarf. "This is literally getting worse by the second. My boots! My coat! *Ugh!*"

She stomped at the slime coating her navy blue boots. Her poor wool coat was saturated in several dark, muddy spots.

"Now I have to call someone to get unstuck so I can get the goddamn pole and fix the goddamn tent and *uuugggggghhhh,* goddammit!"

She wrestled with her coat pocket until her phone was free. Two texts from Mom and one from Hannah sat onscreen, but she ignored them.

"You know what I should be doing? I should be replying to Sammie's work person email. Tell them to sign me up. I'll be in Brooklyn come hell or high water or muddy ditches."

She clicked on her email.

An error has occurred. Please try again.

She refreshed her account, but got the same error message.

"*Fine*," she told the uncooperative device. "I'll call for help first if that'll make you happy. But then I'm sending that email."

Her eyes grazed over the top corner of the screen. No bars. No hint of a wireless network.

No service.

"Why is there no service? There's always service here."

She glanced around as dusk settled over the open land, the evergreens. Lanford Creek burbled up ahead.

"Seriously, phone, we are not in the middle of nowhere."

She turned it off, waited ten seconds, then turned it on again.

Still no service.

"This is . . ." She shook her head in utter disbelief. "I'm losing my mind. It's like I'm cursed."

She marched down the side of the road, holding her phone high. No bars.

Might as well trek to the creek. She'd never had problems getting reception there during Beautification Committee events.

She reached the small gravel lot. No bars. Walked around, staring at her phone. Wandered in a circle. Wandered back and forth.

No. Freaking. Bars.

Lanford Creek whooshed up ahead, and an owl hooted in the nearby trees. Nobody was around to flag down. At this rate, she should just walk back to town for help.

"What the hell," she muttered, and headed for the bridge.

THE ANGELS

Gabriella parked the RV behind the abandoned pickup truck. Clara sat at the table, intently watching Bailey on TV. She was pacing around a little gravel parking lot.

Gabi cut the engine to keep things on the down-low. Jovi tossed a piece of popcorn into her mouth. "Boy, Mother, you said anything can happen today," she said while chewing. "But *this* . . . Ay, Dios mío."

"What a difference a day makes," Gabriella said. She joined them to watch the action.

Clara was still processing how Bailey had gone from talking about having Maria over for dinner and "dessert" to running off. It looked like not even love could keep her in Lanford Falls now.

"That poor woman," she said. "It's been one thing after another."

Jovi gestured at Clara with a piece of popcorn. "The tree fiasco could've been prevented."

"It could have been *corrected*." Clara glared at her drag mother and sister. "Either one of you could've blown the tree into position before it fell."

"The way you were waving it around, it might have swung back and fallen on the crowd," Jovanna said.

She had a point. Still . . . "We could've turned the electricity back on."

"They got it working."

Gabriella squinted at the TV screen. "We needed to see how Bailey would react to the situation. Well, *situations.*"

Clara dropped her arms on the table. "Her reaction was to flip out on the one person keeping her here."

"And then drive all wild and plop in the mud. That was pretty funny." Jovanna chuckled, then sobered when Gabriella shot her a look.

"You're preventing her phone from working," Clara said. "I know you are, Gabi. Don't pretend like you're not."

Her mother gave a dainty shrug. "She can't do that job interview. That's not where her destiny lies."

"Right now, her destiny's lying in a ditch." Clara nodded toward the pickup truck.

"Her destiny's not the truck. It's the town."

"She's suffered enough, Mother. She needs help. *Real* help. No more nudges."

Gabriella bobbed her head. "I agree. It's time."

Finally, the chance to truly get involved. Clara slid off the bench to grab her coat. No, wait—her snow-white faux fur wrap. It paired perfectly with her gold lamé gown.

Bailey George had better get ready for her life to be transformed.

Jovanna leaned forward, pointing at the screen. "Uh, you might want to put a rush order on that."

Clara turned to see Bailey walk onto a wooden footbridge. She was too focused on her phone to pay attention to the conditions. The icy patches and freezing water beneath.

"Oh dear," Gabriella said.

Oh no. Clara tossed the wrap over her shoulders. "Send me to her."

"Don't slip and push her into the river," Jovi said.

Their mother nodded at Clara. "You're ready for this. We'll be watching and talking to you if you need us."

"I won't let you down," Clara said, as much for Gabi's benefit as her own.

"Get those wings, Clara Angel." Jovi fluttered her arms.

"I will."

Gabriella raised her hand. "Good luck, and don't muck it up."

Then she snapped her fingers.

CHAPTER FOURTEEN

"No baaaars," Bailey sang into the quiet. "No bars for meeee."

She walked along the bridge, holding her phone toward the sky. Cheery strands of white lights wound around the side rails, mocking her with their energy usage. "Iiii haaaave noooo seeeerrrrviiiice."

Someday, she'd laugh about this. When she was sitting in her cool Manhattan apartment, watching the snow fall gently over Central Park. Because obviously she was going to have an apartment facing Central Park.

Her boots slipped on a bit of ice. *Oop.* She lowered her phone. Better put it away just in case. Dropping it in Lanford Creek would be the craptastic cherry on top of the day. There should be reception at the other end. There had to be.

Whoa, this bridge was really slick. Melted snow from the railings had frozen in big patches.

She made her way more slowly. A strong gust of wind pushed her from behind. She lost her footing. Oh, shit.

The lights flared intensely and she swore someone said, "Not again."

She spun around and fell to her knees. *Oh God oh God oh God.* She could in theory slip between the railings and fall into the creek.

Something gold sparkled in front of her. She grabbed on to it.

Silky material. An open-toed, strappy gold heel. A long pair of legs.

"Hold on, honey," a voice said. "I've got you."

What the . . .

Two beautifully manicured hands reached down and helped her to her feet. Bailey looked up at . . .

A drag queen.

A gorgeous drag queen in a classic caramel-colored wig and slinky golden gown and furry white wrap.

What the hell was a drag queen doing out here?

"Are you okay?" she asked, steadying Bailey with a firm grip.

"Uh, yeah, I guess. Thank you."

"No trouble." She smiled. "I'm so glad to finally meet you, Bailey."

"Um, I, uh . . . Huh?" Bailey blinked several times. Nope, her eyes weren't playing tricks.

"You don't know me, but I know you. I know a lot about you."

That wasn't creepy or anything. Bailey eased her way back. "Wait a second. Kurt sent you." She nodded to herself. "That's something he would do. He and Arnie sent someone to look for me and thought it'd be funny if it was you."

The queen shook her head. "It wasn't Kurt or Arnie. I'm here for you and you alone."

Bailey took a big step away. Officially super creepy now.

"Where are my manners? You're gonna think I'm a serial killer." She raised one arm and struck a pose. "I'm Clara Angel, of the legendary House of Angel."

Bailey shrugged her arms. "Bailey George, from the unknown House of George."

Clara Angel smiled, revealing a dazzling set of teeth. "Maria's right. You're funny."

Of course. Now it made sense. "You know Maria."

"Can't say I've had the pleasure," Clara said. "She is darling, though. I see why you like her so much."

What the hell was going on? "Are you here for the festival?" Bailey asked. "Are you one of the vendors?"

"No and no."

"Then how do you know me and Maria?"

Clara waved her hands. "This can happen. You're not sure what to make of me, showing up like this. I don't blame you for being confused. Let me explain."

She cleared her throat. Bailey took another step backward. Great time for her phone not to work.

"The Angel family is comprised of my mother Gabriella, my sister Jovanna, and yours truly. We travel around, bringing joy and helping people along the way."

"By putting on drag shows," Bailey said.

"That's a part of it. We've also been blessed with a little"—Clara wiggled her fingers—"magic."

"So you do magic in your shows? Magical drag acts?"

"No, sweetie. We have the power to transform lives. We were called to your cute little town. And you, Miss Bailey George, have been chosen by the universe for a life transformation."

Bailey bobbed her head. "Ohhh, you're with that TV show that does makeovers. I get it. I was nominated, probably by Kurt and Arnie, to get a fancy makeover, and—"

"I told you, Kurt and Arnie aren't involved."

"Then it was Hannah. My sneaky sister."

"Nobody put me up to this," Clara said. "I've been sent here for you."

"By who?"

"Well, specifically Gabriella. But she's guided by a higher power. The essence that connects all living things."

She had to hand it to Clara. The performer was committed to her shtick. "So you're, what," Bailey said. "Magical drag queens?"

"All drag queens are magical." Clara set a hand on her collarbone. "Some more than others."

No. No way. Bailey stumbled across the bridge in a daze. "It's a concussion. I have a concussion from when the truck hit the ditch."

"I sure hope not," Clara said, coming after her.

"Then the stress has finally gotten to me. I've snapped. You're a figment of my imagination."

"Wrong again."

They walked onto the woodchip path. Bailey turned to see if the Ghost of Christmas Insanity had dissipated. But there she was in all her glory.

She poked Clara in the chest. Clara looked down in amusement. "Those aren't real, honey, but I am."

Oh God oh God oh God oh God . . .

"I know this seems odd, but I'm here to help you." Clara tilted her head. "You're not happy. You haven't been for a long time. Life has certainly thrown you some curveballs."

"Seriously, how do you know that?" Bailey said, her voice wavering.

"I told you. We've been watching you. I mean, watching *over* you." Clara snorted. "It's not as bad as it sounds. We followed you around this week to see what we could do to bring back your love of Christmas. Your love for Winter Wonderfest. You're nearly there. You just need a little more nudging."

"So you and your friends have been following me around?"

"Sure have."

"To . . . bring me Christmas cheer?"

"Uh-huh."

Bailey scrunched her face. "And *how* is that not as bad as it sounds?"

"Because we're going to help you live your life to the fullest."

This was either the most bizarre pitch for a multilevel marketing scheme, or she really was losing her mind.

Bailey glanced over her shoulder. Cars whizzed by in the distance on Main Street. "Listen, Clara. I'm sure you put on a heck of a show. But I seriously doubt a drag queen, however fabulous—"

"Thank you."

"—can magically transform my life."

"That's where you're wrong," Clara said.

"And anyway, if you're here to help me, where were you when I needed a replacement act for our finale?"

"I tried to talk Gabi into—"

"And when I lost the checks? Any idea what happened to those?"

Clara shook her head. "No idea. I've just been watching *you*."

"Right, right." Bailey made quote marks with her fingers. "'Watching over me.' Could you have also watched the food tent and the Christmas tree?"

"The tent was not my doing. But the tree . . ." Clara looked away.

Bailey crossed her arms, waiting. Clara avoided all eye contact. "What about the tree?" Bailey said.

Clara drew a circle in the woodchips with her strappy heel. She mumbled something that sounded like, "I might have made the tree fall."

"You what?"

She huffed and dropped her arms. "I made the tree fall. I was trying to stop it from swaying, but I'm still working on manipulating the elements. I'm not Storm from the X-Men."

"Ah. You pushed the tree over with magical wind manipulation." Bailey tapped her temple. "That's what I thought it was."

"I was trying to help. I wanted to help with the tent, but Gabi didn't want to interfere."

"Yeah, well, judging by what you did with the tree, I'm glad."

"I came in here with a little too much force," Clara said. "With the wind on the bridge. Sorry about that."

"That was you? Why didn't Donatella—"

"Gabriella."

"Why didn't whoever keep you from almost blowing me into the creek?"

"She's busy jamming your phone. That's why it won't work."

Bailey released a little cry and pulled out her cell. Still no service.

Clara rolled her eyes up like she was listening. "Well, you are," she muttered, and not to Bailey. "She has a right to know."

Main Street wasn't too far. She could make a run for it through the snow. Clara wouldn't be able to catch her in that tight gown and heels.

"I'm working on it," Clara muttered, then refocused on Bailey. "We didn't want you sending that email. The one about the job interview."

"How do you . . ." Nobody knew about the interview other than Sammie.

"Sorry about the phone. And the wind. Both times. I'm still getting the hang of things."

"So the masters of the universe sent *you* to help me?" Bailey nodded. "That checks out. A drag queen who performs civic duties but doesn't perform onstage."

Clara planted her hands on her perfectly round hips. "Oh, I can work the runway."

"Then work it back to town and leave me alone." Bailey headed for the road.

"I can't."

"Why not?" *Because I'm imagining her in my stress-addled brain.* Clara trotted after her. "I need your help."

"I thought you were here to help *me*," Bailey pointed out.

"We can help each other. Ouch! Slow down. These boots aren't made for walking."

She couldn't help but turn. Clara hopped from foot to foot at the edge of the woodchip path. For an imaginary friend, she appeared to be in real pain.

Whatever the reason, she was there, freezing her toes off to talk to Bailey. "How can I help you, Clara Angel?" she asked. "Get you a ride back to town? Help you find your family? Although . . ." She flapped her arms. "If you're angels, why don't you just fly to each other?"

"I wish," Clara drawled. "That would make travel so much easier. We drive around in an RV that has seen better days."

"Very *Priscilla, Queen of the Desert* of you." Maybe she was a lost soul looking for her people in hospitable, queer-friendly Lanford Falls.

"And, tragically, I don't have my wings. I haven't been able to earn them."

"Sure." Bailey gave what she hoped was a compassionate nod.

"That's what I need your help with. If I rekindle your Christmas spirit, I get my wings. Not actual wings. Beautiful, feathery wings to wear in our show." Clara draped her arms behind her, letting her furry stole drop. "Gabi and Jovi have them. I stand between them on stage dreaming of the day I can wear them too."

This was some elaborate delusion. On whose part was hard to tell at this point. "Your reward is a costume?"

"Not just any costume," Clara breathed. "Think Vegas showgirl, but better. White feathers flecked with silver and gold accents. They're spectacular. They're all I've wanted since I was in baby drag."

Bailey took a step toward her. "Okay. I think I've got it. If you talk me into sticking around for the holidays, your drag family will let you don we now your gay apparel."

Clara cocked one exaggerated eyebrow. "Fa-la-la all you want, but I'm serious. You don't belong in New York. You belong in Lanford Falls. There's so much goodness here for you. Because of you."

Someone *had* to have put her up to this. Mom would go through the elaborate plan of hiring a drag queen to tell Bailey not to go. Hannah had to be in on it too.

"I do *not* belong in Lanford Falls," she said. "And you're doing a bang-up job reminding me of that. The festival's gone terribly. I've ruined it for everyone."

Clara shook a finger in disagreement. "You made the festival what it is. A wonderful event that supports the town."

"I almost destroyed it. With your help. Thanks, by the way."

"Today has been a challenge, but think back to years past. I'm curious why you decided to work on the festival in the first place."

"Nobody else volunteered," Bailey said. "We were in danger of losing the festival and all the stuff that goes with it."

Clara cocked her head. "What stuff?"

"The influx of cash. Tourism. Publicity. Keeping our housing market healthy."

"And fun. And the joy it brings to so many people."

Like building Tropical Dominatrix with Maria. "I guess."

"And the memories." Clara leaned in. "Mistletoe Grove memories."

"Hey, now. That's private." Bailey's cheeks warmed. How did Clara know about that?

"Think of how many other couples have shared a kiss there. Or gotten engaged. I asked universal wisdom. Seven proposals have happened there."

"It's a perfect engagement spot." She'd always figured it would be where she'd propose to the woman she wanted to share her life with.

"Winter Wonderfest made them happen. And you"—Clara tapped Bailey's shoulder—"make Winter Wonderfest happen. If it wasn't for you—"

"Someone else would've done it eventually," Bailey said. "I just had this conversation with my family. I'm the sucker who won't stop volunteering for things."

"You've got it wrong. You're the *reason* these things happen."

"Because I feel enormously responsible for what happens around here. I have a legacy to protect."

"Your father's?"

"Yes."

"Is it just an obligation, or do you truly care?"

"An obligation." Bailey gave a firm nod, even though she didn't fully believe her answer.

"Really?" Clara's smirk told her she didn't believe it, either.

"I mean, yes, I care. But look where that's gotten me. Everyone else gets to do what they want, live where they want, while I'm stuck here."

Clara studied her for several long moments. "You really don't know all the good you've done."

"Yeah, I've really set the world on fire," Bailey drawled.

"You've made such a difference to so many people. Lanford Falls is a much better place because of you."

Unexpected tears pricked her eyes. "But what about what Lanford Falls has done to *me*? I'm tired and grouchy and resentful. And I don't want to be like that. I even pushed someone away who didn't deserve it."

"Maria," Clara said.

"Yeah. I feel terrible. I've been a jerk to everyone lately. They would've been better off if I hadn't stayed this week."

"That's not true."

"Okay, *I* would've been better off. I would've had a great, restful vacation. Something I need. I would've met the people Sammie works for and maybe gotten the job because of it."

"That job is not who you are," Clara murmured.

This was getting annoying. "How do you know that?" Bailey asked.

"Because I know."

"Because the universe told you? Sorry to burst your bubble, but the universe has been a total douchebag to me."

Clara shook her head. "It doesn't make mistakes. Sometimes it needs a little help, but everything has happened to you for a reason. You are where you're supposed to be."

"No, I'm not," Bailey fumed. "Why do you keep saying that? I was just born here. I ended up getting stuck here. I wish I'd never stepped foot in Lanford Falls. I'd be so much better off if I hadn't been born here."

"What's that?"

"I said I wish I'd never been born in this damn town."

"A wish, huh?" Clara rolled her eyes up again. "Can I do that?" She listened or whatever for an answer. "I can? The whole shebang? Cool." She smiled at Bailey. "Hang on tight."

She rubbed her hands together. The snow surrounding them began to swirl, higher and higher.

What the shit was going on?

Snow enveloped them, almost blinding in its intensity.

Clara snapped her fingers. Everything went silent.

Bailey blinked, adjusting her eyes to the sudden darkness. It had gotten *dark*. The lights had gone out on the bridge.

No, wait. Yellow caution tape blocked off a creaky wooden bridge that was falling apart. She went to take a step, but the snow was up past her ankles. The woodchip path was nowhere to be seen. Just a lot of snow.

"Umm . . ." She looked around, trying to figure out where they were. "Is my delusion making me think we're somewhere else?"

"We didn't go anywhere," Clara said. "You got your wish, Bailey George. You weren't born in Lanford Falls."

CHAPTER FIFTEEN

Well, this night had taken a bizarre turn. A drag queen magician had, what, hypnotized her? Yeah, it had to be hypnosis. Though why anyone would go to such lengths for a pair of stage wings was beyond Bailey.

Clara stared at her expectantly. "You got your wish," she repeated. "You weren't born here."

"Oh . . . kay . . ." Bailey inched through the snow. "I guess I'll just head on back to town, then."

"Go wherever. You have your freedom. You can go anywhere. Do anything you want."

"I think I'd like to head back to reality."

She paused at the bridge. It was all busted up and looked like it hadn't been used in years.

"You can't go that way," Clara said, then laughed. "Obviously."

"Can you unhypnotize me or whatever? I have things to do."

"You're not hypnotized. This is real."

The tattered ends of the caution tape flapped in the breeze. "I don't understand why the bridge looks like this," Bailey said. "I was on the committee that spruced up the creek."

233

"The Beautification Committee doesn't exist. You weren't around to get it going."

"No, I was. I went to all the meetings, and do cleanups along Lanford Creek twice a year."

Clara gave a delicate shrug. "Not anymore. You weren't born here, remember."

Yeah, okay, Clara the fallen angel. "Look, I need to get back to the truck so someone can—"

"What truck?"

"The one that's stuck in the mud."

"There's no truck there. You didn't drive away from Winter Wonderfest because there is no Winter Wonderfest."

She didn't have time to argue with Clara. "My phone had better be working. This isn't funny anymore."

Bailey fished around her coat pocket. Empty.

She tried the other pocket. Empty too.

"Where's my phone? Where's . . ." She checked the right pocket again. "Where are the treats Kurt gave me for Lulu?"

A sad smile touched Clara's lips. "Lulu's not your dog, honey."

"No way," Bailey stated. "Lulu is *mine*, and she always gets treats from Kurt."

Clara adjusted her furry stole. "You never adopted Lulu."

That was a load of crap. She'd never let anything happen to Lulu. She held out a hand and said, "Give me my phone back. I have to get to the tent place before it closes."

"Where would I be hiding your phone?" Clara stretched her arms wide, then glanced down. "Don't get any ideas. I'm tucked within an inch of my life."

"Ugh, fine. Whatever. I was going to walk anyway."

Bailey turned and headed toward Main Street. Her coat swung from the movement.

It was clean. Not a spot of muck on the hem. Her boots too. That was weird. The snow must've cleared off the mud.

Traffic was nonexistent up ahead. Not a bad thing, if it meant people were no longer fleeing the festival.

She trudged out of the snow and onto the side of the road. Clara whimpered and moaned, holding her gown with both hands. "Will you slow down?" she implored.

Bailey rolled her eyes. "Next time you get sent to ruin someone's day, wear boots."

"It doesn't usually take this much to help someone," Clara said. "I'm going the extra mile. Literally."

Hmm. Main Street was unusually unlit. Something was missing. A dull metal street sign read *Lanford Falls. Population: 3517.*

That wasn't accurate. Over five thousand permanent residents lived in the Falls.

Darkness stretched toward the highway. Where *were* all the cars? And where was the big welcome sign that always had a spotlight shining on it?

Clara caught up to her. "Looking for something?" she wheezed.

"The light must've gone out by the *Welcome to Lanford Falls* sign."

"Oh, the one that doesn't exist?"

"The one I coordinated to have made for our senior class fundraiser." Clara smoothed out her dress. "Nobody coordinated that."

This was just . . . weird. Bailey shook her head and started walking again. She'd get back to town and ditch Clara and have a good, stiff drink. Probably two.

An old farmhouse came into view. That couldn't be right. It had to be the lone streetlight casting shadows on the dog park.

Only the closer she got, the clearer the structure got. It was the abandoned farmhouse that had been there when she was young. The barn looked one bad storm away from collapse.

She stopped in front of the decrepit house. "This makes no sense."

"What doesn't?" Clara asked beside her.

"This house." Bailey gestured to it and the barn. "This farm had been abandoned for . . . I don't know how long. Once the town acquired the property, we razed the house and built the dog park. It was the ideal use, with the open land."

"Who suggested the dog park?"

"I did. To honor my father."

Her heart twinged. The dog park had been the perfect way to honor Dad's memory. Not having the park meant : . .

She met Clara's gaze. The queen nodded. "You weren't here to suggest it."

And James George Park didn't exist.

What was going on? This was some strange, elaborate way to . . . to . . .

To what? Make her feel guilty? She didn't need help in that department.

Bailey moved north, staring at what was left of the barn. She'd been there the day local builders came and dismantled it to use the reclaimed wood. All of this should be gone.

Where was Lulu going to play with her pals? Where were she and Maria going to let their dogs . . .

Well obviously, they'd be fine. This wasn't real. It felt real, but was just some bad trip. A bout of psychosis. Spoiled hot dog meat from lunch.

She crossed the side street and was met with a literal brick wall. "What fresh hell is this?" she wondered, looking up at the expansive barrier of gray bricks.

She peered down the length of what should've been the affordable housing subdivision. "Did someone put up a new fence?"

"Some*one* did," Clara said.

The homes were completely hidden. It didn't make any sense. Where were the yards filled with festive decorations? Heck, where was the sidewalk? There was only a big, imposing wrought-iron gate in the middle.

Her sense of dread mounted with every step. The gates were shut tight. Motion sensor floodlights flared, and she had to shield her eyes until they adjusted. A cursive *F* adorned the center of one gate. A cursive *P* decorated its mate.

Beyond the gates sat a garish mansion. Gray stone. Gray door. Gray everything.

Gray. Felicity Potter's favorite color.

FP.

This was . . . "Felicity Potter's house?" Bailey said. "She doesn't live here. A bunch of families live here."

Clara hugged her wrap across her body. "Are you starting to see a pattern? No Bailey means those homes didn't get built."

"I clearly remember this project. I remember everything. How come I know these things happened, but they aren't here?"

"Because *you* weren't here."

"But I . . ." Bailey trailed off, at a total loss.

The unfamiliar house sat dark, cold, lifeless. Wait a second. Felicity had fought against having the subdivision built. She'd wanted to put up a couple of showy, pricey homes, but Bailey had led the charge to stop it. Felicity had never forgotten it.

"Supposing . . ." Bailey said, then held up a hand. "And I mean just *supposing* this is true . . ."

"Because it is," Clara said with a nod.

"Wouldn't someone else have stopped her? The subdivision was a win-win project for the town. More families, more revenue, plus it was the right thing to do."

"They needed someone who wasn't intimidated by Felicity Potter. Not many people are willing to stand up to her."

"I have. So many times."

"Sorry, my dear," Clara said. "You and Ms. Potter have never met."

A new thought sprang to mind, worse than some big, ugly house. "Where do the families who had homes here live?"

Clara clasped her hands, growing solemn. "Not in Lanford Falls. They couldn't afford it."

"That's terrible," Bailey murmured.

This was all too much. It couldn't be real.

Clara stood there, looking gorgeous in the harsh lighting. The wind rustled her cascading wig. It was cold and biting against Bailey's face.

She pinched her wrist. Yup, her fingers were freezing. This was somehow very real.

Narrowing her eyes, Clara said, "You're getting to the part where it sinks in. I made your wish come true. You can turn around and leave Lanford Falls forever."

Bailey shook her head slowly, then more emphatically. "I don't know what's going on, but I need answers. I'm going to find my mom and get this straightened out."

"Ooh. That might not be a good idea."

Reaching town was more critical than ever. She made her way quickly up Main Street.

Clara tiptoe-jogged after her. "Bailey, I'm telling you it won't be what you think."

Bailey cut across the road to get to Mom's house. Then did a double take.

Main Street was dim. The streetlamps were on, but that was it. No greenery wrapped around them. No cheerful decorations in the shop windows. A couple of the streetlights were even burned out.

The brightest thing was a neon sign inside the bookstore. Only it was a bar. And the clothing shop next door was a personal injury lawyer. The slogan painted on the window declared *We'll get you the*

settlement you DESERVE. The antique shop that had been there forever had a *For Lease—Potter Enterprises* sign on its newspaper-covered
windows.

She walked on numb legs past familiar buildings with the wrong
businesses. Where were the art galleries? The fudge shop?

Her heart hammered as she crossed the side street just before
George Family Homes. The concrete was all busted up on the sidewalk. Their neighboring jewelry store was also for lease.

She paused in front of what should've been her office. A jagged
lime green and blue sign jutted out from the brick façade.

Smokey's Vape Shack

There were no workstations visible through the tinted windows.
No quaint reception area with a gleaming Christmas tree. Instead,
display cases and shelves ran along the walls. A young man slumped
on a stool behind the cash register, intent on his phone.

This had to be a mistake. It *had* to be.

She pulled the door open with a trembling hand. The employee
didn't look up. It definitely didn't smell like the citrusy diffuser that
normally greeted clients. A burgundy curtain blocked access to where
the offices should be. It was all wrong.

An older man in a Smokey's Vape Shack T-shirt plodded from
behind the curtain. Holy shit.

"Uncle Bill," Bailey said, rushing to him. "Thank God. What's
going on?"

Uncle Bill recoiled, holding a small cardboard box like a shield.

"What happened to the office? Why is everything different?"

"What are you talking about?" His gruff voice sounded even
brusquer.

"Dad's company. George Family Homes." She splayed her hands
on her chest. "It's me, Bailey. How do you not know me?"

"I don't know you," Uncle Bill said, and skirted past her. "George
Family Homes. Huh. Haven't heard that in years."

"You work there. With me. You've worked there since it opened."

He dropped the box on one of the display cases. "That place closed after Jim George died. Going on . . . I dunno, seventeen, eighteen years."

"It didn't close." Bailey moved to stand in front of him. "We saved it. You wouldn't let the other employees sell out to Felicity Potter."

"Potter owns this town," Uncle Bill said. "She poached the whole staff. Left me to rot."

"No, that's . . . that's not what happened to . . ." She trailed off, growing dizzy.

"What do you want?" He jerked his chin toward the cash register. "The kid'll get it."

The young man blew out a puff of air. He looked up, shaggy hair hanging in his eyes. "I'm the assistant manager, dude. You get it."

Wait . . . "Zack?" Bailey realized. "Zack Walsh, from the madrigals."

Zack curled his lip. "What's a madrigal?"

"What about the concert? Why aren't you getting ready?"

"No concerts around here, lady." He leaned back to look out the picture window. "Why is a drag queen stalking you?"

Clara stood outside, talking to herself. Or to angels, or the voices in her head, or whoever.

Bailey laced her fingers beneath her chin and pleaded, "Uncle Bill, please. Tell me this is just some elaborate scheme. You're playing a joke. This is a set, and all the workstations are behind that curtain."

"The only thing back there is inventory." He gave her an up-and-down assessment. "I don't care what floats your boat. I'm not your uncle. Don't even know how you know my name."

"'Cause you've been around since the Stone Age," Zack guffawed. "Shut up, kid."

"You shut up. I can have you fired, old man."

Uncle Bill glanced at Bailey again, then bent down to busy himself in the display case. He genuinely didn't know her. He wasn't a good enough actor to pull this off. And why was Zack being so mean? He seemed like a good kid.

She strolled over to the curtain, pretending to casually peek around it. Just a storage area filled with boxes and cleaning supplies. Both offices were totally gone. No hint of George Family Homes other than where the restroom was located.

"Lady," Uncle Bill groused. "If you're not gonna buy anything, you should get out."

His cold tone chilled her to the bone. "I don't know what's going on, but I'm going to talk to my mom. She'll straighten this out."

"Do that. You got the wrong guy. I don't have a sister."

She opened her mouth to tell him she knew that, and he was her honorary uncle anyway. What was the point in arguing? He thought she was a stranger.

She exited the shop, icy wind smacking her face. Clara joined her on the sidewalk.

"He didn't recognize me," Bailey said, still not quite believing it.

"How sad," Clara said.

"He could've kept the business going. Why is he working here?"

Even as the words left her mouth, she knew why. Uncle Bill didn't have the people skills, which was why Bailey had needed to step in. Plus, he'd said Felicity took all their employees. Where were they now? Where were their current employees working? What happened to all the clients they'd helped over the years? Did they move to Lanford Falls or not?

What an insane ripple effect. Too vast, too overwhelming to comprehend.

Clara patted her arm. "It's a lot, isn't it? How many lives you've touched."

"There's just so many people. But one matters the most." She started toward the corner.

"Where to now?" Clara asked.

"To see my mom. And Lulu, because no matter what's going on, Lulu is my baby."

"Hon, I keep telling you that's not—"

Bailey whirled around. "You have a drag mother, right? A drag family, you said?"

"Yes. A mother and sister."

"And you love them and they love you?"

Clara smirked. "Most days."

"Then you understand why I have to see my mom. She'll know me. We'll figure this out together."

"If you insist," Clara sighed. "Lead on, Rudolph."

Bailey shot her a wary glance. Those Angels really had been following her if they'd overheard that reindeer conversation with Maria. Or maybe it was a coincidence. Anything was possible in this alternate reality.

They walked down a dark side street, devoid of any seasonal décor. Same thing when they reached the residential area. A couple of houses had strings of outdoor lights and Christmas trees in their front windows, but nothing like normal. It almost looked like mid-January when the stragglers hadn't yet taken down their decorations.

Mom's house would be welcoming. Mom's house would have warmth radiating from it and bright exterior lights. Hannah and Reuben loved to help her hang them the day after Thanksgiving.

It was getting awkward wandering the streets with someone who knew an awful lot about her, but not vice versa. So Bailey asked, "How long have you been doing drag?"

"I've been dressing up in one way or another most of my life." Clara smiled. "A lady never reveals her age."

Bailey cracked a grin at that. "And your family? How did you meet them?"

"We were drawn together down in Miami. Like attracts like. Our energies vibrate on the same level."

"That's pretty funky woo-woo."

"The universe is a pretty funky woo-woo place." Clara nudged her with an elbow. "Think about your friends. How you're drawn to be with certain people."

"Hmm. Solid point."

"And Maria. You two found one another again."

Her heart thumped with possibility. Had fate brought Maria back? "That's not the universe. That's her taking a job and moving back to town."

Clara screwed up her eyes. "Ohh, you're right." She looked down at Bailey. "Sorry, I meant that *was* how your life went. Until . . ." She waved around them. "Your wish."

"Right, right. My wish."

They passed one of the beautiful old Victorians. It looked freshly painted. A *For Sale—Potter Real Estate* sign creaked in the breeze. It must've just gone on the market.

Clara shivered and rubbed her arms. She really wanted to get those wings to put herself through this.

"Why does wearing these wings mean so much to you?" Bailey asked.

Her tall companion considered the question. "It's not so much the wings, but what they represent. In order to get them, I have to truly help someone. Make a difference in someone's life. I've had small successes, but nothing that transformed someone's life. That would warm my heart clear through. Each time I don those wings, I'll remember the gift I was able to give to someone deserving."

"Can't say I'm the most deserving person," Bailey said.

"You'll see. If you haven't started seeing it already."

The dog park, George Family Homes . . .

They passed another house with a Potter Real Estate sign in the yard. And there was one across the street. "There are a lot of houses for sale," she noted.

"Who would want to live here?" Clara said.

"Tons of people. Watch my phone light up after Winter Wonderfest."

"The phone you don't have. And a festival this town doesn't have."

Bailey patted her coat pockets. "Yeah, about that. When we're done with this, give me my phone back."

"I don't have it." Clara displayed the ends of her stole. "You're completely free of any attachments."

Bailey raised an eyebrow at her. "This is getting old, Clara."

The fabulous queen simply chuckled.

She almost walked past Mom's house. No lights outside. No wreath on the door. Just a tabletop tree flickering in the gaps between the vertical blinds. The house itself looked dingy and unkempt. One of the shutters was missing. The driveway had a huge crack running down its length. Still, what a relief to be here. To finally get some answers.

"Brace yourself," Clara said. "This is not the childhood home you remember."

Of course it was. This was home base for the George family.

Bailey trotted across the unshoveled walk to the front porch. She tried the door, but it was locked.

"Mom?" she called, knocking loudly. "Mom, it's me."

No answer. Crap, what if she wasn't home?

She tried the doorbell, which didn't seem to be working. Then knocked again. The foyer light went on. Thank God. The shadow of movement danced behind the peephole.

"Mom, it's me," she said. "Come on. Open up."

A dim light went on beside the entrance. The door opened a tiny bit. "You must be lost," Mom said. "This isn't the right house."

"Seriously?" Bailey moved to push the door open. No, better not. Everyone was acting so strange. She didn't want to freak her mother out. "Donna George. You live here."

The door opened another fraction of an inch. Mom peered at her with deep wrinkles around suspicious eyes. Her hair hung gray and stringy. Did she stop going to the salon? "Are you from another collection agency?" she said. She sounded so tired.

"No," Bailey said. "I'm trying to figure out what's going on. Everything's messed up around town."

"You're one of Potter's lackeys." Mom pointed a finger emphatically. "Trying to scrape up the scraps."

"Mom, *no.*"

"Why are you calling me Mom?"

"I saw Uncle Bill, and he didn't recognize me, but I figured you would know your own daughter."

"Who's Uncle Bill?"

"He was at a vape shop, which was totally wrong—"

"You're one of those druggies hanging out at Smokey's." Mom started to close the door. "Don't you try to rob me, druggie!"

Bailey shoved her boot in the doorway. "Mom—Donna. I'm not a druggie, or a bill collector. I'm family."

"You're no family of mine."

Her insides churned from hurt, from disbelief. How could her mother act like this? Something was very, very wrong.

She could tell Mom was getting scared, so she said, "Fine, I'll leave you alone. Just let me get Lulu."

"Who?"

"Where's Lulu?" She looked over Mom's shoulder. "Lulu! Come here, Lulu Bear. Where's my girl?"

Mom's eyes ballooned. "What are you doing? Who's Lulu?"

"Who's yelling out there?" a familiar voice said. *Hannah.*

Her sister yanked the door open. Bailey's stomach clenched even tighter. Hannah's hair was up in a messy ponytail. Her stained sweatshirt and drab sweatpants were two things she'd never be caught dead in.

"Yes?" she said in a clipped tone.

"Hannah, it's me." Bailey longed to reach out, to hug both of them and make this go away.

"Me who?"

If their mother didn't recognize her, no way Hannah would. "Bailey. I'm Bailey George. I grew up here with you."

"Wrong house, weirdo." Hannah leaned against the door. "We're the only ones who live here."

"You live here?" Bailey said. "Not in Syracuse with Reuben and your dogs?"

"The only Reuben I know is the sandwich at Nick's." Hannah shared a look with Mom. "Look, if you're a collector or a drugged-out robber, we don't have anything worth taking. The house is in foreclosure."

"But that's not supposed to happen," Bailey said.

"That's what happens when you can't afford to pay the mortgage," her sister said.

Mom choked out a mirthless laugh. "Potter can't wait to get her hooks into it. You tell her I hope she rots in Lanford Creek."

"Greedy old wench," Hannah grumbled.

Cobwebs dangled off the usually pristine foyer ceiling light. The floral wallpaper Mom had replaced forever ago hung on the walls, faded and peeling in one section.

This was all Bailey's fault. "I'm so sorry," she told them.

"That's life," Hannah said with a shrug. "Happy holidays, weirdo."

She slammed the door in Bailey's face. The click of the deadbolt sounded. Then the porch light went out.

Uncle Bill didn't know her. Her mother and sister didn't know her.

What was going on?

CHAPTER SIXTEEN

Bailey plodded down the driveway in a daze. Clara waited patiently for her, but she couldn't speak a single word. She was so profoundly *sad*. The grief she'd seen in her mother's eyes. The wear and tear on Hannah.

"Didn't go well, huh?" Clara said.

"It was awful," Bailey whispered. "What happened to them?"

"Donna had to take a leave of absence when Jim George passed. Then the school eliminated her art teacher position. Hannah couldn't afford to go to college. They've had to make do with what local jobs can be had."

"If Hannah didn't go to college, she didn't start a business doing what she loves. And she never met her husband."

Clara shook her head. "No, sweetie."

"And Mom." Bailey began to pace. "She's supposed to be comfortable and happy. That was one of the reasons I took over George Family Homes. So she wouldn't lose the house."

"Things have been difficult."

"Come on, Clara. This isn't fair. I never wanted anything to happen to them. They should be doing okay. They're strong, resilient women."

"Sometimes life gets overwhelming," Clara said. "They simply couldn't handle everything."

Bailey stopped pacing in front of her. "This is a really mean trick."

"It's no trick. It's just the way it is."

Thoughts whirled through her mind. Everything she'd done at the office, fighting off Felicity, working hard for the people she cared about. It hadn't been a chore. She'd done it out of love and a desire to give them as much as they gave her.

"I need a drink," she said.

"I'm up for that," Clara said, then muttered, "Oh hush, Gabi. One appletini."

She continued arguing with "Gabi" as they walked along the sidewalk. There were consequences for the choices Bailey had made. Some bad, like being stuck in Lanford Falls. But that had been the focus for too long. One bad thing. And it wasn't even bad. What about all the good things? Mom and Hannah thriving, and Uncle Bill too. The dog park . . .

Where was Lulu, anyway?

No Bailey, no Lulu.

Her heart cracked wide open, sending a surge of blood through her veins. What had happened to Lulu? And Rosie? And Maria?

"What's Maria doing?" Bailey blurted out.

Clara's mouth froze in an O. "Uhh . . ."

"You know what?" Bailey held up a hand. "Don't tell me. She won't know who I am, and I can't take another hit."

Seeing beautiful Maria without a big smile would do her in. Then again, she'd left Maria earlier with tears in her eyes.

I'm such a fool.

She wanted Maria in her life. Wanted to return to normalcy so she could whisk her away to Mistletoe Grove and show her just how much she liked her. Hopefully, this nightmare would end soon. She had to apologize to Maria. Do a lot more than cook her spaghetti, like take her out for dinner to . . .

To where? The best restaurants in town didn't exist anymore.

Her heart, already split in two, crumbled to tiny pieces. This whole week with Maria had been the best surprise—the best gift—Bailey had received since their first kiss.

A kiss that maybe never happened now.

She picked up speed to get to Main Street. The usual friendly glow didn't emanate from that direction.

When they hit the shopping district, more neon signs beckoned patrons into several bars. At least there were options on where to get said drink.

"You know what strikes me odd?" Clara said. "It's so quiet. There's no foot traffic."

She was right. Most businesses were closed up for the night. "Things should be open," Bailey said. "During Winter Wonderfest weekend, they stay open late for the influx of tourists."

"Bailey, you know there's no Winter Wonderfest. The last time the town had it was—"

"Eleven years ago," she finished.

"Twelve," Clara said.

"Right. Twelve." Bailey had taken it over after the poorly planned festival that nearly ruined its reputation.

"There wasn't enough interest to keep it going. The town has grown more gloomy every year." Clara touched her fingers to her chest. "What a shame."

A lone car drove up Main Street. Its headlights reflected off a large garage door.

Hold on. That should've been Yvette's flower shop. Above the garage were modern condos with, from what Bailey could tell, vaulted ceilings.

The oldest buildings in town had been replaced with condos. Just like Felicity Potter wanted.

Because Bailey wasn't around to stop her.

"You got your condos, Felicity," she murmured.

"What's that?" Clara said.

"This used to be family-owned stores. They were here for generations. And a well-known gallery that showcased local artists. What are they doing now? What's my friend Yvette doing?"

"The same thing everyone else is. Surviving as best as she can."

"But not thriving."

"Unfortunately not."

Those poor families. Their employees. All the artists. She had to walk away from the ugly metal-and-glass structure. It was totally out of place in the middle of the charming downtown.

Caffeinated Corner didn't sit on the corner, and there was no Pride flag. It was a pawn shop with tacky yellow signage Kurt would hate. Oh no. Did Kurt work there? That would suck. He'd hate it.

She plastered herself against one of the windows. The scruffy man behind the counter gave her a dirty look. Okay, not Kurt. Maybe he was okay.

The village green was dark, other than a buzzing streetlight illuminating the entrance. Bailey went over to it anyway, needing definitive proof.

From what she could see, the green was little more than two park benches and a gravel path. It looked like someone had built a snowman that got kicked over.

"That's annoying." She pointed it out to Clara. "Some kid made a snowman to bring a little joy to this place, and it got destroyed."

"Winter Wonderfest could have brought so much joy," Clara said. "Think about all those couples who didn't share a kiss under the mistletoe. Or get engaged."

Anger spread through Bailey's chest. "Okay, I get the point. I suck for not being here."

Clara rubbed her back. "This isn't to make you feel bad. It's to show you all the good you did. And what Lanford Falls looks like without you in it."

"It looks like shit."

"It does. There's a wide, Bailey-sized hole."

"But . . . this isn't fair," Bailey said. "My friends and family shouldn't have to suffer so I can get what I want."

"And what is it you want?" Clara crossed her arms.

"Freedom. The chance to try new things."

"You have that now."

"Not like this. I don't want it like this."

Clara took a step closer. "Things were pretty good with you around. Not just for them. For you as well."

"I had my dog," Bailey said. "And my family."

"You had friends." Clara looked down Main Street. "All the people you're worrying about. Friends who gave you free coffee, and trivia nights, and who gladly stepped in to help when you needed them."

"Yeah, but . . ."

"But . . . ?"

Groaning, Bailey said, "I've never gotten to live anywhere else. Do anything else."

"Let me ask you something." Clara settled her hands on her hips. "Since you can finally do whatever you want, what do you want to do first? More than anything?"

I want to go home. "Well, I suppose I can't go anywhere without a wallet or keys *or a phone.*"

She waved that off. "I can get you where you want to go. Where to?"

Home. Speaking of, who lived in her house? Ugh, it was probably abandoned and filled with rogue squirrels.

"I'd like to get a drink. Do you have any cash?" Bailey gestured at Clara's ample round bosom. "Some bills stuck in there?"

"Not without a gig."

"Fine. Let's just go to Martin's. If he recognizes me, he'll know I'm good for it. If not, he'll kick us out." Martin's didn't serve booze, but they had pancakes and syrup. Essential sugar and carbs.

As they crossed the street, she was glad to see Gruber's still there. At least her two summers of employment hadn't altered the course of its history.

She caught sight of Mr. Gruber sweeping the floor. He looked as sad and dreary as the rest of the normally cheerful store. Did he still charm his customers with colorful stories, or had those gone away with everything else?

By habit, she looked outside Martin's for the placard menu. It wasn't there. The door said *Nick's Bar & Grill*.

"Nick's?" Bailey said.

"It's a little different than what you remember," Clara said.

Loud classic rock greeted them inside. It still had the old diner décor, only the counter had been replaced with a bar. At least she could get a drink now.

She searched for familiar faces. Where was Marty? Where were the patrons? Instead of packed tables, a smattering of lone people sat here and there.

Miss Josephine sat in a booth against the windows. She looked so small, like the red vinyl might swallow her whole. She spooned some soup with a shaky hand.

"Can I get you something?" a man said from behind the bar.

It took her a second to recognize Kurt. His tight black T-shirt didn't hug sculpted muscles, and his ever-present smile was faint, forced. "Hey, Kurt," she said anyway.

"Uh, okay." He gave her the confused look that had become all too familiar. "You two can sit wherever you want. Domestic beer is half-price tonight."

"You're a bartender? You said you'd never do that again after working through college."

"Did we go to school together?" Kurt asked, tossing a hand towel over his shoulder.

"You could say that."

"Well, y'know, the tips are good. One of the better jobs in town." He glanced at Clara. "You can sit down."

Clara shuffled to one of the barstools. "Thank you. My feet are *dying*."

Bailey sat beside her. She couldn't stop staring at Kurt. At the food prep area behind him. At the smoke wafting from the grill in the kitchen. "What happened to Martin's?"

"The guy who owned it had financial problems. I guess he sold it to cover his debts."

"So Nick the night manager bought it?"

"Potter Enterprises owns the building. He leases the restaurant." Kurt leaned against the bar. "You need to order something. If Nick sees you just sitting here, I'll get an earful."

"Appletini, please," Clara said, then muttered to herself, "Just one, Gabi."

Kurt smiled, a glimpse of his old, familiar self. "This is a beer and liquor kind of place."

Bailey tried to shake the fog from her head. "Felicity Potter owns the town, Marty's God knows where, and you're working at a bar that doesn't serve appletinis. I bet you're not married to Arnie, either."

His mouth set in a grim line. "You know my ex-boyfriend?"

"I know both of you."

"If you're friends with Arnie, you are *not* welcome here."

"What do you mean?" Bailey asked, genuinely at a loss.

Kurt snagged the towel and wrung it in his hands. "Mister hotshot deputy sheriff ran off with our yoga instructor. He broke my heart *and* closed the only yoga studio for miles."

"Aw, Kurt, I'm sorry," Bailey said. "I . . . didn't know."

She'd clearly made him uncomfortable. Maybe it would be best to leave. Plus, the white man in a trucker hat at the end of the bar was sneering at Clara. This version of Lanford Falls didn't seem as welcoming as the old one. It for sure wasn't a haven for artistic types.

The door to the kitchen swung open. Nick came out in a well-worn and stained white apron. "Ho ho ho," he said, holding a platter. "Santa's come early, kids."

He used metal tongs to toss bright orange hot wings on each diner's plate. He plopped two beside Miss Josephine's soup bowl. "Oh, no thank you," she said. "I can't eat those with my dentures."

"Take 'em out and suck on the bones. It's Christmas." He offered one to the guy at the bar. Then he approached Bailey and Clara. "Compliments of the chef."

"What are you doing?" Bailey asked him.

"I'm giving out wings."

"If only it were that easy," Clara grumble-muttered.

"No, thanks," Bailey said.

Quirking his thick eyebrows, Nick said, "You don't have drinks, and you don't want food. I suggest you order something or find somewhere else to loiter."

Loiter? Who even said things like that?

Clara touched her arm and leaned in. "We should go. I don't think he'll be happy to learn we have no m-o-n-e-y."

"No money?" Damn, Nick had overheard. He pointed the tongs at the door. "This ain't a charity."

"But you're giving out wings, Saint Nick," Bailey couldn't help saying.

"Even Santa gets paid in milk and cookies."

"Come on." Clara tugged on her coat sleeve.

Bailey slid off the barstool, aching from the puzzled looks Nick and Kurt were giving her. She followed Clara toward the exit, watching Miss Josephine struggle with her soup bowl. Someone should be helping her. Everyone in town took care of her.

That is, they did. Lanford Falls wasn't that place anymore.

At the door, Bailey turned and caught Kurt's eye. "I'll fix this if I can," she told him.

He made a face like *What a looney tune.*

She could barely walk along the sidewalk, her legs having turned to lead. "My very gay best friend is working at a very straight bar."

"He was never able to get things in order to open the café," Clara said. "You helped him with that."

"I did," Bailey murmured. A wistful smile pulled at her lips. "We had so much fun doing it. We literally skipped out of the bank when he secured the loan. And oh man, he made such a mess painting the walls. We laughed so hard, we were in tears."

"It sounds like you were good for each other," Clara said.

"Yeah." Bailey hugged her arms tightly. "I guess I forgot how much Kurt means to me. He's always been the one who gets me out of the house and reminds me to have fun."

"He wanted you to be happy."

"He really does."

"All your friends wanted you to be happy."

"They do."

Clara sighed deeply. "Too bad that's just a memory for you. These people never got to know you."

"So you keep saying." *So I keep discovering.*

Ironically, Potter Real Estate looked exactly the same. Next door, an equally imposing office proclaimed it was Potter Enterprises. Felicity was eating up the town, bit by bit. She'd probably try to change its name to something ridiculous, like Pottersville.

"If this is what Lanford Falls is like now, I should be glad not to live here," Bailey said.

"Sure." Clara sidestepped a sloppy pile of shoveled snow. "None of this is your problem, and that's what you wanted. To be free of this town."

"I mean, it wasn't *that* bad." Memories floated about like snowflakes. Her morning coffee runs and chats with Kurt. Lulu romping at the dog park. Helping Miss Josephine. Trivia night. The thrill she got each time a client bought their dream home. Listening to Mr. Gruber's stories, and cleaning up Lanford Creek, and Mom and Hannah. So much with Mom and Hannah.

And Maria. Going around town with Maria. Sharing stories with Maria while making ornaments. Maria at Mistletoe Grove, both as a teen and an adult. Maria and the joy and passion she radiated.

"Clara." Bailey was almost afraid to ask. "Where's Maria?"

Clara's face pinched. "Oh honey, I don't think you want to know."

"I do. She just came back into my life. I couldn't have screwed hers up that badly."

"Well, remember that ripple effect of you not being here . . ."

Worry snaked through Bailey's bloodstream. "Did she never leave, like Hannah?"

Clara looked up, as though searching for guidance. "I think I'd better show you. It's easier that way."

They approached Town Hall. The large pine tree in front didn't dazzle with lights. A new metal sign proclaimed *Lanford Falls, New York. Felicity Potter, Mayor.*

"Really?" She didn't know whether to laugh or cry.

"Oh, Ms. Potter is mayor," Clara said over her shoulder. "You should've guessed that by now."

"I want my friend to be mayor," Bailey said. "Ellis is a fantastic mayor."

"Ellis ran against her, but as I said . . ."

"People are afraid of Felicity."

"Mm-hmm. Who'd vote against her?"

Shit. Her biggest fear had come true. Without someone keeping Felicity in check, she'd run rampant over the town. It had always felt like a burden, but if this was the alternative, it was more important than Bailey ever realized.

Clara stopped near the library. "Maria's still working here?" Bailey said. "At least one thing's going right."

Clara didn't say anything.

Bailey followed her gaze. It was the same historic building with *Lanford Falls Public Library* chiseled above the doors. But there was a sign to the right of the stone steps. A business directory. Like this was an office building.

"What's going on?" Bailey breathed.

"I hate to tell you this," said Clara. "The library closed a few years ago. Budget cutbacks. It was converted to office space."

She could scarcely push the word through the lump in her throat. "Maria?"

"Maria never moved back to Lanford Falls." Clara shrugged. "She had no reason to."

"So she's . . ."

"In Concord. Single. No pets."

"No." Bailey shook her head. "Maria always wanted to move home. That was her dream, and it came true. And to be honest, I think I was maybe part of that dream. I think she was hoping we would reconnect. And we did."

"No, sweetie."

"*We did.* You can't tell me I'm gutted over something that never happened. What we have is very real."

"I wish it was." Clara touched Bailey's shoulder. "I truly wish it was. But *your* wish did not include Maria."

This infuriating wish. People said off-the-cuff things like that all the time. It didn't mean they genuinely wanted them. Didn't mean Bailey wanted to have never stepped foot in Lanford Falls.

Maria never moved home. Maria isn't happy the way she should be every single day of her life.

Tears pooled in her eyes. She had to turn away from the library. "Everyone I love is miserable."

"Things could be better for them," Clara said.

"I'm hurting all of them."

"Your presence is greatly missed."

Maria wasn't going to do her projects and presentations. She wasn't going to meet Bailey at the dog park. They weren't going to have coffee or dinners or dates or anything. They would never kiss again. Never sleep together. They couldn't start something. Couldn't try. And that just *hurt*. She'd thrown away the chance to be with Maria.

Clara looped her arm through Bailey's. "You see, Bailey?" she murmured. "You had a pretty fabulous life."

She really did.

And now it was gone.

THE ANGELS

Clara studied Bailey closely for a response. She'd gone all in, reminding her of the good things in her life.

Bailey cleared her throat, tears shining in her dark eyes. "Can you give me a minute?" she said, untangling their arms. "I need to be alone."

"Of course." Clara stepped away.

Bailey walked to a nearby bench and sank onto it. Poor thing. Life transformations were exhausting. People really didn't see the impact they made every day, in big and small ways.

Looking up at the night sky, Clara asked, "How am I doing, Gabriella?"

"Girl," Gabi's voice echoed in her head. "You are killing it."

"This town is so depressing," Jovanna chimed in. "I had to wrap a blanket around myself to ward off the chill."

"Her heart is changing. Can you feel it?"

Clara tuned in to Bailey's core. A small fire had been ignited and was smoldering. Growing. "Yes. She's starting to believe again."

Clara could also feel, more than ever before, her wings were within reach. Which was wonderful, no doubt about it. But just as wonderful was going on this journey with Bailey. It was tough to stand back and observe, but Bailey was worth it. She'd been a good challenge. She needed something as extreme as this to bring back her holiday spirit.

"Nice touch making Felicity Potter mayor," Gabi said.

"I thought you'd like that," Clara said.

"Can we work on that woman next?" Jovanna said. "She could use a strong cup of spiked eggnog."

"A little nudge might be in order," said Gabriella. "I'll consult universal wisdom."

"I'll do it for you." Jovi whistled loudly. "Yo. Felicity Potter. Eggnog enema. Cool? Cool."

Their mother sighed. "If you need a project that badly, why don't you organize your wigs?"

"Because I'd rather help people."

"Mm-hmm."

Clara waved her hands to shush them. "Can we focus on Bailey? This is a critical moment. Whether she chooses to stay or go."

"It's up to her now," Gabriella said. "You've done all you can."

Bailey wiped beneath her eyes. She looked positively wrecked.

There was still one thing Clara could do for her. "She needs a friend," she said, and walked toward the bench. Her feet ached in protest. "Remind me to consider better footwear next time."

"Hey, Clara," Jovanna said. "Next time, wear boots."

She shot her sister a dirty look, which Jovi would catch on TV. Then she sat beside Bailey on the cold metal bench. Bailey slouched against the back, eyes red, face raw.

"What's on your mind?" Clara asked gently.

Bailey plucked at the cerulean blue scarf peeking out from her coat. "There's no dog hair. It had Lulu fuzz and Rosie's short hairs all over it. I never thought I'd miss dog hair on my clothes."

"I'm sure you didn't."

She flopped her hands in her lap. "Everything I wanted was right in front of me, but I didn't see it. I was too busy looking ahead. At this life I thought would be so much better if I'd gotten the chance to live it."

Clara nodded in understanding. "Looking at the destination, not the journey."

"Yeah." Bailey rolled her head to look at her. "That's exactly what it was. Not paying attention to the right here, right now."

"It's the journey that will bring you joy. I think a lot of people forget that."

Bailey wagged a finger. "You're very good at what you do. Whatever it is you do."

"Deliver sickening looks and universal wisdom," Clara said.

"That you do." Bailey dropped her head back and released a deep groan. "I can't believe I messed things up with Maria. Twice. Once when I left her at Winter Wonderfest, and now this. She's everything someone could ask for in a partner. She's so sweet, and funny, and kind, and so beautiful it almost hurts. And she was right in front of me and I missed it. Now it's too late."

The hope inside Bailey pulsated. Clara could feel it growing stronger.

Bailey looked at her, pleading with her eyes. "Is it too late?"

"No, honey," Jovanna said in Clara's mind. "It's never too late."

"No, honey, it's never too late," Clara said.

"Hey, that's my line."

A great flood of emotion washed over Bailey, so powerful it flowed into Clara.

"Ah, there it is," Gabriella said.

It was the release when a life transformation took hold. Bailey's heart had changed.

Clara had felt it before, but never to this intensity. She'd finally altered someone's life all by herself. It was almost intoxicating. No wonder Gabi didn't want her to have an appletini.

A slow smile spread across Bailey's face. Clara matched it with her own.

Both of their deepest desires were about to come true.

CHAPTER SEVENTEEN

It wasn't too late. She could get her life back.

Bailey sat up straight. "Okay, then. What do we do? It's Christmas, right? The time for miracles and stuff. Can you sprinkle some holiday magic over the town?"

"That's a different kind of magic." Clara touched her heart. "Your magic lives in here. It's more of a feeling. A state of mind. You already have it. You've just forgotten about it."

"So . . . I have the power to change this?"

"You do."

"How? Do I make another wish? Okay, I wish that—"

"Hang on. I'm not a genie, granting wishes over here. It needs to be your deepest desire."

Tears stung Bailey's cheeks, but it felt good. Invigorating. Like her senses were waking from a long winter's nap. "It is. I know what I really want now."

"Can you feel it?" Clara asked.

A renewed energy, a sense of purpose, a deep and profound love coursed through her veins. "I can."

"Then tell me what it is you want."

"I want Winter Wonderfest back. I want everything back. I want to live in the Lanford Falls I know and love. With the people I love. Everyone." In case it wasn't implied, she added, "Maria, Lulu, Rosie . . ."

"Are you sure?" Clara raised her eyebrows. "You could go visit Maria. You still have a shot at freedom."

Bailey shook her head so vehemently, her hair swung over her shoulders. "Maria belongs here." Her heart pounded as the truth became crystal clear. "*I* belong here. And if I haven't messed everything up, maybe we belong here together."

Clara's smile nearly lit up the darkness. "I was hoping you'd say that," she said, her voice thick with tears.

"I know it sounds silly, but I believe in this town. What we have is so special. I don't want to give that up. I'm not giving up on my family and friends, or even Winter Wonderfest." Bailey laughed at those words coming out of her mouth.

"That doesn't sound silly at all."

"And I want you to get your wings!" She leaped off the bench and grabbed Clara's hands, pulling her up. "I want you to dazzle the crowd in your glorious wings. You deserve them. I've been a huge pain in the butt."

They danced in a circle, hopping and laughing and being free. It wasn't about physically leaving Lanford Falls. It was . . . What did Clara call it? A state of mind. That was it exactly. Being content and happy with the present and not always looking to an outdated vision of the future.

"You know all those things I said were chores?" Bailey said, slightly breathless.

"Uh-huh?"

"They were gifts. Ways for me to give back to the community. My dad taught me the value of that. I've been honoring his memory by doing them." Her heart twinged, but with happiness. "It wasn't my duty. It's been my pleasure, like it was for him."

"That's a beautiful way to see things," Clara murmured.

"Helping Kurt, and Hannah, and my mom, were ways to show them I love them." More thoughts tumbled out of her mouth. "I hope I can help Maria with whatever she needs. We can start a frickin' adult choir if that would make her happy. I just want her to be happy."

She stopped dead in her tracks. "Clara, I think I love Maria."

"I think you do too," Clara laughed.

"I do. I love her." Bailey let out a jubilantly crazed laugh. "I'm in love with Maria! I have to tell her. Now would be a great time to have my phone." She patted her coat pockets, just in case.

"If you told her right now, she'd think you're off your rocker."

"Oh crap, that's right. I need to get back to *my* Lanford Falls." She squeezed Clara's arms. "Can you fix this? Can you take me back?"

"Are you sure that's what you really and truly want?"

Bailey looked her square in the face. "Never more sure of anything."

Clara took a step back. "All right. Hang on to your panties."

She slapped her hands together and rubbed them thoroughly. The snow piled behind the bench began to twirl around them.

I'm going home. I'm going where I belong. Bailey danced with excitement.

The snow stalled and dropped to the ground.

"Come on," Clara grumbled. She clapped her hands twice and tried again.

The snow chugged upward against its will. "Uh, Clara?" Bailey said, nerves mounting. "You *can* fix this, right?"

"I'm working on it. This snow thing is giving me guff."

"Do you have to do the snow thing?"

"No, but it creates a nice dramatic effect."

"Clara!" She was jumping out of her skin with anticipation. "I don't need dramatic effect. Just do it already."

Clara gave her a dirty look. "Fine."

She snapped her fingers.

And then Bailey was blinking from sudden bright lights.

They were on the wooden footbridge. The intact bridge lined with Christmas lights.

"Are we back?" she whispered.

"We're back."

"Yes!" Bailey raised her arms high and gave a joyous whoop. "I'm back!"

Her rubber boots were caked with dried mud, and . . . "My coat's all gross," she noted in delight.

Familiar weight hung in its pockets. She shoved her hand in the left pocket. "My phone." Then she checked the other one.

"Lulu's treats," she said, pulling them out. Never in her life had she been happier to see dog treats. They meant she had a dog to give them to.

"Lulu is yours again," Clara said, adjusting her stole.

"I'm never letting her go again. I need to see her." Bailey tucked the precious treats in her pocket. "I need to see everyone and make sure they're okay."

"They'll be glad to see you."

"Come on. We have so much to celebrate!"

She grasped Clara's hand and started down the bridge. Clara didn't budge.

"This is where I leave you," she said.

"You have to come with," Bailey said. "Your family can meet us there."

"You don't need my help anymore."

"I guess not, but we can still hang out." Strange as it seemed, she liked talking with Clara.

Her fabulous new friend shook her head. "I'm afraid that's not how this works."

"Well, shit." Bailey let go of her hand. "Can't you break the rules?"

Clara looked skyward, listened, then shook her head again. "Not this time."

What a bummer. Clara had really done her a humongous favor. Seeing all the things she'd touched through a different lens was quite humbling. Bailey's place in Lanford Falls was bigger than she ever imagined, and she would never take that for granted again.

"Thank you," she said. "For everything."

"For bringing my special brand of holiday magic?" Clara teased.

"Yes. I'm gonna be scratching my head about this for a long time. Whatever this was, you made me believe in holiday magic again." Bailey gave her a bow. "So thank you, Clara Angel of the legendary House of Angel."

Clara dipped into a grand curtsy. "The pleasure is all mine, dearest Bailey."

"You helped me so much. I hope I helped you with your wings."

"I think there's a pretty good chance." Clara playfully poked her. "Remember this feeling. Keep it in your heart, and spread lots of cheer."

"I will," Bailey assured her.

"Now get out of here and find Maria. Go snog with her under the mistletoe."

She laughed with gleeful abandon. "I probably shouldn't lead with 'I think I want to spend the rest of my life with you.'"

Clara wrinkled her nose. "Save that for later."

She blew Bailey a kiss, and then was gone. Disappeared off the bridge.

"You sure know how to make an exit, Clara," Bailey said. "And an entrance."

For a moment, she could only stare at the lights winding around the railings. The creek babbled below, but other than that, it was silent.

Had it been a dream? A stress-induced hallucination? Maybe Clara had been a product of her subconscious. Or heck, who said angels weren't real?

It had been a gift, most of all. A gift she was going to put to good use.

The woodchip path stretched toward Main Street like a beacon. She took off running. There wasn't time to worry about the truck. She needed to get back to Winter Wonderfest. And Maria. She had to find Maria.

Cars whizzed by the *Welcome to Lanford Falls* sign. Lights twinkled around the second one touting *Home of Winter Wonderfest.*

"Yes!" Bailey pumped her fist.

The dog park was quiet, but it was there. Dad's park. "Hello, dog park," she called. "I'm so happy you're here."

She sent love up to Dad. Without a doubt, he was smiling down with pride.

The festive houses were all back. She waved at a blow-up Santa in one of the front yards. "Hi, Santa!"

Pure adrenaline coursed through her body. *I have to get back to Wonderfest. I have to find Maria.*

Downtown looked exactly as it should: merry and bright and bustling with activity. Bailey jumped and threw her arms in the air. "Lanford Falls is back!"

The library was a library again. The tree outside Town Hall glimmered to the top with multicolored lights. The proper wooden sign proclaimed Ellis Thompson was still mayor.

Across the street, George Family Homes was where it belonged. "Goodbye, Smokey's Vape Shack."

She hurried down the sidewalk, sharing season's greetings with the people she passed. Every step brought confirmation that the Falls was just as she'd left it. No, better. Each storefront was a delight to behold. It almost felt like she was seeing it all with a fresh perspective, like she'd gotten new glasses and could see more clearly.

The placard in front of Martin's listed its fun seasonal dishes. Bailey patted it with a chuckle. Mr. Gruber wasn't behind the counter in his store because he was at the festival.

"Oh my God, the cart," she remembered. Had that whole disaster been just a short while ago?

Kurt stood outside Caffeinated Corner, locking the door. The Progress Pride flag was a most welcome sight.

"Kurt!" Bailey yelled, sprinting across the road. She waved at the SUV sitting at the stop sign. "Sorry! Kurt!"

He turned and raised his eyebrows. "What happened to you?"

"Long story."

"You're filthy."

"I know." Bailey disregarded her coat and boots. "I have to tell you how much your friendship means to me. I'm so glad we get to hang out and play trivia, and you give me way too many free coffees that I'm going to start paying for . . ."

"Not necessary," her pal said with a smile.

"And for loving Lulu and giving her treats. And . . . you're just the best. You and Arnie." She flicked a glance at his left hand to verify the presence of his wedding ring.

Kurt's brows met in the middle. "Have you been dipping into Mrs. Claus's special brownies?"

Giggling uncontrollably, Bailey said, "Maybe it's a contact high from the vape shack."

"What?"

"Never mind." She yanked him into a tight hug. "I love you, buddy. I'll see you at the festival. But right now, I have to find Maria."

"Okay." He looked at her with a mix of amusement and alarm. "Love you too, Bails."

They shared a wave, and she dashed off toward the village green. She stopped at the entrance, overwhelmed by the joy radiating from within. Laughter and conversation. The sweet scent of sugary snacks. And lights—so many twinkly, sparkly lights. No more darkness.

"Welcome back, Winter Wonderfest," she murmured.

Ooh—the Christmas tree lights were all on, and the star had been straightened. "The tree's okay," she said to an olive-skinned, middle-aged man walking by.

"It's okay," he echoed.

The crew had fixed everything while she was gone. "Nice job," she said.

"Mom!" a familiar voice called. "I found her."

Hannah emerged from the crowd, concern etched on her face. "Han!" Bailey cried, swooping in to give her a hug.

"Where have you been? I texted you like ten times. We were starting to get worried."

She pulled back but held Hannah's arms, studying her sister and her coordinated red hat, scarf, and gloves. "I'm fine. Better than fine. I feel amazing."

"Okay, but where were you?"

Mom joined them, and Reuben holding Lulu's leash. "Mom!" Bailey crushed her in a huge embrace.

"Hi—*oof*," Mom wheezed.

"I love you," Bailey said, then broke the hug to see Lulu. "Hey there, Lulu Bear. How's my girl?"

Lulu's full-body wiggles in her green sweater caused Bailey's heart to overflow.

"I love you, monster. You'll always be my girl."

She cuddled and cooed to her sweet doggie. Her brother-in-law had on the most fantastically ridiculous blue-and-white sweater with a giant cartoon reindeer face. "I'm so glad you're part of the family," Bailey told him.

Reuben's dark eyebrows scrunched in confusion. "Thanks. I am too."

"Where were you?" Mom asked. "Nobody could get ahold of you."

"I was around. I . . . had some phone trouble." Bailey kissed the top of Lulu's head and stood.

"You should text the guy with the park district," Hannah said. "What's his name?"

"Vince," Mom said.

"Yeah, him. They fixed the food tent."

"They did?" Bailey looked toward the large white tent. It appeared to be upright and in use once more.

"They jerry-rigged a new pole to replace the bent one." Her mom brushed her hair back. "You look different. Is everything okay?"

"Everything is wonderful," Bailey said, smiling so wide it hurt. "I'm so glad I didn't miss the festival this year. It's really magical."

She giggled to herself. *Magical, indeed.*

Mom shook her head. "Vince wanted to tell you not to go to the rental center if you weren't already there."

"I never made it. Oh, but I should tell him about the truck. I drove it into the mud."

"You got into an accident?" Mom felt her forehead. "Did you hit your head?"

"I don't think so. Maybe. Probably not." Bailey laughed again.

Hannah touched Reuben's arm. "She has a concussion."

"I'm fine. Really. My mind's clear." Bailey looked to each of them. "Have you seen Maria? I need to talk to her."

Mom gestured in the direction of the stage. "The last time I saw her, she was over there with—"

"Thank you!" Bailey snagged Lulu's leash. "I'll find you for the concert. I can't wait for the madrigals!"

Her family rightfully thought she had head trauma. Better than when they thought she was a lunatic on the doorstep. Had that even happened?

She smiled down at Lulu in her green turtleneck sweater. At least things were back to normal. And Maria was nearby.

Maria.

People were beginning to assemble in front of the stage for the concert. Bailey weaved between them, searching for the gorgeous Christmas elf she was rather helplessly in love with.

Ellis spotted her and waved. "Did you talk to Vince?" she asked.

"No, but I heard they fixed the tent."

"They worked some kind of magic and made it safe and secure."

Magic was all around tonight. "I'm glad," Bailey said. "Sorry again about the checks."

"It's in the past." Ellis moved her hands in a straight line. "Don't you worry about that. Everyone's been paid."

"Thank you for trusting me with the festival."

"You saved our butts."

"I mean all these years. But especially this year. I'm so happy I didn't miss it."

Ellis gave her the *Is Bailey high?* face everyone was making. "I'm happy you stuck around too."

"Let's have that lunch next week. You name the day and place. My treat." Before Ellis could protest, Bailey said, "I want to buy my friend lunch and catch up with you."

They squeezed hands. "I'd like that," Ellis said.

"Great. Where's Maria? I heard she was around here."

"She was back there with the high school kids." Ellis pointed behind the stage.

"Come on, Lulu," Bailey said. "Let's go find Maria." She took a few steps away, then said, "Hey, Ellis? I'm really glad you're our mayor."

Ellis made a face that said *Yeah, she's definitely high.* "Thanks, Bailey."

The madrigals were bunched in small groups, harmonizing quietly and working on choreography. They wore red tops and black bottoms and had their striped LFHS scarves around their necks. Maria and Zack Walsh conferred with Sound Tech Guy.

Her pulse zinged and ringed and cheered. Maria glanced over and saw her, all softness and warmth and coziness in her fuzzy winter white hat and holly green coat. Bailey grinned and quickened her pace.

Maria scowled deeply. "Where have you been? I almost sent a search party to look for you."

"I had phone trouble." *Because magical drag queens were preventing me from using it.*

She stepped away from Zack. Bailey opened her arms to envelop her in a hug, but Maria punched her in the arm.

"Oww." Bailey rubbed the tingling spot.

"I thought you were on your way to the city, you were gone so long."

"I'm not going anywhere."

Maria looked down at Bailey's coat. "You're covered in mud."

"Slight problem with the pickup truck."

"Uh-huh." She crossed her arms. "You had car *and* phone trouble?"

"I did. It's been a weird night."

"Oh. Well, I'm glad you're okay."

"I'm fine. Only . . ." Bailey glanced at the teenagers. She gently guided Maria away from them. "I owe you an apology. I was a Grade A jerk. I had some time to reflect on what matters, and—"

"What you said really hurt," Maria said. "That you were done with me."

Bailey's heart lurched. "You didn't deserve that. I'm so sorry."

Maria gazed at her warily. "Go on."

"I thought I would never find true happiness here, but I was wrong." She smiled. "I love it here. Lanford Falls *is* home. I understand why you wanted to move back. It's a special place. It means more to me than I allowed myself to admit."

Maria's eyes widened.

Bailey touched her arm. "This week has been perfect. I really loved setting up for the Wonderfest with you. And you were right. Nobody should ever settle for you. You're the most amazing person, and I consider it an honor that you want to be in my life. And . . . maybe more."

Her breath stilled as she awaited Maria's response.

She softened and patted Bailey's hand. "You didn't get the job," Maria said, sympathy in her voice.

"It's not that. A good friend reminded me of what was right in front of me. A life filled with fun and the people I care about."

"What about adventure and excitement? You won't get that here."

"Who says I won't?" Taking a risk, Bailey laced their fingers together. "Singing with you was the most fun I've had in years. I love being your partner for trivia and making inappropriate snow ladies. I have a feeling doing anything with you will be an adventure. And I have it on good authority you enjoy taking vacations."

A slow smile pulled at Maria's lips.

Without the mental gunk clogging her head, memories came more sharply. The times she'd seen Maria over the years at past Wonderfests, always taking an extra few minutes to talk with her. Passing her in the hallway at school and sharing a smile, their secret kiss just between them. And yes, even prom night. Maria had looked like the star of a teen romantic comedy.

"You wore a sparkly red dress," Bailey remembered. "To prom. A halter top. It was short, and had a full skirt. You had your hair up in a fancy bun."

She met Maria's surprised gaze.

"You looked beautiful. I'm sorry I never told you. I was still stinging from your rejection, and distracted by everything else, but I noticed."

Maria's mouth hung open. Her hand sat limply in Bailey's.

There was no going back now, so she said, "I always noticed you."

"Good." Maria's adorable nose wrinkled as she smiled. "That was my plan. Glad it finally worked."

"It took a while to figure out, huh?"

"About seventeen years."

Bailey let out a huge laugh. "Whoa. I'm pretty dense."

"You are rather ridiculous." Maria grinned down at Lulu. "Right, Lulu? Is your mommy ridiculous?"

Lulu wiggled in agreement.

"But that's what I like about her." To Bailey, she said, "You're a good person, Bailey George. You've held the weight of the world on your shoulders long enough. It's okay if you want to let it go."

"I will, but not how you think. I'm still going to be here for everyone and volunteer for things, but because I like doing those things. Only I don't want to handle Winter Wonderfest next year. But that's so we can enjoy the day together." Whoops, that last part had slipped out.

Maria looked like she was about to burst from jubilation. "So you plan on being around next year?"

"Absolutely."

"And might you be interested in helping me with the Art Walk? It combines art and history, two of your favorite things." Which of course Maria knew, because she was amazing.

"That depends," Bailey teased. "Can I be your committee head of food and entertainment?"

"Obviously, since you keep bragging about your excellent culinary skills."

They shared a laugh. Bailey tugged her closer, though Maria had already taken a step in. Maria slid her other hand around Bailey's and the dog leash.

"Maybe we can start up the community choir again," Bailey murmured.

"Maybe. Though I do like dueting with you."

"We can still duet."

Maria waggled her eyebrows. "Make beautiful music together?"

"Exactly," Bailey chuckled. *But seriously, YES. God, yes.*

"We could carol at our parents' houses on Christmas Eve. Unless that's too presumptuous," Maria rushed out. "I didn't mean we—"

"I would love to spend Christmas Eve with you." *And Christmas Day, and New Year's Eve, and . . .* "Honestly, I can't imagine a more perfect Christmas than spending it here, with you."

Maria squeezed her hands. "That does sound perfect."

"But we should probably start with that dinner date tomorrow night."

"Right. Dinner date first."

Dinner date before telling Maria she loved her.

Bailey looked into those chocolate brown eyes. *I love her.*

Someone coughed politely nearby. Sound Tech Guy. "Sorry to interrupt," he said, visibly embarrassed at ruining this lovely moment. "Just wanted you to know everything should be set."

"Thank you," Bailey said, tearing her gaze away from Maria even though she really didn't want to.

Maria checked her watch. "It's ten to seven. I've been helping the madrigals get ready. I really should . . ."

"I really should . . ." There were festival items on the checklist and conferring with everyone and a host of things Bailey should be doing.

Hang on. "Has Jane been in charge since I've been gone?" she asked.

"Yes, and she's stuck faithfully to the schedule."

"And Pete and Tom? Everything good with them?"

"Everything's good with them," Maria said.

She trusted her committee—her friends, really. And Ellis had paid everyone. And Vince and the park district crew were on top of things. "You know what? The festival is in good hands. Let's make sure the kids are ready to rock and roll."

Maria smiled and wrapped her arms around Bailey. Bailey pulled her close, reveling in the feel of Maria against her. The faint scent of perfume clinging to her coat. They still had a chance. This could happen. *They* could happen.

Maria lifted her head. "Who did you talk to that changed your mind?"

"If I told you, you'd never believe me."

"Felicity Potter?"

"Not that unbelievable," Bailey laughed. "A friend visiting from out of town."

"I'm not sure if I should thank them or ask them how serious you are." Maria's arms loosened. "I'm a little worried, to be honest."

Crap. "You have every right to be cautious," Bailey said. She had to put in some serious good faith effort. "I'll do everything I can to assure you I'm here for the long haul. Starting with cooking you a tolerable spaghetti dinner while our dogs wrestle."

"You're gonna have to do better than a tolerable dinner," Maria said.

"I'll use fresh pasta and sauce. The refrigerated kind. And I'll make a salad. And . . . I'll give you a long massage. I give good massages."

"I do like massages."

"Oh, and we'll start the day with peppermint lattes. Kurt doesn't work on Sundays, but I'll pay, so yours will be free. You'll never pay for another cup of coffee. I promise."

Maria's lips pursed into a wry smirk, as though she believed Bailey despite her ridiculousness. "Let's continue this conversation later."

"Definitely," Bailey said. "Meet me at Mistletoe Grove?"

Maria nodded. "To be continued at Mistletoe Grove."

She tiptoed up and dropped a kiss on Bailey's cheek. Bailey rested her chin against the side of Maria's forehead and breathed deep. *I'm home.*

"To be continued," she said.

CHAPTER EIGHTEEN

Once they'd assured the teens they were going to wow the crowd (and let them pet Lulu for good luck), Bailey and Maria walked along the side of the stage. "There's a surprise for you in the food tent," Maria said.

"Tables? Chairs? People?"

"Yes, after some convincing by Ellis that it was safe. But it's something else. I'll show you."

Their hands found one another and twined. Little pulses of electricity danced between their fingers.

Bailey smiled at Miss Josephine nestled in a folding chair. The owner of the hardware store tucked a heavy wool blanket around her while his two young sons chatted her ear off. His wife held the older woman's plate of cookies. Miss Josephine loved her cookies. Nice to see her being fussed over.

They were almost to the paved path when a dying moose call boomed through the air. Maria looked in its direction. "We've been spotted."

Rosie dragged Maria's dad toward them. Lulu yapped and strained against her leash. Mr. Hatcher wisely let go before he fell over.

That unmistakable gleam lit Rosie's eyes, so Bailey simply opened her arms and accepted the body slam of a canine embrace. "I missed you too," she grunted.

"Worst dog ever," Maria sighed.

"I love your enthusiasm, Rosie girl." Bailey kissed the top of Rosie's head. The overzealous dog slapped her big tongue across Bailey's face. She looked pretty cute in her bright red doggie coat.

Lulu yapped again and shoved Rosie down. They proceeded to chew on each other's faces, as one does when one is a very strange dog.

"Thanks for bringing her," Maria said to her parents.

Mrs. Hatcher made a shooing motion. "She's your problem now."

For some reason, that was endlessly funny. Bailey laughed hard and stopped herself from telling Maria's mother not to worry. Rosie would be spending a lot more time with the George family.

Speaking of . . . "If you want to watch the concert with my mom and sister, they should be over there somewhere." Bailey pointed at the gathering crowd. "Maria and I have some official Wonderfest business, but then we'll join you."

The Hatchers thanked her. Bailey took both dogs' leashes and tugged them forward. Maria tilted her head inward as they walked. "Getting our families together, huh?"

"Subconsciously, yes, I guess I am." Bailey shrugged. "Hannah and my mom adore you. They can work on your parents on my behalf."

"My parents like you."

"They like Dan's old friend. Are they going to . . ." *Like me as your girlfriend?*

"They like you," Maria insisted. Then she giggled. "Oh man, is Dan gonna be thrilled."

"I think he'll be happy his sister is in good hands."

"Plus, he won't mind hanging out with you."

Bailey made a face. "As long as he doesn't try to fart on me."

"I can't make any guarantees," Maria laughed.

279

Dan could pass whatever bodily expulsions he wanted if it meant Bailey had a future with Maria. He'd always treated Bailey like a sister. What if . . .

What if someday . . .

They reached the food tent, buzzing inside with activity. "No doggos allowed," Bailey said.

"Especially you, knucklehead." Maria rubbed Rosie's curiously sniffing nose. "Look against the far wall."

Bailey craned her neck until she spied Mr. Gruber and his son standing behind a table. Their hot chocolate urns looked a little dinged up, but were dispensing cocoa to waiting patrons.

"They felt terrible about the runaway cart," Maria said. "They're giving away free hot cocoa. I stashed our mugs in your bag. Jane has it, so I'll run in and get it."

"Great. Thanks." Not that the tree falling over had been the Grubers' fault.

Maria made her way to a table near the entrance. Jane and Vince sat with the park district crew, everyone enjoying much-deserved dinners. Maria said something and gestured toward Bailey. They all looked over and said hello.

Ooh, at some point, she'd have to tell Vince about the pickup truck. After the concert. But before Mistletoe Grove.

Jane hopped from her seat and hustled out of the tent, clipboard in hand. "Everything's on schedule," she said. "But I'd be lying if I said I wasn't glad to give this back to you."

The dogs greeted her in the hopes Jane had brought them snacks. "Thank you," Bailey said, glancing at the satisfying checkmarks on the list. "For holding down the fort, and handling so many things this week."

"Are we having a committee meeting?" a man said.

She turned to see Pete and Tom. "I was just telling Jane how much I appreciate all her help. Thank you both as well. We managed to pull this off because you gave so much of your time and energy. I'm incredibly grateful for you guys."

They insisted they were happy to help, and Bailey deserved the lion's share of thanks. "Susan said she'll be back in action next year," Jane said. "And you're all invited to be on the committee."

"I have every confidence in you." Bailey raised her eyebrows. "But if anyone has an unplanned emergency surgery, I'll be around to help."

A few taps on a microphone sounded through the stage speakers. "Good evening, Winter Wonderfest," Ellis said. She stood stage left in front of a mic stand. "Today has been one for the books. Thank you for your good humor and patience while the festival gremlins had a little too much fun."

The audience laughed. Bailey could only shake her head.

"Let's have a big round of applause for the Town Hall staff, our hardworking park district employees, and all the volunteers who gave countless hours to make today happen. In particular, I want to give special thanks to the Winter Wonderfest committee, who really stepped up when they were needed. Thank you from the bottom of my heart."

Appreciative claps and whistles rippled through the crowd.

Ellis shielded her eyes. "Bailey? Where's Bailey George?"

Hoots and hollers enveloped Bailey as her friends pointed her out. She tried to hide inside her coat. Lulu and Rosie pranced from the attention.

Ellis waved at her. "Everyone, please turn and thank Bailey George. To say she was thrown into the fire this week is an understatement. I don't know what Lanford Falls would do without you, Bailey. Thank you."

A huge roar went up. It startled her. Bailey gave a weak gesture of acknowledgment, overcome with emotion. She'd seen that Lanford Falls and was very, very glad to be in this one.

Kurt and a de-Santa-ed Arnie clapped above their heads in the crowd. "We love you, Bails!" Arnie called.

Tears welled up from deep inside. "I'm so thankful for all of you," Bailey said.

Ellis announced that due to unforeseen circumstances, Dusty Dreams would not be performing. (The circumstance being Dustin's douchiness.) "However, we are thrilled to have our very own Lanford Falls High School madrigal singers. I listened to them practicing, and let me tell you, we are in for a treat."

The crowd hummed with approval and excitement.

"Enjoy the music, and happy holidays."

Maria reappeared with their red tumblers and Bailey's messenger bag. "Just in time," Bailey said, placing the clipboard in her bag. "They're about to start."

The teens filed onstage. Maria adorably cheered like they were her own children. They stood in a straight line, heads down. Then Zack popped his head up and broke into "Underneath the Tree."

The other teens snapped their heads up and joined in. Their harmonies were tight. They broke into some jazzy, in-place choreography.

"Oh my God," Bailey murmured. "They're good. They're like, *really* good."

"They *are* good," Maria murmured back.

They watched in awe as their replacement act put their all into the performance. Talk about a blessing in disguise. Bailey sipped her warm cocoa with one hand while adjusting the leashes in the other.

Yvette and Paul walked past. "You pulled it off," Yvette said.

"We sure did." Bailey smiled at her committee. Mostly Maria. "I'm looking forward to the next trivia night."

"You two make a great team." Yvette didn't bother hiding her double meaning.

Maria leaned into Bailey's side. She leaned back.

The jazzy madrigals finished the song. Bailey whistled and clapped along with the audience. Maria reached for Rosie's leash and said, "Let's sneak over to our families."

They weaved through the crowd as the kids performed their Mariah Carey holiday song medley. Hopefully Mrs. Walsh would let them shake things up after this.

Lulu spied Uncle Bill beside Mom and strained to reach him. He took her leash without being asked. Rosie considered jumping on him, but then felt his animal-loving aura and rammed him with her boxy head instead. He took her leash as well.

Maria looked confused, so Bailey explained, "He's a dog whisperer."

"What?" she said above the noise.

Bailey leaned down to her ear. "He's a dog whisperer." Her lips ached to inch closer to that most tempting earlobe.

"Hi, Maria." Hannah waved, a wide grin stretching across her face.

"Hi, Hannah. Mrs. George." Maria gave them a little wave.

"It's so nice to see you," Mom said. "Welcome home."

"Thank you. It's good to be home." Maria slid a glance up at Bailey, who could only smile in response.

She tried to watch the teens perform "This Christmas," but kept getting interrupted by townspeople thanking her for helping out this year. Former clients, Beautification Committee volunteers, families living in her favorite subdivision. She assured each one of them it'd been her pleasure.

Nick caught her eye in the crowd and tipped his fuzzy Santa hat. Saint Nick, indeed.

During a break between songs, Hannah said, "You sure are feeling the love tonight."

"Hear, hear." Reuben held up his cup of cider.

"It's a reflection of all the love I've received," Bailey said.

"Let's have a toast." Hannah raised her cup. "To my big sister Bailey. The most-loved person in town."

The Georges and Hatchers cheered, "To Bailey!"

They clinked metal tumblers and paper cups. Bailey drank her cocoa, meeting Maria's tender gaze. She was definitely feeling the love from her family, but from Maria too.

Her heart pounded wildly. Maybe it wasn't so impossible to think the here and now was the start of their future.

The madrigals performed two of their standard classics while Maria hummed along. Bailey held her hand, then wondered how long she'd been holding it. Their handholding just kept happening naturally.

She took in the smiling faces, the wreaths people had decorated, the lights, the tall tree with a not at all crooked star, Uncle Bill cooing to the dogs. What a perfect moment. She snapped a mental picture to remember this feeling.

Clara would be so proud of me.

She sent thanks to Clara, wherever the fabulous queen was.

As the madrigals prepped for another song, someone cleared their throat loudly behind her. She was shocked to see Felicity in her severe hat and coat.

"What are you doing here?" Bailey said.

The dour woman looked so out of place amid the merriment. "I, umm . . ." She cleared her throat again. "I found this. I believe it belongs to you."

She held an envelope out. Wait a second . . .

Bailey snatched it and glanced at its contents. "The checks! Where did you find this?"

"In the diner."

"I searched everywhere at Martin's. Where was it?"

"It had . . . fallen into my newspapers." Felicity avoided her gaze.

Bailey eyed her suspiciously. "Have you had this all day?"

"I discovered it after returning home."

"And you're just now giving it to me?"

"The important thing is you have it now." Felicity stood to her full height. "I recognize the financial benefits of the festival. I appreciate all you have done to make this town a vibrant place to live."

Wait, what?

Maria's eyebrows met in the middle. "Have you two been smoking the same thing?"

Bailey shared a long look with Felicity. Did she also have a visit from an angelic someone?

"Thank you," Bailey said slowly. "That's kind of you to say."

The older woman gave a firm nod. "That's all." Her lips pursed as she noticed Uncle Bill and the dogs. "I'll be on my way. Far too much noise here."

Hmm. Maybe Clara hadn't paid her a visit. "There's free hot cocoa in the food tent," Bailey said anyway.

That seemed to pique Felicity's interest. "Is it Gruber hot cocoa?"

"It is."

She didn't reply, but did turn and head in that direction. Maybe there was hope for her after all.

Maria tapped the envelope. "I can't believe she had this all day and didn't say anything."

Uncle Bill harrumphed. "I bet she stole it. 'Fell into my newspaper' my left butt cheek."

Normally, Bailey would agree. But she told him, "At least she gave it back. Cut her some slack. It's Christmas."

"There's nothing merry about her."

"She was actually nice to me. You heard her. She sees the good things in town."

Maria took the envelope and tucked it securely in Bailey's messenger bag. "There must be something in the air tonight," she said, and Hannah concurred.

Mom smiled. "Whatever it is, I'll take it."

"Can't a person find a little Christmas joy?" Bailey said, which made everyone laugh. She and Felicity sure were rediscovering what they'd lost.

The madrigals broke into "I Saw Three Ships" with a hip-hop flair. "They are so talented," Maria said. She touched Bailey's arm. "Y'know, if you're not taking that job in the city, you could recommend Felicity Potter for it. Eliminate the competition in town."

"Sammie would never go for it," Bailey laughed.

Hang on. She never did reply to that email. Thank goodness. Well, thank the House of Angel.

She pulled out her phone. Her screen was filled with missed texts and calls from her time in Alternative Lanford Falls. She went into her email and replied to all so Sammie would see it. The words flew effortlessly from her fingers.

Thank you for the opportunity, but I am not seeking new employment. I'm very happy where I'm at.

Maria caught her grinning at her phone as she sent the email. "Just had to decline an interview in the city," Bailey told her.

Relief flowed through her bloodstream. It was the right call.

"So that job's off the table?" Maria asked.

"It's not even in the room."

She bobbed her head. "Noted. That's one step toward making me think you're sticking around."

"Like I said, I'm not going anywhere." Bailey dropped a loose arm across her shoulders. She wasn't sure how much PDA Maria might be comfortable with in a crowd.

Maria wrapped her arm snugly around Bailey's waist and squeezed. Well, that answered that.

They cuddled as the madrigals gradually filed offstage while doing a reprise of "Underneath the Tree." Once the stage was empty, Maria untangled her arm so she could applaud. "They did so well. We should have them back next year."

"Absolutely," Bailey agreed. "Only we'll give them more time to prepare."

She didn't mind talking about next year's festival like she might be a part of it. Susan could one hundred percent be in charge, but a small committee role—with Maria—would be pretty okay.

"Looks like that's it," Mom said. "You survived. Congratulations, honey."

"Now it's time for close-up and cleanup," Bailey said. "The real fun part. Who wants to help?"

Reuben and Hannah muttered to each other about having to let the dogs out, while Mom just laughed. Mr. and Mrs. Hatcher pretended to be distracted by something in the distance.

Uncle Bill handed over the dogs. "I'm going home."

"It was good to see you," Bailey said, as if she didn't see him almost every day. "I don't know if I tell you enough, but I'm so glad you stayed on and kept the agency afloat. I could never have done it without you."

He gave her a rare smile. "It's what your dad would've wanted."

Warmth pulsed through her chest.

"And by this point, I've got so many vacation days, I'd be a fool not to stick it out."

"True," Bailey laughed. "You've earned them all."

"So have you." Uncle Bill winked at her. "Use them, okay?"

She was hyper aware of Maria standing beside her. "I will."

The stage lights came back up. A recording of a choir singing "Hark! The Herald Angels Sing" played through the speakers.

"Do the madrigals have an encore?" Bailey asked Maria.

"Not that I'm aware of."

The song changed to a thumping beat. A pale, curvy drag queen in a glittery white leotard appeared on one side of the stage. A statuesque Black queen, her leotard a shimmering silver, appeared on the opposite side. Both had large sets of closed wings on their backs.

Wings. Drag queens in wings.

They lip-synced to the song, engaging the crowd with grand arm and hand movements. Maria clapped and cheered with glee.

A third queen sashayed onstage in a brilliant gold leotard.

"Clara," Bailey whispered.

She had on a full blonde wig and bold makeup. And she was wearing her wings.

"You did it." Bailey couldn't contain herself and waved like a maniac. "Way to go, Clara!"

Clara searched the audience until she saw her. She waved back as she mouthed the lyrics.

"Holy shit, she's real."

Bailey looked at the other queens. Clara's family. That meant the whole journey to the dark side had been real.

"Where did they come from?" Maria said.

"Heaven?" Bailey guessed. "They are Angels."

She stood entranced by the show. Clara was a fabulous performer. She shimmied and hammed it up to the delight of the crowd.

The song slowed and quieted. The queens staggered themselves across the stage.

A swell of trumpets sounded. Their wings unfurled to reveal gleaming white feathers.

The crowd gasped.

The queens raised their arms to the sky. It was as though the stage lights made them glow. Or maybe it was their own special brand of magic.

The tempo returned to dance-worthy. They paraded back and forth, displaying the beautiful wings. The lights caught the silver and gold threading through them. They were indeed worth everything Clara had done to get hers.

Dear Clara. She looked so happy. Beyond happy. She had to be bursting with as much joy as was coursing through Bailey.

She drew Maria into her arms and snuggled her from behind. Maria rested her head on Bailey's shoulder. They watched the Angels dance in perfect sync. Rosie and Lulu plopped at their feet, tongues lolling from their mouths.

Tremendous gratitude overwhelmed her. This was pretty damn perfect.

The performance came to a glorious end with Clara posing in the middle, arms wide. The audience went wild.

The queens held their positions for several long moments before breaking apart. Clara stepped back, but the tall queen in silver urged her toward one of the microphones. She seemed genuinely surprised, then delighted.

"Thank you, Lanford Falls," Clara said. "We wish you a very happy holiday season. And remember . . ." She looked in Bailey's direction. "The true measure of success is in love. Surround yourself with love and good friends, and you'll achieve beautiful things."

Tears coated Bailey's eyes. She blew Clara a kiss.

Clara gestured to her wings, which made Bailey laugh and nod vigorously. Clara blew her several kisses with both hands. Then she waved to the audience and trotted offstage.

Maria turned in Bailey's arms. "Do you know her?"

"That was Clara. My dear friend from out of town."

"You didn't tell me your friend was a stunning drag queen."

"She's a whole lot of things," Bailey said.

Somewhere in the crowd, several people began to sing "Auld Lang Syne." It caught on, with more folks joining in. There was a fair amount of "*nah nah nah*" for the lyrics they didn't know.

Bailey stared at the beautiful woman in her arms. An old acquaintance she thankfully never forgot.

"You have cool friends." Maria gave her secretive little smile.

"Yes, I do." Bailey lowered her head and nuzzled Maria's nose.

"If you think I'm a cool *friend* . . ." There was no mistaking the intent in her eyes, in her tone. "Just you wait."

CHAPTER NINETEEN

A quiet stillness surrounded Mistletoe Grove. With general cleanup done for the evening, the village green was deserted. Bailey unclipped Lulu's leash to let her explore the edge of the pine trees.

Maria looked down at Rosie. "Stay with Lulu, you naughty monster."

She released the hound, who bounded over to sniff the same spot of snow as Lulu. Bailey hung Lulu's leash on the arbor. Maria hung Rosie's beside it. Side by side, just like their dogs. Just like them.

Staring up at the sky, Maria said, "What a beautiful night."

Bailey inhaled the crisp air and looked at the stars winking in the inky darkness. "Beautiful night," she agreed, her breath coming out in a puffy cloud.

"I lost feeling in my feet an hour ago, but other than freezing—"

"You're cold? Come here."

She led Maria under the arch, beneath the kissing ball. Bailey pulled her close, rubbing her back. She rested her slightly warmer cheek against Maria's chilly forehead. "Better?"

"Mm-hmm." Maria melted against her, tucking her arms around Bailey.

They held each other, sharing body heat, enjoying the ease of being together. But really, they were here for one very important thing.

"So." Bailey lowered her voice. "Fancy meeting you here."

"We have a habit of running into each other here every two decades or so."

She chuckled and said, "I hope we can increase the frequency. A lot."

Maria hummed and raised her head. "I think that's doable."

Their lips met in a slow, sweet kiss. She tasted of rich hot cocoa and lip balm and wintertime.

Bailey trailed her fingers along Maria's cheek, gently drawing her mouth up. The kiss deepened, awakening the part of her that had always been reserved for Maria. Fate or the universe or kindhearted drag queens had brought them together once more, and she was holding on this time.

"Happy Winter Wonderfest," Bailey murmured.

"Happy Winter Wonderfest."

"It's going to be an amazing Christmas."

"It already is." Maria's smile thawed the chill in the air. "I got my Christmas wish early."

Bailey grinned. "I did too."

They kissed, and kissed, until a familiar weight pressed against their legs. Laughter broke them apart. That, and Rosie shoving herself between them. She smiled up like she required all the attention. Lulu stood outside the arbor, all but rolling her eyes at the needy youngster.

"The absolute worst," Maria said, poking Rosie in the head. She bent down and told her doggo, "But I love you."

Bailey motioned for Lulu to join them. "The absolute best," she cooed to her baby. "And I love you."

They petted both dogs, glancing at one another through their lashes. The push to tell Maria *she* was the absolute best was as strong as the vibe pulsing off Maria.

Maria loves me.

Maria loves me, and I love her.

Wow.

Maybe they'd say it tonight. Maybe they wouldn't. But Bailey knew it, and Maria knew it. Even their dogs were acting like they knew it and were psyched to be best buddies.

They shared a smile, excitement surrounding them as boundless as their future together. Maria set a hand on Bailey's chest. "Do you have any plans for New Year's Eve?"

"Nope."

"No?"

"None at all."

Maria bit her lower lip. "New York could be a fun adventure. Watch the ball drop and everything."

Bailey looked around at the twinkle lights, the greenery, the pine trees and path that led back to town. "I'm exactly where I want to be."

"Really?" Maria seemed surprised but elated.

"Really. Maybe I'll host a party for my friends and family."

"That sounds nice."

Bailey gestured downward with her chin. "Besides, I think these two will want to ring in the New Year with us."

"These two will want to do everything with us," Maria laughed. "But if you want to stick around for New Year's, that's okay with me."

"For New Year's." Bailey raised her eyebrows. "Though maybe for Valentine's Day . . ."

Maria raised her eyebrows too. "I'm very much okay with that."

They reached for one another at the same time, meeting for a joyous kiss. Lulu barked at something in the evergreens. Possibly a magical drag queen.

Bailey pulled Maria into her arms. Their kisses spoke of all the holidays to come. Of meeting every year from here on out at Mistletoe Grove. Of caroling together and decorating trees and snuggling on the couch while Lulu and Rosie snoozed in front of the fireplace. Of the things they'd do in front of the fireplace on a cozy pile of pillows and blankets while the dogs snoozed on the couch.

Of one hell of a fabulous life.

ACKNOWLEDGMENTS

This book went on a *journey*, my friend. So many people and some unexpected twists and turns helped get it into your hot little hands.

Bryn Donovan, this book would not have happened without your persistence. Thank you for never, ever giving up on it. I'm so glad to call you my friend!

Eva Scalzo, agent extraordinaire, I'm thrilled we finally connected and that you found this story a permanent home. I love working with you and our Zoom calls, and can't wait to see what the future holds!

Holly Ingraham gave this book its second chance, and I am forever grateful. Big thanks to you and the terrific team at Alcove Press for bringing Bailey, Maria, and Clara's story to fruition.

Louisa Maggio, I am obsessed with this gorgeous book cover. You captured the cozy feel of the story perfectly.

The Panera Supper Club and Chicago-North Romance Writers, you are my people. In particular, Rachelle Paige Campbell, Julie Hamilton, Beccan James, Pamala Knight, Shannyn Schroeder, and Kelly Smith. You're the ones I tell aaallll my news first, good and bad. And there were a lot of ups and downs with this book! Thank you for riding the waves with me.

My parents and brother are awesome and hilarious and grounding. I can't imagine going on this journey without you. Ditto to all my friends and family who are as excited when I have book news as I am!

Camille Pagán, your coaching and guidance continue to help with the wild ride of this wacky author career. Thanks for everything.

Emilka Orlowski Kapa, thanks so much for helping me with the Polish food and language. I can smell the golabki, and pronounce it, too!

My newsletter subscribers! I love you! I get a little thrill each time someone new signs up or replies to one of my emails. You are all awesome and make me feel so authorly.

I also want to thank everyone on Twitter who retweeted, DM'd, and commented when I posted about this book losing its first publisher. I was overwhelmed by the support and encouragement. Thanks for helping out my queer little Christmas story.

And I have to thank every contestant who has ever been on *RuPaul's Drag Race*, and Mama Ru herself. Also much love to Bob, Shangela, Eureka, and all the wonderful participants on *We're Here*. You have shared your stories, your talent, your laughter, and your tears. Thank you for your fierceness, your fearlessness, and bringing your art to the world. Any time you want to do a makeover on a short white bi girl who's secretly a lip sync assassin, I am *available*!

As always, I am immensely grateful to you, fabulous reader, for choosing to spend your precious time and money hanging out in a world I created so it doesn't just exist in my head. Thank you for supporting love for all.

This book is a love letter to a few of my favorite things. The art of drag. Christmas movies, music, and TV specials. High school choir. Adorable rescue dogs. Celebrating queer joy. And, of course, *It's a Wonderful Life*.

Acknowledgments

I remember the first time I watched the movie as a teenager. I was struck by the simple but powerful lines Clarence says to George when he points out that each life touches so many other lives. And when someone isn't around, they leave an awful hole. That sentiment has stayed with me all these years later, and honestly, even gotten me through some dark times. Your life matters. *You* matter. Don't ever let anyone make you feel otherwise.

The movie was released over seventy-five years ago. And while so much has changed in that time, much remains the same. We live in a world where I can openly write a book about drag queens and two women falling in love, which is amazing. Yet there are places where such things are frowned upon, and sadly, far, far worse. Drag performers reading stories to children and public drag performances should be in the news for celebrating love, diversity, positivity, and living your truth. Period.

I long for a world more like Lanford Falls. Let's each do our part to get us there.